THE
HOLY FAMILY

a novel

Alan Michael Wilt

Tucker Seven

Boston, Massachusetts

Sail, Baby, Sail was written by Alice C. D. Riley in 1899.

ISBN: 978-0-9883727-0-2 (paperback)
ISBN: 978-0-9883727-1-9 (digital)

Cover photo: © Demurez Cover Arts/Ricardo Demurez
Cover design: Brad Norr, bradnorrdesign.com

Published by Tucker Seven
www.tuckerseven.com
www.alanmichaelwilt.com

For my family

1

Thanksgiving Day

A hint of early morning light peeks through the long thin opening between the window shade and the sill as I roll to the right and slightly open my eyes. Not bright enough to wake me fully, it still whets my curiosity about the day I am about to face. I slip out of bed softly so as not to wake Justine. It's just past six o'clock, and though she used to be the earlier riser, these last few months she has been sleeping later, especially when it is not a work day. I close the bedroom door behind me and go downstairs to the living room.

The south-facing window seems to await the sunrise, when the early light will leap the treetops of Central Park, run down our street, and angle through the glass and sheer curtains. I hope that the air will be cool and crisp today, and that later, when we drive our Camry across the Hudson River to New Jersey, the air in my hometown, Manasawga, will smell good, even taste good, and when I breathe it deep into my lungs it will invigorate and renew me.

It has had that effect in the past, especially on days that I have felt worn down by work, or by Manhattan, or by life.

I go into the kitchen and drink a small glass of orange juice, then return to the bedroom and slip back into the bed, careful not to jostle and wake Justine. She is sleeping on her left side, I am on my back, and I allow my left thigh to brush up gently against her. She has not been much for touching lately, but this slight sensation sends ripples through me just as it has for twenty-five years. As I begin to doze again Justine turns, then turns some more, and I feel her breath on my neck, then her lips, then I am wide awake as she kisses me and swings her leg over to straddle me.

"Marty," she says, "oh honey it's been such a time" and we make love, a gentle, rocking lovemaking as if we are floating in water, and then just remain in a wordless embrace until we fall asleep again. It is eight o'clock when we wake to the smell of coffee brewing downstairs in the kitchen, the automatic coffee-pot unfailing in its only task.

A little later I am eating a light breakfast and sipping coffee in the kitchen and Justine comes in and pours a cup. "I think just coffee for me," she says, whether to me, or to the coffee, or to the kitchen sink, I am not sure. She sips a little off the top and then walks out of the kitchen.

I finish my cereal and then pick up my mug to go into the living room and join her. She has not gone to the living room, but is standing at the top of the stairs, outside the closed door of the bedroom our daughters shared from the ages of eight and ten until they went off to college—Janet first, to Rochester and later to Minnesota to pursue a doctorate in geophysics, and Celia to Vassar a couple of years later with her paints and brushes.

I take a breath, thinking I am going to say something, but instead I continue into the living room. I stare out the window again toward Central Park and it occurs to me, not for the first time, that this is our first holiday with neither of our girls home with us.

I told my parents we would get out to Manasawga as early as we could to help prepare Thanksgiving dinner. They are in their mid-seventies now, Mom and Dad, and still like to put out the spread. I made two pies, pumpkin and apple, yesterday, and we stow them in paper bags behind the driver's seat of the old Toyota. Justine typically likes to drive, but she ignores the keys when I hold them out and gets into the passenger side.

Traffic is light going down Ninth Avenue and into the Lincoln Tunnel. We quickly cross the Hudson River, the tile walls a blur as I maintain a steady seven miles an hour over the speed limit. Traffic is sporadic on Routes 3 and 46, and on Route 80 I just stay in the center lane and cruise. Justine stares out the passenger window. There is not a cloud in the sky but she stares intently at something up there. As we approach the exit that will take us into Manasawga she shifts her weight and leans, placing her hand on my right thigh and then her head on my shoulder. It is awkward to drive this way, but as a single tear drops from her eye and rolls down the sleeve of my jacket I hold steady and make the final turns with one hand on the wheel, the other holding Justine's.

It is almost noon and the aroma of turkey greets us as we open the door and walk in. After hugs and hellos we hang up coats and unpack pies and look for ways to help in the kitchen. My mother tells us that my brother Dan, divorced, and his six-teen-year-old son will be here, and my sister Marie and her husband and the youngest of her boys. My sister Jeanette is having dinner at her mother-in-law's, but her oldest son Tom is having dinner here. "He's got a new girlfriend he wants us to meet," my mother explains. "Then they're going to granny-number-two's house for dessert, I guess." Tom lives in Philadelphia where he works as an accountant, and this is his first trip home with his new girl. He met her just after the last time we saw him, in late August.

Dinner is just about ready when Tom and his girlfriend walk through the door. He puts on a big show of introductions. Her name is Rachel and she is a knockout—too hot for an accountant is my first thought, but I bury that quickly and shake her hand when Tom gets around to saying "My Uncle Marty Halsey and my Aunt Justine." Rachel may be overcompensating, or just nervous, but she speaks a tad louder than she needs to—I want to say to her, Use your Inside Voice, but I don't—and saying again and again what a delight it is to meet everyone and how blessed she feels to be with us for Thanksgiving dinner.

The minor tsunami of Tom and Rachel's entrance subsides as quickly as it had swept in, and there is a moment of awkward silence before my mother directs everyone to the take a place at the table. I save a seat for Justine to my right while she helps bring dishes of steaming food to the table. "I'll get that, Ruth," Justine says, hefting the large platter of carved turkey before my mother can get to it. When we're all seated, Tom and Rachel are directly across from Justine and me and I can see that my mother is about to tell my father to start passing the turkey, but Rachel speaks first.

"I'm just so thankful to be here," she says, "I'm just so grateful to the Lord for bringing me to this table of fellowship with all of you. Maybe we could all—you know, share a moment to say what we're thankful for this year?"

I can see my mother's demeanor stiffen—we're not grace-sayers, or thanks-expounders, and are especially not interested in faith that is worn on the sleeve. And Mom wants the food to be served while it's hot, which is just plain common sense. There's another awkward silence, and when I take a breath to speak Justine pinches my knee and gives me her "uh-uh, don't go there" look, but I go anyway.

"I'm terribly thankful that we can eat and talk about thanks at the same time, so let's get this food moving around the table while it's hot. Get that turkey going, Dad!" Everyone starts talking and reaching at once. Rachel seems a little crestfallen, but Mom is clearly relieved and smiles as she scoops some pearl onions onto her plate. Tom senses Rachel's discomfort and says, as he serves food onto both his and her plates, "Well, I'm thankful that Thanksgiving doesn't happen during tax season, so I can be here with my family." Marie raises her glass of pinot noir and says "To family," and we all respond in kind with the glasses of whatever we are drinking.

Dinner continues with small talk, bad jokes, and gentle ribbing among the siblings and relations around the table. Rachel, the odd-girl-out, tries to keep up, her blue eyes flashing from person to person as she tries to follow the family dynamics and inside jokes. She occasionally looks at Tom in hopes of an explanation, but the look on his face says, Later, I'll explain that later. Every now and again she chimes in with a "Thank the Lord for that" or "That's such a blessing from the Lord." When my sister tells us that a drunk driver sideswiped her parked car on the street in front of her house, Rachel exclaims, "Thank the Lord there was no one in the car!" Hearing that the drunk was caught and arrested, she gives us a big "Praise Jesus!" Marie, through gritted teeth, asks whether Jesus has anything to do with the goddamn insurance agents who have been making her life a living hell ever since the accident. Rachel is taken aback and after a moment excuses herself and asks for directions to the bathroom.

When she is out of earshot, Tom says, "I'm trying to break her of that, guys. It's how she was raised. She's not really like that—fundamentalist. Not like you're thinking, anyway."

I give him a look and say, "So she's okay with sex before marriage, you mean?"

I can see I've embarrassed him, and I'm not sorry. He glances over at his grandparents, who are both chuckling, and says, "Hey, she's not even against gay marriage." Marie just rolls her eyes and says, "Yeah, praise the Lord. Whatever."

Justine has been quiet throughout dinner, making only brief remarks here and there. No one mentions Janet or Celia, or asks how things are going for us in Justine's graphic design business and my talent agency. As dinner ends we take a break before dessert, breaking into smaller groupings having separate conversations. I hear bits and pieces. Rachel has come down from the bathroom and stands beside Tom, a strained smile on her face. She participates less, and when she does her voice is softer than before. She and Marie avoid eye contact and move as if they have the same magnetic charge. I ask Justine to come outside to the front yard with me for some fresh air, and she takes my hand as we go down the front steps. I lean against one of the cars in the driveway and she leans against me, her back to my front, and I wrap my arms around her and kiss her on the temple.

"Warm enough?" I ask.

"As long as you hold me like this."

"I'm holding."

She says, "Well, thank the Lord for that," a perfect replication of the timbre of Rachel's voice, and we both burst out laughing. The familiar scent of her becomes suddenly strong and sweet, as if laughing has released some essence of her that had been held back. She turns and faces me, kisses me full on the lips and then burrows into my shoulder.

"That felt good. Laughing," she says.

"You smell so good," I say.

We stay like that until we hear the front door open. Tom and Rachel are leaving to go to his other grandmother's house. Tom approaches with his hand extended and gives me a firm handshake that turns into a hug, then goes straight for the hug with Justine.

"It's good to see you, Uncle Marty. Aunt Justine. Nice and cool out here."

"Glad you could come for dinner," I say. "I hope the job is going well." Tom nods as Rachel reaches out to shake our hands.

Taking one of our hands in each of hers, Rachel looks from me to Justine and says, "I didn't know. Till just now. I—I'm so sorry for your loss." Justine offers a sympathetic smile, knowing how hard it is for people sometimes to say these things, but her eyes darken when Rachel looks straight into them and says, "God is with you. He really is. Have faith. And he has his reasons—"

But before Rachel can finish her thought Justine turns roughly away and starts walking toward the backyard, pulling me by the hand as she goes. I follow her without a second thought or a look back, gathering her against me as she steers us along the brick path that goes around the house. Our moment of laughter is long gone, replaced by Justine's retreat into a much darker place where tears fall from her eyes and her lips tremble and she is here but not here, with me but not with me, and I feel utterly lost.

❖

At the age of eighteen I was an agnostic half-lapsed Catholic kid from New Jersey. Thinking it would be a good idea to get as far away from Manasawga as I could, I spent my freshman year of college near Atlanta, Georgia. The college was associated with a mainstream Protestant denomination, which did not figure largely in the school's recruitment literature. This was the Bible belt, though, and I was consequently immersed, without warning or preparation, in a fundamentalist Christian religious culture. I doubt that I even knew the word "fundamentalist" before that.

As the weeks and months passed I was subjected to frequent calls to accept Jesus as my Personal Lord and Savior. The self-described spirit-filled Christians who populated the dormitory offered a God who really, really loved me, but would unblinkingly send me to hell—along with Socrates, Plato, the Buddha, and every other human being who lived before Jesus, or failed to ever hear about him, or whose personal relationships with him did not live up to the criteria proclaimed by the wet-behind-the-ears twenty-year-olds who tormented any and all at the drop of a hat, chapter, or verse, or the mention of the satanical pope in Rome, with their testimony and witness.

It was enough to drive a person to drink, which would have been a more likely option if the campus had not been dry despite the state's drinking age of eighteen. It was enough to drive some people to Jesus (upon which occasion all would hear great rejoicing on the dorm floor, no matter the hour. Imagine being awakened at two o'clock in the morning by joyful shouts of "Dickie accepted the Lord! Dickie accepted the Lord!" Poor Dickie, finally brow-beaten into salvation in the middle of the night). It was also enough to cause, in some, a state of fear that led to a sort of emotional paralysis over the potential fate of eternal hellfire if it turned out that these guys were right. I have to admit that I fell into that category, at least for a while. Some of my classmates, who earned my envy, were able to just ignore it all and go about their secular business of getting an education.

One night I caught a ride to an off-campus watering hole in town with a guy, Clay Pelton, I hardly knew. He lived down the hall, on the other side of the communal bathroom. The bar, a dive called the Triple H, couldn't really be called a bar, since all they served was weak beer from leaky taps. I didn't know what the H's stood for, but I was smart enough not to mention that I hoped it stood for Hubert H. Humphrey.

Clay was a few years older than me, but a freshman, and drove an old pickup truck. We made small talk on the way to the Triple H, and with all his references to Mama and Daddy and his gal back home I figured he was just the standard good ole boy. He wanted to give the college thing a try, he told me, to learn something about business in order to help his daddy run the family's farm more efficiently and profitably.

By the time we each had a couple of beers we were talking as if we had known each other for years. Across the concrete floor of the Triple H we could see an argument brewing—the very large owner of the place was trying to defuse two hot-headed townies in the act of provoking a college kid. The owner poured each of the locals a beer and took them outside to drink in the fresh air. Through the noise and music I said to Clay, "Man, I don't want to be in here when a fight breaks out."

Clay smiled and shook his head, then patted something inside his jacket pocket. I could see a rounded shape, and Clay said, "I got all the protection we need," and I thought, He's got a gun, Jesus, he's got a gun. Wide-eyed, I pointed at his pocket and said, hoping not to be heard over the noise, "You've got a gun?" Clay shushed me with a gesture and then laughed. He pulled the object out of his pocket—a portable medical supply kit that included a pair of bandage scissors, which had provided the illusion of the outline of a trigger. "You think I'm dumb enough to bring a gun to a shithole like this?" he said, laughing. "Just messin' with you, Mart, just messin'. Back home I drive ambulance, volunteer. I'm thoroughly trained to use these scissors, and to patch up those redneck motherfuckers after they break each other's faces open while they're praising Jesus." He laughed again.

I said, "Clay, something's been really nagging at me the whole time I've been here in Georgia. Tell me what you think, and I don't mean to offend, but, what do you think about all

15

those spirit-filled Christians in our dorm? You know, Dave Gladwell and Scott Radner and those guys."

"Pure bullshit," he said. "Absolute pure bullshit. Those assholes are preaching a fairy tale."

"So you're not—"

"Not now, not ever. My family is famous in Troup County. One of my great-granddaddies ran with a real godless crowd and passed it down like blue eyes in our DNA."

He told me more later, in the quiet of his truck on the way back to campus. Clay's great-grandfather and grandfather had passed down copies of the Bible, Qur'an, Bhagavad Gita, and Dhammapada. "All marked up with marginal notes by grampas, aunts, uncles, you name it." Other books were added as the decades passed. The Book of Mormon, Christian Science writings, and most recently, Clay said, "We've got a copy of some recent nonsense called Scientology—a real doozy. Almost as apeshit crazy as Thomas Aquinas!" He laughed explosively at his joke. "It's the best goddamn library of religion in Troup County. Better than any goddam church has." From the time he was a child he was required to read and understand these books. "Daddy said, 'I reject them, but you make up your own mind,' and I'm glad to say I came to the same conclusion as the old man."

I took all this in, but still needed to apply it to the emotionally manipulative tactics of the born-agains in the dorm. I had never before felt guilt about sexual fantasies and masturbation, but in Georgia the preacher-boys had turned up the volume on guilt and its best friend, fear. What if these Christian pricks are right? I wondered. What if my failure to say "yes" to their Jesus consigns me to an eternity of the hell they so gleefully describe? "Man, they really get to me sometimes," I said to Clay. "Are they right? Am I going to hell? I mean, I toss and turn and worry—"

Clay shook his head back and forth. "They start talking at you, just walk away. They have an answer for everything, but it's just a script, it's just fiction, no matter how true they claim it to be. They don't respect where anyone is at but themselves. Walk away." He took a long pull on the beer he was finishing in the dorm parking lot. "Besides, if the alternative to the hellish eternity they promise to unbelievers is to be forever in the presence of dicks like them, I'll take the devil's company."

I breathed more easily from that point on, but Clay had not provided a definitive answer for me to the question of God. Despite my claim of agnosticism, I still had this spiritual streak in me. I had not entirely given up on God, just on the various versions of God that had been offered by priests, nuns, and, now, these post-pubescent college boys who claimed to have exclusive keys to the magic-Jesus formula. Back home I had resisted going to church on Sunday. It was boring and meaningless. Reciting prayers was deadly dull and the homilies of the priests rarely touched on anything that mattered to me. I prevailed by sheer stubbornness and in my junior year of high school I was excused by my mother from the Sunday obligation.

"Nature is my God," I would claim whenever conversations with peers or family went down this track. A walk in the woods was my preferred mode of worship, and though I was shy and unlikely, anytime soon, to be considered a potential sex partner by any of the girls I knew, I fantasized about a future relationship that would last a lifetime and be worthy of the adjective "sacred."

Clay Pelton had shown me the answer of atheism—in his case, a very well-informed atheism. He had far more knowledge about religion than I could claim despite having been brought up as a church member. I stared at the wall in bed at night thinking about that word. Atheist. Definitive. I didn't have it in me to be definitive. If I said, "I am Catholic," the statement was open to a whole range of interpretation. It might mean that I was loyal to the pope and his riches in Rome. It might mean I identified with rebellious priests who got arrested while protesting the Vietnam War. But "atheist"—that would remove all ambiguity and put me in a category as clear as "red" or "blue," and that was not a place of comfort for me.

❖

By the time Justine and I go to bed, after a quiet drive back to Manhattan and an evening with classical music playing softly in the background, Justine seems to have pulled out, or nearly so, of her darkness. I had gone there with her, though not quite so deep. I have been following this woman since the first time I laid eyes on her more than twenty-five years ago, but like an animal sleeping closer to the burrow's entrance I tend to stay nearer to the surface in order to protect those who are further in—and, no doubt, to protect myself from that deeper darkness. Before she turns off the bedside lamp she lies with her face about eight inches from mine and we gaze at each other. Not with longing or devotion, but simply studying, as if to confirm a simple and lasting presence. After a few minutes she allows herself a wry smile, which I mirror. She inches closer, and as the tips of our noses touch we kiss lightly on the lips.

"Brand new start tomorrow," she says, her voice something shy of a whisper.

"And all the tomorrows after that," I say.

Friday

The day after Thanksgiving has always been for us a day to stay in, away from the crowds of shoppers looking for bargains. We might watch a movie or two, or play board games with the girls, or read stories to one another. But this is the first year with just the two of us, and though we video-chat online with Janet for half an hour around lunchtime, that only makes the absence of the girls more acute. We finally decide to leave the apartment and walk over to Central Park despite the heavy pedestrian traffic we anticipate. "Let's walk uptown," Justine says as we cross Central Park West. I am not surprised. Not many blocks downtown are the Dakota Hotel and the Strawberry Fields memorial to John Lennon, two places that always make Justine sad. She is wise enough to walk away from such places when she knows she will not be able to bear them.

We step into Central Park at West Ninetieth Street and walk far enough into the park to put the traffic sounds at a good distance. We find a bench and sit facing the Reservoir. I put my arm around her shoulders and pull her close. The sunlight glints off the thin new ice and the buildings that tower over the bare trees on the east side of the park. Justine turns her head and kisses my neck, nibbles my ear lobe. I can't help but smile and start to react in kind.

"The fresh air makes you frisky?" I say.

"I've got to get back on track."

I nod. "I know. I know."

From the roadway behind us we hear singing, the high voices of two or three teenage girls crossing the park from east to west. Their song is a cross between a jump-rope rhyme and Broadway show tune. Hearing it, Justine's eyes turn momentarily dark, like yesterday, but she takes a deep breath and looks up into the cloudless sky, daring the sun to shine on her.

"That's always something," she says, "talking to Janet with video. Seeing her face from so far away. Like science fiction."

Janet is at a climate research station in Alaska, above the Arctic Circle, for the winter. We won't see her again until next April, when we'll travel to Minneapolis for a couple of weeks of reunion, Twins baseball games, and theater. We talk from time to time via an internet video connection but mostly keep in touch by email.

"It's good to see her as well as to hear her voice," Justine continues.

"Yes. I love how much she loves what she's doing."

"Someday maybe I'll get smart enough to understand what she's all about, what her work is all about. Her research papers are impenetrably technical."

"But she loves it," I say. "And it matters. I love it that she managed to become a scientist among all us artsy types. Someone has to actually have a grip on physical reality and how it works."

We sit silently for a while. The shadows get darker and deeper as the sun descends, the air a little colder. Justine feels inside her coat pocket and finds a ski cap. "You look like a Russian spy, a regular Bond girl," I say when she puts it on.

"Russian spies need warm ears, the better to hear with." She says it with a generic Cold War spy-movie accent.

I'm glad that she responds to joking with joking, and that our conversation out here on this park bench has been accompanied by light touches and kisses.

"That girl yesterday, that Rachel," she says. The sudden change of topic catches me off guard, but Justine does not wait for me to say anything. "So young. So sure of herself."

"Like we were when we were young," I say, not sure if I have struck the right tone.

"I wanted to tell her, I have a daughter who is as sure of herself as you are, but she's spending the winter at the Arctic Circle to make her case." I laugh quietly, trying to generate a sound that tells her she has made an excellent point. "And Celia," Justine continues, her voice a little softer, "no self-esteem issues there, ever, but she'd never tell you what to believe." She pauses and then says, with pretentious evangelical earnestness, "Have *faith*."

Justine stops as abruptly as she had begun, and buries her face between my neck and shoulder. I feel warm tears, but she makes no sound. The sun is just touching the horizon when, finally, we stand up and walk out to Central Park West toward home.

We divert to Popover Café, a favorite of ours, for an early dinner. Salad and white wine, and we share a cup of rich cocoa for dessert. At home I check the phone—no messages—and then hear bathwater running.

"I think I'll soak for a while," Justine says quietly when I stop at the door. She's reaching into the linen closet and brings out a towel and some scented candles. I watch from the doorway as she places the candles along the edges of the tub and lights them, then goes past me—with a brief pause to look at me—to the bedroom to undress. After a moment I walk downstairs but stop and turn when I reach the bottom. Looking back up the stairs I see Justine glide from bedroom to bathroom wearing her long winter bathrobe, her hair piled neatly atop her head, with a few locks dangling around her face. She leaves the door ajar and I hear the sound of rippling water as she eases into the tub. Then silence.

I step lightly back up the stairs. In the bedroom I take off my jeans and flannel shirt and put on a pair of pajamas. I can smell the scented candles from the bathroom—lavender, I think, though I'm never too sure about scents—but I still hear nothing else. Taking the slightly open door as an invitation, I stand in the threshold and look at Justine, the flickering candles providing the only light in the room. Her eyes are closed, like she is meditating, but she senses my presence and looks up at me. She has been crying again, silently, but smiles through it and beckons, says, "Come here," patting the edge of the tub.

I sit on the floor beside the tub, close enough to touch her. She takes my hand and presses it flat against her stomach, her womb, and holds it there. She doesn't say anything, doesn't need to. I know what this shared gesture signifies: Janet and Celia—their conception in love, their first home, their passage into the world we all know and love together as a family. It is the same posture of hands as when she would guide me to feel our babies move inside her when she was pregnant.

With her other hand she wipes a tear from her cheek and says, "I'm such a waterworks today. But you—" She doesn't finish her sentence.

"You know how it is with me." I'm not a crier. Justine knows the story, it has come up before. Until I was fourteen or so I could cry freely and easily. Family fights, feeling cheated or slighted, and I would run up to my room, spilling like a broken water main. One day, during one of these episodes, my brother, who is a few years younger than me, ridiculed me, savagely, it seemed to me. In my room, behind the closed door, the tears stopped, almost completely, perhaps for good. I haven't cried—really cried—since then. Sadness and anger and grief have not opened my waterworks, leaving me to face those feelings in a dark, dry canal. And it's been nearly forty years. My brother can weep openly, even at the death of a dog. But I don't hold it against him. There is more to the loss of my tears, I am sure, than being called a crybaby by a younger brother.

Now, though, I see the tears falling from Justine's eyes, I see her face framed by her still-strawberry hair. I see her breasts, which have suckled and nurtured our babies and have been my playground. I feel her hand on mine, still pressed against her womb. My eyes well up and I cry, really cry, and it is now Justine who must comfort me. She stands up in the tub, pulling me up beside her as she wraps us both in her warm long robe. She guides me to our bed, where we lie down and hold each other as though it might be for the last time.

Saturday

Justine and I are quiet in the morning. We seem to have chosen not to talk about the day and night before. Despite or because of everything, I can't say which, I slept deeply and long, and it seems that Justine did as well. I am still tired, though, but she looks and acts refreshed. Her eyes are brighter and her face less drawn than they have been in recent weeks. Across the kitchen table she sips coffee and pushes the newspaper aside before crossing the room to the counter. She unplugs her phone from the charger and sits back down, poking the screen as the little machine beeps and buzzes.

She frowns as she reads, sighs as she punches the tiny keyboard, then puts the phone down and slides it to the middle of the table dismissively and shakes her head.

"I should go in to work for a while," she says quietly. "Loose ends need attention." The studio of Justine Damont Graphic Design is on West 58th Street. "It's a bitch being the boss," Justine says. "But just for a couple of hours." I know that she has been feeling guilty about working short days and taking days off ever since August, sometimes leaving her staff shorthanded with no warning. I know she wants to get back on track. I have done my best to be available when she needs me, even when I'd come home from work and find her staring blankly out the window at a grey sky and I felt she was barely aware that I had sat down beside her. During the same time, I have packed in full days of reviewing clients' contracts and consulting with my staff about software upgrades or upcoming theatrical seasons and opportunities, and then going to some Off-Broadway show to scout for new young talent, some triple-threat with potential for a career that will need to be managed by someone like me.

Work has been my escape, as much as Justine's has been to stare into grey space without being compelled to graphically transform it into a sales tool or information kiosk or made-to-order decorative item.

"I should probably do the same," I say, even though it is not true. But I don't want to be in the apartment alone, don't want to sit in a coffee shop or go to a museum. Nor do I think it would make sense to tag along to Damont Graphic Design. "Let's get a cab, I'll drop you off at DGD, then I'll go down to Spender and Halsey. There were plenty of loose ends on my desk, too, when I came home on Wednesday to bake those pies."

Forty-five minutes later I am punching in the security code to get the elevator to take me up to the third floor. The building has undergone huge changes in the thirty years since I first took the old Otis elevator up that same shaft. Back then the Stuart Spender Talent Agency occupied just three rooms on the floor—the reception area, Stuart's cavernous office, and a room of equal size divided up among a few part-time associate agents—despite the fact that Stuart could have afforded more space and employed more help. He worked out of file cabinets that used the alphabet as only an approximation of an organizing principle, but he and Martha, his one full-time employee, and common-law wife, could put their hands on anything they needed without having to think twice about it. He had been in business for about twenty years when I met him and had built up an impressive roster of clients and an astonishing track record of successes. There were failures, too, a reality Stuart knew how to take in stride—no one was better than Stuart at stroking the ego, in the best sense of the phrase, of an actor on a losing streak, whose priorities need to be adjusted in order to survive and learn how to move on.

Thirty years later, Spender and Halsey Talent Management takes up the third, fourth, and fifth floors of the building. Fifteen agents and support staff keep the place buzzing, whether they're working on casting a Broadway show or a Caribbean cruise ship's comedy and dance revues. An equal-sized office in Los Angeles handles our television and movie business.

Today, though, the place is dark and quiet. I switch on some lights after punching in more security codes and sit down at my desk with the cup of coffee I had bought at the shop a couple of doors down on 23rd Street. I stare at my faux-old-fashioned desk, where loose ends do in fact wait—resumes and head shots, a pile of scripts, audition schedules for regional theatres, envelopes I have not yet opened.

But I don't look at any of that. I open the bottom drawer of my desk and take out a framed 5-by-7-inch photograph of the four of us—Justine, Janet, Celia, and me—taken by a neighbor last summer when we were all together at the cabin we rent every August up near Saratoga. It's one of those pictures—posed but candid, the spontaneity of the moment in which it was taken producing a portrait that is just off, but perfect, each face caught exactly as it always appears in memory. The camera had been put aside at summer's end, stashed in an overnight bag where I had found it just a few weeks ago and discovered this photo. I printed and framed it and put it in my drawer, hidden like a flask of whiskey, because I couldn't bear for it to be on my desk, in sight at all times.

I gaze at the photograph for perhaps several minutes until I can no longer see it through the water that blurs my vision. I turn it face down and stand up with a sense of purpose, even though I don't know which way my next step will take me. Horns blow out on 23rd Street, followed by frustrated shouts. Jaywalkers and angry drivers, no doubt, but I don't care. I go from my office to the outer office, toward the exit, and, starting with Stuart Spender's earliest clients, circa 1961, I slowly traverse the perimeter of the room and spend a moment with each actor's photograph—head shots, candid shots, performance shots—that line the room, allowing the time to pass until Justine calls to say she's ready for me to hail a cab and meet her at her studio.

❖

I graduated from the state college in Montclair, where I had transferred after the year in Georgia. Three years later, I was living in Manhattan in a tiny loft, by myself, after having spent nearly two years crammed into a slightly larger apartment with three other theatrical types all trying to burst onto the acting scene while working unpredictable hours at restaurants, diners, bookstores, and offices as temporary receptionists or file clerks or toilet cleaners and floor sweepers. Our lives had all the elegance of dried gum on the sidewalk, but whenever one of us had a moment—now there's a theatrical term—a moment of success, like a callback to an audition or an actual appearance on a stage, however small the role or audience or stage itself, we could sense the flavor of the big time even if we couldn't actually taste it. These moments kept us going, convincing us we were just one little turning point away from achieving our goal of being noticed and known for being good at our chosen craft, and of being empowered to devote ourselves entirely to its development.

We were not averse to the possibility of fame, if it happened to accompany success at our craft, but a sense of propriety led us—for the most part—to keep those hopes nonverbal.

I had a few roles in tiny productions here and there, but when I was in the chorus of a dinner theater production of *Bells Are Ringing* up in Connecticut, I inexplicably caught the eye of an agent who had been dragged to the show one Saturday night by the leading lady's aunt. The agent visited backstage after the show and was introduced to the lead by the aunt, who shamelessly recited a litany of her niece's musical theater triumphs since the age of seven to demonstrate the girl's triple-threat ability. The niece smiled prettily and slyly rearranged her low-cut blouse to reveal just a tad more cleavage. The agent chatted with the girl but his eye wandered around the room. When there was nothing left to say he handed her his business card and said, "Call the office and we'll make an appointment to talk about what I can do for you." He excused himself and told the aunt that he needed to get to the station to catch the train back to the city. "Just let me hit the head over here for a minute, and I'll meet you in the parking lot."

I had heard this conversation as I milled through the crowd, making my way to the men's room, and walked in just ahead of him. I was standing at the urinal getting unzipped when he stepped up to the urinal next to me. With what I would soon learn was his characteristic panache, he looked straight at me and said, "You weren't trying to, but you stole the scene on the subway. Strong comic presence." He backed away from the urinal and washed his hands at the sink. He reached into his jacket pocket and placed a business card on the edge of the sink. He said, "Stuart Spender, Spender Talent Agency. Call me, and let's talk. I'm serious." I was still pissing but tried to turn toward him. "Let's save the formal introduction for my office," he said. "Call." He left. I finished and studied his card. It looked legitimate. His named sounded familiar. The lead's aunt didn't seem to be the type to hang out with charlatans or perverts, and anyway, considering all the agents who had declined to represent me, I could not turn down an invitation like this. I pocketed the card and left to go out for a late dinner with my cast mates.

I overslept the next morning. As soon as I eyeballed my alarm clock it was obvious that I had turned off the buzzer in my sleep. Mass at St. Luke's had started a half hour ago and there was no point in trying to get there now. I was dismayed, not out of any sense of the so-called sin of missing Sunday mass—which had frightened me as child, but which now seemed to be an example of overreach on the part of the church—but because I genuinely missed participating in the ritual. I had come a long way from my teenaged rejection of all things Catholic. My rejections and affirmations were now more selective and informed. I studied and read and audited classes in theology and the history of Christianity. Most important, I had become part of a congregation of like-minded individuals, couples, and families.

Instead of mass, I engaged in a longer than usual session of centering prayer, a meditation technique I had learned several years before—in Georgia, ironically—that leads to the experience of the quieter areas of the mind that are perhaps more integrated and closer to God, that perhaps even provide a glimpse of, for lack of a better word, the divine.

Feeling refreshed I went out to a diner a few blocks from my place and ordered coffee and a stack of pancakes. I brought with me a book I had picked up somewhere along the line on the business of acting. If I were going to call Stuart Spender this week, I felt I should develop a clearer idea of what an agent actually does and how a client should work with one. Back at my apartment I continued reading until it was time to leave for Connecticut for the late afternoon performance. Still disappointed about missing mass, I waited in front of my building for the *Bells Are Ringing* stage manager, who had a car and lived nearby, to pick me up for the drive to Darien. I napped as he drove, and at the end of the night I was glad to have a break until Wednesday and the final weekend of performances.

I called Stuart Spender on Monday and he invited me to come in on Tuesday at lunch time. His office was over a men's clothing store in a very active block on West Twenty-Third Street. His secretary greeted me by name before I even introduced myself. "You must be Martin Halsey," she said, "from *Bells Are Ringing*. Mr. Spender is just finishing a phone call.

I'm Martha. Welcome." I thanked her and started looking at the autographed photos of actors and actresses, presumably Spender's clients, that lined the walls.

"It's quite a gallery," Martha remarked. "Mr. Spender represents a cross-section of talent from stage and screen. He's got his share of stars, but he helps a lot of chorus girls and boys and character actors stay busy all over the country." She stood beside me and waved her hand in the direction of the photos. "There are regional theaters and summer stock outfits that don't even think about putting out a casting call without calling Stuart first. Mr. Spender, I mean."

Spender suddenly strode into the room and extended his hand. "I'll take that handshake now. You hungry? I am. It's lunch time. Martha, please call Giannelli's and have them send up a pizza, pronto. Whaddaya like, Martin? I'm a pepperoni man, let's try that. Coke or Seven-up? Coke helps settle my stomach after lunch, so let's go with Coke." Martha was already making the call. "Don't forget to tell them pronto," Spender said to Martha. He winked at me. "I give them autographed photos now and again of famous actors. They put them up as if they've had them as guests at their little pizzeria. Best pie south of Forty-Second Street, though."

He ushered me into his office, pointed to a chair, and sat down at his desk. The window behind him looked out on Twenty-Third Street and I could hear shouts and horns honking from the street below. He spread his arms, indicating his paneled office which, like the outer office, was covered with photos of clients. "Nothing fancy, but it's effective. I know everyone in this business, and if I don't know them it's because I don't want to know them. How are you feeling about your career?"

I hadn't expected such a headlong rush of conversation, but figured I had better keep pace with Spender. "Well, I'm working right now—*Bells* has one more weekend—but there's nothing else on the horizon. I went to three calls last week, but I doubt that anything will come from them. I haven't seen the trades yet this week, so I don't know what's coming up. It feels good to be working, though, that's for sure."

"What's your day job?"

"I work part-time at the Drama Book Shop and deliver, uh, pizzas for Costa's in the west eighties. Best pie *north* of Forty-Second Street." I said it in my best TV-pitchman tone. Spender grinned. "Then there's occasional work for caterers, and Ma and Pa Halsey send me a check every once in a while. When they can."

"For which I trust you are very grateful."

"That is correct."

Spender sat with his hands clasped in front of him, then rubbed his palms together. "Okay, audition time. I saw presence the other night, but heard no solos and just two or three lines. Show me who you are. Sing to me. Before we get our mouths full of pizza."

As if on cue, Martha entered the office with a paper cup of water from the cooler in the outer office. I thanked her and sipped from it. "I learned this in high school, when I did not get the part of the minstrel in *Once Upon a Mattress*, but made sure everyone knew I had it down cold in case the kid who did get the role came down with laryngitis or met with an unfortunate accident." I launched into the ballad "Many Moons Ago," looking over Spender's head and singing out the window to Twenty-Third Street. I couldn't help but sense that both Spender and Martha were giving me their full attention, but when I finished neither of them applauded or said anything.

After a pause Spender said, "Now act. A monologue."

I took a moment to breathe and assume my character and took off on Hamlet's "O, what a rogue and peasant slave am I" soliloquy, which may have been pretentious but was the only one of my eight or ten audition monologues to come to mind on such short and sudden notice. I had worked and worked the soliloquy over, tearing it apart like a literary critic and then putting it back together as an actor, and it was somehow wholly new every time I did it—so far, though, to no avail—in front of directors casting Shakespeare and even, once, in a room with Joe Papp of the Public Theatre.

This time Martha applauded, tiny claps of her small hands that I could barely hear over Spender's grunts and groans as he noisily opened a file cabinet and took out a dog-eared pile of papers stapled in the upper left corner. He handed it to me brusquely and said "Read the part of Joe, right there on page one, you start it off."

"Cold?" I asked.

"Freezing."

I read the part, trying to at least not stumble over the words, unable, in this crazy moment, to really grasp at all what I was saying. As my first lines ended, Spender launched into the lines of whomever it was Joe was talking to, two characters clearly engaged in an important and volatile conflict. Spender worked without a script, and I kept one eye on him and the other on the page as I tried to hit all my cues. The scene couldn't have lasted much more than two minutes, but as soon as it ended Martha refilled my cup of water, and handed a fresh one to Spender. "A lot of good energy, gentlemen," she said. "Very good energy."

"Yes, that was a great deal of fun," Spender said. "You managed to do more than just keep up. I could see you thinking. I love it when I can see an actor thinking."

"Yes, you do," Martha said.

I downed my cup of water in a single gulp, hoping that the relief I was feeling was the correct response to their comments.

The door to the outer office opened and a young man walked in carrying a pizza and a soda bottle. "Anthony," Spender said, "my favorite of all the world's pizza men." They conversed for a moment in Italian and Spender handed him some cash. "Keep the change my friend, keep it." With grand gestures he walked Anthony to the door and bade him farewell—yes, bade him farewell. Stuart Spender did not merely say goodbye. And then it was the three of us in the office again—Stuart Spender, Martha whose last name I did not know, and the young, perspiring, utterly confused Martin Halsey, trying to make sense of everything that had happened in the last twenty minutes.

We ate our pizza slices quietly at first, but after finishing one Spender opened a desk drawer, took out a thin sheaf of papers, and pushed it across the desk to me. "That's an agency contract. Everything is spelled out there. I have an appointment uptown and must go outside and hail a cab. Stay, eat. Martha will answer any questions you might have about the terms." Without another word he strode out the door. Martha refilled my empty glass of Coke.

Just like that, I was an actor with an agent.

My cell phone rings as I turn the corner to face the wall of actors' photos from the most recent era of the Spender Halsey Agency, the actors who have become clients in the twenty-first century, many years after Stuart's death. Most of these know Stuart, if at all, by reputation—but his name still means something in the business, and it is up to me, as Stuart's partner, to honor and maintain it. We had very different styles, Stuart and I, very different ways of relating to people, sizing them up, judging their strengths and weaknesses. But we both were in the business because we loved to see people do excellent and amazing work in a place—the stage—that we had discovered, separately and decades apart, was too frightening a place for us to stand ourselves. But with passion and strenuous effort we worked to bring braver people than we were into circumstances where they could strive to excel in the holy arts of what Vincent Crummles, in *Nicholas Nickleby*, so dramatically refers to as "the theatrical profession."

The phone has rung three times before it registers on me to answer it, and when I do Justine tells me she's hungry and suggests that she grab a cab and come down to my neighborhood so we can go to the First Date Diner. I say okay, finally realizing that it has somehow gotten to be two o'clock. We hang up and I wait a few more minutes before walking to the diner we call the First Date Diner because it is the place where we had our first date. It was called the Primrose Coffee Shop back then, and has had a lot of other names in the decades since. We don't bother to keep track, but we still like to go there from time to time, regardless of the cuisine or ambiance, because it marks a special time for us. The last I can remember it was a Chinese eat-in or take-out spot, but I have not actually noticed since the last time Justine and I were there three or four years ago.

The place is now a shop in a coffee chain, identical to hundreds of others all over the country. Justine and I arrive almost simultaneously. She is crestfallen at the sight of the place. "Hardly a place for a meal," she says. "Cookies and muffins. Maybe an acceptable sandwich." Still, she wants to go in. "I'll forgive it because it sits on this corner. I love this corner. It's where I first started to love you."

I kiss her rather than try to find the words for an adequate response. But I am glad, like Justine, to be at this place. We go in and speak faux-Italian as we order plain old coffees and a salad and sandwich to share. "Real mugs, please," I say, "not those cardboard things." I prefer the heft. We choose a table and sit, and Justine tells me that she feels much better now that she has cleared some administrative matters from her desk.

"It'll be nice to go in on Monday and just start right off in creative mode." She leans into the table to try to make contact with my downcast eyes. "I'm really needing that, to kind of get a hold of the reasons I got into this business to begin with."

I nod slightly to let her know I am listening, but I don't have anything to say in return.

"You?" she asks.

"Me?" I ask back. I don't know what she means.

"Did you get any junk cleared from your desk?"

The young woman at the counter calls our order number and Justine tells me to stay put and goes to get it. When she sits back down we divide things up between us.

"So?" she says.

"No, not really. I walked along the walls of the offices, touring Spender and Halsey client photos from the beginning on."

"Memory lane?"

It is only now that I begin to have an idea about what I was doing as I walked meditatively around the office, and I try to put it into words. "More like a ritual. I think I was looking for the heart of my career. I've been working so much, so hard, since summer—"

"Too hard."

"Maybe. Probably. But I feel as though I've been going through the motions, playing a role, doing more acting than half the people I represent. We signed some great deals. That used to really juice me, but now it's just ink on paper. Like the fire's out. I walked around the office and felt no heat, no excitement, no spark. My heart beat no faster at the thought of spotlights and greasepaint and these marvelously talented people I'm associated with."

Justine looks directly into my eyes but remains silent, willing me to continue.

"I know what you're thinking, Justine, that this is not about my career. But as hard as I've been working, I feel like I've got no steam, no fire. But I also have no compulsion to re-stoke my engine, and if I don't do that there is no way I'll perform up to the standard I expect of myself. Or that Stuart would expect of me."

I swirl the coffee in the mug but have no desire to drink it, and have lost any appetite I had for the sandwich. A stiff drink seems more appropriate now, preferably on an empty stomach.

"It's not about your career. You said that, and you're right. It's about you, me, us, everything that's happened and we need to deal with. Will always have to deal with." She seems about to break into tears but keeps it together. "If something has to fall apart, though, I would much rather it be your career than you and me." Her face changes now, fiery and defiant, almost fierce. "But I have more than enough confidence in both of us to believe that neither of those outcomes is necessary, or likely, or anything more than just simply possible."

Justine puts her fork down and reaches for my hand. She squeezes it, hard to the point of painful, for a full minute. Then she says, "If you're heading into a tailspin, you need to be conscious of it so you can pull out of it. Don't get me wrong, I'm not giving you an ultimatum. I'm challenging you. I can't pull you out of it, but I will stand with you just as you have been standing with me." She stops again, eases her grip on my hand and says, with something like the sound of supplication, "We have the strength to remain standing, together. Please let us use it, Marty."

"I don't want to get lost in the dark," I say. "I don't want anything to fall apart. I feel like I've been trying to stay level on a roller coaster the past three months, maybe it's even looked as though I'm succeeding, at least to someone on the outside," and my voice trails off as I lose hold of anything resembling a train of thought. I offer Justine a strained smile. "I don't know what I'm talking about anymore, it's all just words. I hear what you're saying—strong, together. Just—tell me that you'll hold me accountable."

Justine now smiles, her face more relaxed. "Damn straight I will."

"It's so tempting to just go slack."

"That's not your style, you know that. But if it takes a cattle prod, Marty, I'll go get one and charge it up so you won't forget."

"And maybe you could watch my back, too? I always feel like something's coming up from behind me these days."

"Done."

I feel as though I have been trying to dodge bullets for the past three months, not even aware that a few of them have winged me. Now that I'm starting to feel them, I almost want to just stand in their path and let them hit me full on. But I sense a rise in confidence knowing for certain that Justine, who has already taken her share of hits, will be there to help me absorb mine and assimilate them so we can learn, together, how to live with these wounds.

❖

Stuart Spender had been my agent for about three weeks the first time I told him about an actor I thought was very good and who might be a strong candidate for a new musical that was getting a lot of buzz around town for its Broadway potential. Stuart invited him in, put him through his paces, signed him up, and got him a supporting role in the show.

A couple of months later I saw a lovely young actress in a showcase of one-act plays in a public school basement on the East Side. While backstage to congratulate one of my former roommates on his performance, I met the actress. I can't say for sure whether I was trying to impress her because she was very attractive, or trying to give a fellow actor a boost because I thought she was good, and it doesn't really matter. But I asked her if she was looking for an agent and offered to suggest to

Stuart that he come to the next performance. I did, Stuart did, and he signed her up. She worked steadily for years.

Meanwhile I was getting my fair share of auditions but was rarely called back. My one success, a commercial for a local discount furniture chain, fell through before the shoot when the business went suddenly bankrupt and its owner disappeared, only to surface somewhere in the Caribbean several months later. I was in touch with Stuart often, though, and enjoyed dropping in to his office once or twice a week, offering to help out with paperwork or anything else just to listen to him talk about New York theatre and television and movies out in Hollywood and theories of drama and Shakespeare's plays. He had a wealth of knowledge and shared it at the slightest nudge. Four or five actors I had recommended to Stuart had become his clients. When I spoke to family or friends back home I always had a lot to talk about despite the fact that I was doing hardly any acting.

On the morning of what would turn out to be a beautiful autumn day, my phone rang while I was eating breakfast. It was Stuart, inviting me—commanding me, really—to meet him at one o'clock at a fancy Italian restaurant near his office. He said he had some issues he wanted to discuss. I was always ready to meet with Stuart, and a free lunch was a bonus. I told him I had to be at work at the bookstore by three o'clock, and he said that would be plenty of time.

As soon as we sat down Stuart ordered a bottle of red wine and got right to business.

"You're good at this," he said. "At evaluating talent. At discerning how a particular actor's talents and gifts might be best employed. You've brought me several new clients, and they're all off to good starts. When I get you auditions, though, you flop. You want to know what I hear from casting directors about you? You're gun shy up there on stage. You have a good idea but you can't pull the trigger. You're at sixes and sevens with yourself. You have your moments, but you don't sustain."

The conversation was starting to feel like a breakup. Thanks for the memories. He's going to cut me loose, I thought, no more agent. The criticism also stung—I had worked hard, had some small successes here and there, just needed to make my own artistic breakthrough somehow, and then I would prove all of that criticism to be counterfeit and wrong.

"He's afraid, is what they tell me about you," Stuart said. "Afraid."

Stuart took a swig of the merlot, the wine such a dark red that it might as well have been as black as my mood was becoming.

"You remind me," he said, "of me, myself, when I was around your age. I'm an agent because I couldn't handle being an actor. I couldn't put myself out there like that night after night. Once in a while, sure, but I couldn't do it consistently, I don't have that kind of discipline, and I don't have the kind of stomach that can handle the nerves." He paused and drank again. "If you do it right, this is a high-intensity business. It takes a strong stomach. A special kind of intestinal fortitude. Literally, Martin, as well as metaphorically."

"Look, if you're saying that you don't want to represent me—"

"No no no no no," he said. "I'm offering you a job. As an agent. I need more help and I think you're the man who can give me the help I need. Martha agrees. In fact it was Martha's idea, I'm lucky I have her to point out things like this that are apparently too obvious for me to notice."

The waiter interrupted, placed our entrées in front of us, and asked if there was anything else we needed. Stuart politely dismissed him and got back to me, his fork full of pasta and red sauce.

"If you need some time to think it over, take it, but I'd like to know soon." He took an envelope from his inside pocket and handed it me. "That's a formal offer, salary, all that. Martha insisted that we put it in writing. She doesn't think that a nice lunch should be sullied by talk of dollars and terms."

I looked from the letter to Stuart, asking a question with my eyes—*Read it now, or read it later?*—and he responded with a shrug that said *There's no time like the present.* I opened the letter and quickly read it—it was short, to the point, and the numbers were laid out without ambiguity. A steady and healthy salary working for a company that had been active for twenty years sounded like a good wager, especially because it would allow me to continue working in the theatre—something that acting, ironically, was not accomplishing.

"Yes," I said. "I don't need to think it over. I accept the offer. I'll give notice at the book shop this afternoon."

Stuart signaled to the maitre d' and made a thumbs-up gesture. "He's going to call Martha and tell her for me. She was very anxious for you to say yes."

"I'm very happy to assuage her anxiety."

"Thatta boy." We clinked our glasses together and dove into our meals.

Working for Stuart was like spending my days with an unofficial historian of the New York and regional theatre scene of the past thirty or so years, with a bit of Hollywood thrown in for good measure and additional profit. He was as opinionated as he was knowledgeable, but for him it all came down to a single principle: "Keep actors working. It not only keeps the lights on here, it maintains the tradition of our noble profession—the good and the bad, for better or worse—people who need to act need to act, and people who need to be entertained need to be entertained. We're part of making all that happen."

A few weeks after I started working for Stuart, I was with him in his office going over various client histories when Stuart's oldest friend and first-ever client, Ned Flynn, stopped by for a visit. Ned was about my father's age, maybe a little younger, a tall strapping Irish-American with a full, rich baritone voice and expressive face. Not a leading man's face—he had never been an ingénue—but one that could play the guy next door, the petty crook or hit man, the district judge, Touchstone, Malvolio, Willy Loman, or Cyrano de Bergerac. A world-class character actor, he was regularly seen in supporting and guest roles on TV dramas and sitcoms as well as in movies. I remembered him from his soap opera days in the sixties when he played undesirables who led women astray, and I would see him on TV on days I was home sick from school, or on lazy summer afternoons. His presence, in person, was that of an extremely live wire. Stuart kept Ned busy working with uncommon ease on both stage and screen.

"Here he is," Stuart announced, "fresh from Hollywood—what did you just get done filming? I'm losing track."

"Movie yet to be titled. I play some L.A. gangster who winds up at the bottom of Big Bear Lake for ratting out the head honcho. With any luck I'll make it to the final reel before they fit me with my cement shoes."

Stuart introduced us and said, "I've been wanting to introduce the two of you. You're both a couple of serious Catholics."

I was taken aback—I didn't think I'd been wearing my religion on my sleeve.

"Don't look so surprised, Marty. I pay attention," Stuart said. "I understand those sensibilities. I have those sensibilities. Religion and theatre have shared origins—actors, priests, mystics, they're all cut from a similar cloth. Ancient cloth, sometimes threadbare, sometimes smooth as velvet or coarse as a horse blanket."

"But the man has not darkened the door of a church, or a synagogue for that matter, in all the time I've known him," Ned said.

"I prefer the theatre," Stuart said, his look serious. "Where fly space gives you the illusion of heaven and trap doors the illusion of hell. I reserve the suspension of my disbelief for the stage. I have never found it possible in a church."

Ned laughed and then gave me a serious look. "There is no man more honest and loyal than Stuart in this business. Learn that from him, if nothing else. I always say, honesty is Stuart's eleven o'clock number and his loyalty always stops the show. But tell me now, Mr. Halsey, where do you worship?"

What followed was the first of many conversations between Ned and me about Catholicism, faith, values, morals, and eventually disillusionment and the loss of faith. Ned and I came at our religious faith with different sets of expectations—he came from a more traditional background and he and his wife, Molly, had been raising their children in the church since the mid-1960s. I was younger and single and my resurgent interest in Catholicism centered on the church's teachings about social justice and its traditions of ritual and music—its most theatrical aspects—and the literary study of the scriptures. What Ned often took at face value I tended to question and hold up to the light to see how it might look from an unusual angle.

Ned easily discerned where I was coming from and said jovially, "Ah, a young cafeteria Catholic, picking and choosing from the buffet table, right?"

I decided not to be cowed by him because he was older and a client—it seemed to me that if I were to succeed in this career I had to be seen as a peer, not a hanger-on or flunky, and Stuart was always clear about the need to hold our ground and assert ourselves with our clients. "Well, Ned," I said—at Stuart's insistence we had moved quickly to first names—"I honestly can't say I know of a Catholic who is *not* of the cafeteria style. And I would include in that assessment the big guy in Rome."

"Those are fighting words," Ned said in a gangster-style voice but with a sly smile.

"Economic justice," I said. "The church talks a good game, the bishops write articulate documents. But they live in their palatial rectories while church employees—mainly women—are paid minimum wage or worse, and subjected to namby-pamby female role models like the greeting card Virgin Mary—meek, mild, modest."

"Now, now, now, I'm Irish, you know, and we Irish have a special place in our hearts for the Blessed Virgin."

Stuart's eyes flashed from Ned to me and back, gleefully watching our exchange. "Go get him, Marty," he said.

"I do too," I said, "but not Mary Mary meek and mild. I prefer a ballsy, take-no-prisoners Mary who can stick out her unmarried pregnant belly and growl"—and now I declaimed in my best Shakespearean style, like Henry the Fifth at the top of his game—"My soul doth magnify the Lord, and my spirit hath rejoiced in God my Savior. For he hath regarded the low estate of his handmaiden: for, behold, from henceforth all generations shall call me blessed. He hath showed strength with his arm; he hath scattered the proud in the imagination of their hearts. He hath put down the mighty from their seats, and exalted them of low degree. He hath filled the hungry with good things; and the rich he hath sent empty away."

Ned stood and applauded. "Take your bow, young man, that's quite a show. Stu, you done good, I like this lad. I always enjoy a spirited and agreeable disagreement. Advent and Christmas are right around the corner. I suppose you take issue with the Immaculate Conception."

I laughed and said, "You wouldn't be trying to trip me into saying that the Immaculate Conception is a reference to the virginal conception of Jesus, would you? This non-biblical addition to the legend of Mary that magically exempts her from original sin by defining the sexual act through which *she* was conceived as sinless—well, there's a certain amount of charming symbolism to it, I admit, ensuring that the vessel through which Christ is born is pure, but the implication attached to it, that all other sex is sinful—even loving, married, open-to-conception sex—well, I think that's a very poor trade."

Ned had a huge grin on his face. "You've been reading your theology."

"I study a bit," I said, grinning back.

"I understand, you like your logic. I like my belief, my believing it because the church tells me it is so."

His voice had a poignant tone, and though Ned was an accomplished actor I knew that right now he was fully sincere, not playing a part. "It's not really logic versus believing," I said. "Speaking for myself. I prefer the symbols and metaphors layered into the stories to a literal understanding of them. Seven days of creation—not factual, but beautiful symbolism."

"And Jesus himself? Factual? Symbolic?"

"Yes," I said. Ned laughed quietly. "I'm grateful," I said, "for an abiding sense of God in my life. Something present in me, around me, but I can't really, honestly, humanize it the way many believers do. It's especially amazing when I sense it in the eyes of other people. And as it is for Stuart, it is sometimes most apparent to me in a theater, whether all lit up for opening night, or quiet and dark except for a ghost light in the middle of an empty stage."

I took a deep breath and the three of us listened to the sounds of traffic on Twenty-Third Street.

Finally Ned stood up and said, "I sincerely hope that you will be able to attend the Flynn Family Christmas Pageant in December, Martin." He reached into his coat pocket and extracted a couple of small cards and handed one to me and one to Stuart. He winked at Stuart and said, "Fill Martin in on the details, but just not all of them. You know what I mean, eh, Stu?" Stuart winked back. "It's good to see you both, but I must go up to ABC studios and give voice to some villainous cartoon character this afternoon. I'll see you again soon."

When he left, Stuart pointed to the card Ned had given me. It contained the address and phone number of Ned's apartment, along with the date and time of the pageant. "You won't want to miss that," Stuart said. "You won't want to miss it."

The pall that has been cloaking the day seems to lift when Justine promises to hold me accountable. It is comforting, in a strange way, to know that we both recognize the need to watch out for the other, but not to be afraid of being critical if we feel that the other is listing like a damaged ship at sea, or willfully giving in to a slough of despair or lethargy. We are both in businesses where thick skins are an asset, even a necessity, but outside of work we are both vulnerable fair game just like every other man and woman walking the streets of this city today.

The air is cool and the breeze stiff, but we walk a few blocks before deciding it's too cold to continue on foot. I step to the curb to hail a cab but Justine pulls me back by the sleeve and points to the subway station on the corner.

"Let's ride the trains for a while," she says, her grin taking twenty years from her face, "like we used to before the girls were born."

We descend to the platform and catch a downtown train to Brooklyn, then change to one that comes back to Manhattan and transfer to the Flushing line as if we were going to a Mets game, then turn back and come into Times Square, where we switch to the Broadway local, which leaves us a few corners from our place on the Upper West Side.

The trains are moderately crowded and we sometimes sit, sometimes stand, always staying close enough to comment to each other about our fellow passengers. On the way back from Queens, I shame some young men by giving up my seat to a pregnant woman who is hanging onto a strap just inches from them. Justine points out a high school girl with a huge textbook on her lap, mouths the word "Janet," and I know exactly what she means. Some thuggish teenage boys posture for several stops on the way from Brooklyn to Manhattan, but when two men the size of NFL linemen get on at Astor Place it takes just one look before the boys find seats and suddenly look their age again.

When we emerge back into the late afternoon shadows we feel contentedly exuberant, the contentment mine and the exuberance Justine's. Waiting for a light to change, Justine links her arm with mine and presses against me, then while we cross the street she swings into me and bumps my hip like in that old faddish dance from the 1970s. A couple of blocks from home we pass a church—one I've walked by hundreds of times but never entered, Anglican by the look of it, and I slow down, feeling drawn to it and the possibility of solace behind the tall doors.

With the excuse that there is something in my shoe, I sit on the steps. I untie, shake out an imaginary pebble, and re-tie while Justine sits beside me, pressed up close again and making it hard for me to use my right hand. She purposely knocks my hand away from the knot I am tying and says, "Hurry up, Marty Halsey, it's cold out here," and then unties the knot just as I've finished it and says, "You're such a slowpoke." She finally lets me tie my shoe and then pulls me up beside her and says, "That's what I could go for, a nice slow poke," and puts her hand into the back pocket of my jeans and squeezes.

At home we cook and eat and browse through the day's New York *Times*, and all the while Justine is a Chatty Cathy as she recalls the subway ride and talks about her plans for her business and her ideas about doing some more painting, just for herself, and she describes how she wants to use colors in ways she has never done before, that Celia's paintings have given her new ideas and she needs to study them closely, objectively, detachedly.

Eventually she kisses me and asks me to take her to bed. Her word choice charms me—she has been leading all afternoon and evening but now wants to be taken—and I have neither the power nor the desire to disappoint her. Later I am worn out from the exertion of my unplanned, unexpected day of reflection and remembrance at my office, of aimless attentive subway riding, of speaking and listening and lovemaking, and I am still trying to listen as Justine talks and I drift slowly off to sleep, hoping that she understands that I am interested in what she is saying but simply unable to keep up with her as the day fades to black.

2

First Sunday

I wake up in the midst of a startling thought: It is the first Sunday of Advent.

Other than occasional weddings and funerals I have not darkened the door of a church, Catholic or otherwise, in nearly twenty years. But today I have awakened to the thought that it is the first Sunday of Advent, the four-week season that leads up to the Christian celebration of Jesus' birth. I realize that I've been having a vivid impressionistic dream about the days, back in my early twenties, when I faithfully attended mass at St. Luke's Chapel here in New York. As Justine continues to sleep I turn and burrow in beside her, hoping to fall asleep again quickly, to find a dream that will chase away religious allusions. But sleep eludes me and my thoughts take me back to Georgia when I was eighteen.

I had to endure a full year of college in Georgia to get all the transfer credits I needed. It would take something besides stoic self-imposed exile to get me through. I wasn't interested in going as far as Clay Pelton had gone—absolute rejection of God and Christianity. I was probably not capable, at the time, of taking that step. Clay had the background knowledge and evidence to actively and passionately reject them—it had been bred in his bones—while I had been raised with the understanding that Catholic beliefs were simply facts of our family's existence, and despite my doubts I knew that I could not reject them out of hand. So I walked into town one Sunday morning in late February and found St. Mary's, the local Catholic parish. According to the sign out front I was about a half hour early for mass. My ambivalence at home about going to church, I thought, may have had more to do with family baggage and Our Lady's in Manasawga's association with negative moments in my childhood. A new town, a new parish, a new, adult start with no local past or family involvement seemed to be as good a litmus test as I could devise to test the hypothesis that this faith should matter to me.

The sign in front of the church noted that the parish had been established in 1870. But even with a hundred years of history, being here seemed to be about as counter-cultural as anything could be in the Bible Belt. The Catholic church was comparatively exotic and foreign, its dynamic so thoroughly unlike "getting saved"—and with any luck it would not involve any confident young Catholics who were dead certain about the origin and fate of the universe and every individual in it.

I didn't want to go inside until about five minutes before mass was to begin. I sat on a bench across the street, set back from the sidewalk and flanked by an abundant patch of daffodils, early bloomers even in that latitude. I stared at them and wondered if they might be a sign of some kind of new beginning for me. Then I heard the screech of tires and my name was called out from across the street. Scott Radner shouted from the backseat of a blue Dodge Dart, his head stuck out of the open window.

"Martin!" he called. I looked up, startled. "Martin! What're you doin' in town, man?" He had gotten out of the car and was crossing the street. "Dickie and Meg and I are heading to our Bible fellowship meeting. Why don't you come with us? It's right down the street."

"Nah, I'm busy."

"You don't look busy. Did you walk here?"

"Yup."

"Come with us, we'll give you a ride back to campus later."

Several times I had seen Scott and his friends returning from their meetings with new recruits from the freshmen in the dorm. If anyone had swallowed the bait the mood would be celebratory, their voices echoing down the hallway as if the football team had won the big game. If no acceptance of the Lord had occurred, the voices of Scott and company would echo instead with cajoling bordering on harassment, bordering on ridicule. I wanted no part of it.

"I'm fine, Scott." I didn't think it was any of his business why I was in town, so I volunteered no information. He sat down next to me and put on the "I care about you" face of a college junior condescending to a freshman. I cringed at the thought that he might touch me.

"Is something wrong, buddy?"

"I'm not your buddy." I regretted the words the minute they were out of my mouth. It was just the sort of response that Scott would interpret as a cry for help.

He shifted position and put his hand on my shoulder. I flinched and pulled away to the edge of the bench, making sure to move far enough that he could not touch me again.

"Hey, sorry, I didn't mean anything by that, Martin, I just thought this might be a nice opportunity—"

"I'm not looking for a nice opportunity, Scott, I'm sitting here minding my own business. Why don't you go back to your friends and do the same?" I stood up and moved away from the bench, repelled by Scott's creepiness.

"Whatever you say, pal. I'm on my way." As he crossed the street he turned and noticed the proximity of the Catholic church. "Oh, I see," he said. "You're going to go eat flesh and drink blood with the papists." He kept walking and talking. "Nomeenay domeenay patreeay spiritay. That's devil talk, Martin," he said. He turned suddenly toward me again, the smile on his face both mocking and entreating me. "You can still come with us."

I said, "I'll take devil talk over your snake-handling freak show, Scott. But thanks for asking."

"There's no need for that kind of talk, Martin—"

"Fuck off," I said, loudly, and I gave him the finger. The girl in the car, Meg, barked a throaty laugh. Dickie shouted, "Hey, Halsey, there's a lady present, I should bust your—"

"Only one lady? I count three," I said. Dickie started to climb out the driver's door, but Scott gestured to him to get back in the car. A moment later they drove away.

I settled back on the bench and waited five more minutes before walking up to the church entrance. As I entered I reached, out of old habit, for the holy water font, dipped my fingertips into the cool liquid, and made the sign of the cross, forehead to breastbone to left shoulder to right. Avoiding eye contact I took a seat in the sparsely populated rows in the back of the church. I looked around at the familiar trappings—the cloth-draped altar and lectern, the regal chair for the priest between the servile ones for the altar boys, and high above it all a large cross with a realistic figure of the crucified, dead, and remarkably well-muscled Jesus, an image that fell just short of being both gruesome and erotic. I lowered the kneeler and settled onto it for a pre-mass moment of prayer, but no prayers came to me so I closed my eyes and asked myself what I was doing here. Presently there began a dirge-like processional hymn, played too slowly either because the organist was unskilled or her hands were old and arthritic. A middle-aged woman stood at the front and in a reedy voice that was just enough off-pitch to be grating, she led the singing of the hymn. I knew the hymn, and had a decent voice, so I sang my best but felt self-conscious and dialed it down when a few of the apparent regulars turned to look in my direction.

From that point on the mass was much as I remembered it from home. The accents of the priest and readers were southern, but the prayers were the same, and the priest and altar boys navigated the small space around the altar with careful steps and the grace that sometimes comes from careful repetition. I thought about staying put when the time came to receive communion, but at the last moment I walked down the aisle and opened my mouth to let the priest place the wafer on my tongue. I went back to my seat and fell into a sort of natural state of contemplation, perhaps responding to all of the sense memories that had flooded back to me during the past forty minutes, perhaps still feeling a rush from telling Scott to fuck off. I felt spent, and only half listened as the priest said the closing prayers. I waited, after "Go in peace," for the priest and others who had served on the altar to exit the church while the organist played the recessional.

A few people nodded a greeting or said "Hey" as we shuffled to the rear of the church and the single exit door. I responded in kind, but wanted to leave without having to greet the priest so I stayed near a pack of parishioners and slipped out hidden by the clutch of people. A notice on a bulletin board caught my eye, though, and I stepped away from the crowd to read it. On the first Wednesday of each month a monk from a monastery near Atlanta came to St. Mary's to teach some sort of meditative Catholic prayer—the sign said "contemplative prayer," but that told me nothing. The coming Wednesday was the first Wednesday in March. I had research to do in the library later that day, so I would try to remember to look up contemplative prayer and see if it might be worth another walk to town.

The topic attracted my attention, and though I did not expect anything earth-shattering from it, the experience turned out to be potentially life altering. I walked to the church on Wednesday and followed the directions to a classroom in the basement. The monk was middle-aged and looked, for all I knew, as much like a truck driver as a monk. He introduced himself as Brother Henry. For the benefit of the three new people in the room, he explained that he was an old friend of the church's pastor and had asked for special permission from his abbot to teach contemplative prayer at his buddy's church. He sent me and the other first-timers into another room while he got the others started on a session of prayer. After about five minutes he joined us and gave us a brief introduction and explanation of contemplative prayer, and then said, "The only way to understand this, really, is to experience it, so I'm going to walk you through the process and let you see for yourselves."

Brother Henry explained that we would be choosing a "prayer word," or perhaps a short phrase, and that we would sit comfortably and allow our minds to gently focus on the word or phrase. In a soft and easy voice that might have seemed seductive in another context he led us into the proper way of letting the prayer word slow down the thought process. After just a few moments of guidance the word I had chosen—"Amen," with the "a" sound as in "ah ha"—seemed to lead me to a quiet space in my mind that I had never known before. Other thoughts fluttered about like butterflies in a meadow, lightly and randomly, but following Brother Henry's instruction I left them to themselves, peripheral, as the *amen* drew me deeper.

Some time passed, I did not know how much, and Brother Henry, again as gently as a mother handles a newborn, coaxed us out of the inner quiet into which we all apparently had been submerged. We sat, still silent, with eyes open for about five minutes before Brother Henry began to ask us about our experience during the last twenty minutes.

I managed to mutter only "I'm speechless," which evoked a smile from Brother Henry.

"I've heard that before," he said.

"What *was* that?" someone else asked. "Where did I go? Did we all go there?"

Brother Henry smiled. "I'm sure you all had unique and similar aspects to your sessions. If we set the human mind in motion in the proper way, we can journey to places, inside, interior places, such as those that some of the great saints and mystics tell us about in their writings and autobiographies." He went on with some further instruction about how to apply the prayer technique on our own and, after a few questions, invited us to return the next month for another session. "I won't teach you anything new," he emphasized, "because you have already learned contemplative prayer. But there are always questions, always new things to understand about it, but it's not something you'll learn about at school."

"No," I said, still emerging from the daze the prayer had produced. "At school all I hear is that if I don't accept Jesus as my personal lord and savior I'm going to wind up in hell."

Brother Henry smiled again. "That's one way of following Jesus, I suppose, but it's not our way, our Catholic way. In the light of this prayer practice, though, don't be surprised to hear new meanings in the words of Jesus, even meanings that might make you feel more personally connected to him."

We rejoined the others for a final few minutes of discussion, and, before saying goodnight, Brother Henry said a closing prayer. His words sounded spontaneous and unrehearsed, and I walked back to campus feeling light and unburdened, the happiest I had felt since arriving here six months before.

Back in my daily life it was easy to prefer the meditative state of prayer over the fascist Jesus. I was amused to hear the

Christian boys in the dorm warn me against this prayer practice because "The devil might get into your *mind!*"—it was the mid-1970s, we had put men on the Moon, and I was living among people who took *The Exorcist* seriously. I was tempted to stage a frothy-mouthed naked rampage up and down the halls of the dormitory, but Clay Pelton talked me out of it.

"Ignore the bastards" was his simple advice. Clay also suggested that if I practiced the contemplative technique without any reference to Christianity or Catholicism, he would bet his daddy's farm that the benefit to me would be the same. "I've read about this kind of practice, and I've got an uncle, atheist and all, who swears by it, doesn't miss a day. Says the human mind and body are marvels of evolution, but that God's got no more to do with it than with falling asleep at night. It's physiological, he says. Science'll figure out how to measure and explain it someday, and you won't need to drop some silly gods into the equation." I filed that in the back of mind, intending to ask Brother Henry what he thought about it. But I had forgotten about it the next month when I attended another session with him, and in May I was too busy with final exams and preparing to move back home to Manasawga, so I missed the meeting and the chance to ask the question never came.

Several months later, after I had transferred to Montclair State back in New Jersey, I went to a weekend retreat to learn more about contemplative prayer from a priest who had written several books on the topic. The retreat was given at a Catholic retreat house on the eastern bank of the Hudson River in New York—an old estate, probably bequeathed to the diocese by some good Catholic whose family had reached the end of its line. The house was run by a group of nuns who provided gracious hospitality and good food. It was a beautiful spring weekend and all was well in my little world.

In between meetings and prayer sessions I noticed, on a table at the bottom of the main stairs, a paperback book titled

The Man in the Sycamore Tree: The Good Times and Hard Life of Thomas Merton by Edward Rice. I had never heard of this Merton, but as I flipped through the book he captured my attention. He was a monk of some sort—Catholic? Buddhist? The book was filled with photos of Merton and his friends—nattily dressed in one, slovenly in another, seriously hung over in a third. It included line drawings by Merton—naked women, abstract calligraphies, pictures made from words.

As I looked through the book, the diminutive sister who seemed to be the top nun on the retreat center's totem pole walked through the foyer in which I was standing. She smiled at me and said nothing as she took note of the book in my hand. I sheepishly returned it to the table, smiled back, and continued on my way.

Later, I went to the main stairs again to take another look at the book about Merton. The little sister again walked by, greeted me wordlessly, and noted the book in my hands. Later still, I went to the book rack on the landing halfway up the stairs and scoured it to see if there was a copy of the book available to buy. There were plenty of books about St. Francis, the Blessed Virgin, the divine office, and the rosary, but no *Man in the Sycamore Tree*. I was ready with a dollar ninety-five to put in the honor-system cashbox, but I was out of luck. I checked the rack one more time, looking behind every book to see if there was a hidden Merton to be discovered, and as I hunted, the little sister descended from the top of the stairs, greeted me again, and went on her way. I wrote down the title of the book and figured I would look for a copy when I got home.

The next morning, when it was time to leave, I stopped one last time at the book rack. This time, a copy of *The Man in the Sycamore Tree* presented itself. I stuffed my money into the cash slot, picked up my overnight bag and, with the book in hand, walked down the stairs. On the table there was no copy of the book. I looked from the table to my hand, realized it was the same copy, and then noticed that I was being watched by the little sister, who smiled and wordlessly bid me goodbye as I went out the door to walk to the train station.

This was back in the days before a few keystrokes on a computer could bring a person's life to your desktop. Today it's easy to learn about Merton: his Euro-American upbringing, the deaths of his parents, his conversion to Catholicism, the many twists and turns that led eventually to a monastic vocation as a Trappist in Kentucky, his absurd death in Bangkok in 1968. It doesn't take long to gain an appreciation of the breadth of his interests and his depth of understanding and compassion. He was an eclectic's eclectic with an amazing knack for leaving a paper trail.

It's too bad, since Merton's untimely death, that his publishers and monastic order have conspired to turn his literary legacy into an unseemly industry that could fuel the economy of a small country. But I wasn't thinking about that back then. I dove into the books, and like paper catching fire I was captured by the flame and started over, a renewed Catholic.

These memories parade through my mind like a series of grainy photographs and videos rather than a string of words. I'm seeing these places—the Catholic church in Georgia, the mansion on the Hudson River—as snapshots in my mind's eye, and the events, along with the thoughts and perceptions that accompanied them, come to the surface from wherever it is they have been buried or imprinted as physical sensations and sense memories. They play out like a carefully produced stage show, complete with the anticipation, hesitation, and reverence that accompanied the actual experience, but it takes only moments to see the whole show. After a few minutes I know that I am not going to fall asleep again, and though it is early I decide to get up in order to distract myself from these memories. I can think of no good reason to linger with them.

But in the kitchen, pouring a glass of orange juice, the memories extend further, to the Catholic churches I began to attend after that weekend up on the Hudson. I was looking for some sort of spiritual home, I suppose, and thought that if the Catholic church could so capture someone like Thomas Merton, that there must be something real and substantial there, if only I could get past the inadequacies of the religion in which I grew up. I sip my orange juice and think about that serious nineteen-year-old kid that I was. Shy and horny, reverent and confused, looking for some sort of concrete magic to believe in. I almost laugh out loud thinking of the education we received as kids, like when the stern and high-strung Sister Christopher prepared me and my fellow six-year-olds for first holy communion, which also meant preparing us for the sacrament of penance, more popularly known as confession.

Young as we were, we knew what it meant to confess. Some of us had had to confess, by then, that we had eaten candy a half hour before dinner, taking the grave chance that we would "spoil our appetites" and render ourselves unable to eat the meatloaf that Mom would put on our plates. And what a waste that would be.

But to have to kneel in what was in effect a darkened closet and confess to a man whose face was obscured behind a screen—that was something new and different. My parents had never forced me to sit in a closet for any reason. And to confess what? I had a fight with my brother. I didn't clean up my room when my mother told me to. I took an extra lollipop at the barbershop.

When Saturday rolled around and it was time to go to confession—in order to receive holy communion at mass the next day—my siblings and I were always hard-pressed to come up with any sins. The fights and arguments we had had since the previous Sunday? Gone and forgotten. And if not forgotten, certainly not something we would consider a sin. We were just kids, we were just acting like kids. "You talked back to me on Wednesday," my mother might remind me. Forgotten. She couldn't remember what it was about, either, so how could I go into that dark closet and confess something I didn't even remember had happened? But inevitably that's what I did. "I talked back to my mother. I fought with my brother." Week after week of seeking forgiveness for nothing more than being a normal kid.

Sister Christopher's biggest challenge was probably teaching us the Act of Contrition, the prayer that we were required to recite in the dark closet before Father Zeccarello could dole out our penance of three Hail Marys and two Our Fathers.

Sister wrote the prayer on the blackboard:

O my God, I am heartily sorry for having offended thee and I detest all my sins, because I dread the loss of heaven and the pains of hell. But most of all, because they offended thee, my God, who are all good and deserving of all my love. I firmly resolve with the help of Thy grace to confess my sins, to do penance and to amend my life. Amen.

Then she walked us through it, bit by bit, pointing at the words on the board with a length of chalk.

"Repeat after me: O my God, I am heartily sorry."

"OhmygodIamhardlysorry."

"Not 'hardly,' 'heartily'. O my God, and I am heartily sorry."

"OhmygodIamhardlysorry."

"Heartily. Say it."

"Hardly."

Sister wrote it on the board in capital letters with a dash between each syllable.

"Heart. Ih. Lee." She smacked the chalk against each syllable as she said it.

"Heart. Uh. Lee."

"Much better," Sister said. "Again, slowly, O my God, I am heartily sorry."

"Oh. My. God. I. Am. Hardly. Sorry."

Sister Christopher had a short temper, but she breathed deeply and tried another tack.

"In this prayer, we tell God that we are very, very sorry for having done things that He doesn't like. So we say 'heartily,' which means we are sorry with all our heart. If we say 'hardly,' that means we are only a little bit sorry. We don't want to tell God that we are only a little bit sorry, do we?"

"No, Sister." Only a few of us committed to that response. The rest of us had no idea what she was talking about.

It went on like that. "For having offended Thee" was repeated with muffled and muddled pronunciation signaling the fact that we did not know what we were saying, despite the words on the board that Sister was now underlining as well as striking repeatedly with her diminishing piece of chalk. "Offended means to have hurt someone or made them angry."

"Who did we make angry?" a blond girl asked.

And Sister Christopher explained how when we sin we make God angry, which led to further questions about how we sin and why it makes God mad, and how does God know what every one of us is doing, and where does God live until finally Sister put an end to the questions and explanations and just worked on rote memorization, promising us that one day we would understand all the words and meanings much better than we did now.

As the hour came to a close she had apparently reached the end of her rope with regard to six-year-old children. After all, she taught them all day until three o'clock, and on Thursday afternoons was subject to another hour's worth of us, the ones who walked over to Our Lady of Mercy from the public school several blocks away for our weekly indoctrination in the faith. Determined to achieve perfect memorization before our parents started picking us up at a quarter to five, she drilled us and drilled us until finally she stood in front of the class, erased the prayer from the chalkboard, and commanded us to recite the prayer from beginning to end. "I want nothing less than perfection," she said, and in retrospect I can only guess that her choice of a non-worldly line of work, together with a charming naiveté, allowed her to believe that such a thing was possible.

We started our final run-through confident, even putting three syllables in "heartily," but by the time we got to "deserving of all my love" we were half a classroom of mumblers, half of silent word-mouthers. Still, after a great deal of uncertainty surrounding "Thy grace to confess my sins, to do penance," we finished strong with "amend my life amen." At this moment Sister Christopher abandoned her station beneath the classroom crucifix, walked around the teacher's desk at the front of the room, strode up the center aisle, and, grabbing me by the left bicep, hoisted me out of my chair and shook me like a dog shakes a rag toy. I don't know why she chose me, whether I was a random representative, or perceived as a ringleader, or whether I was just the first of thirty kids who were about to get the same treatment. But then the bell rang, which seemed to wake Sister from a sort of stupor, and she let go of my arm. I believe I fell about foot and a half to the floor, landing safely on my feet and feeling somewhat as I imagine a boxer must feel when he takes a punch squarely to the nose.

As if nothing unusual had happened, Sister Christopher dismissed us from class. "Go home and be good boys and girls, and practice your Act of Contrition. Your parents can help you. Next week we will test our memorization. Good night." She stood at the classroom door and as we filed out. I tried to slip by invisibly, afraid she might shake me again, but she smiled sweetly and patted my shoulder as I tried to rush by without running, which was not permitted in the hallways. "Goodnight Martin," she sang. "I'll see you all again next week."

It was a menacing thought—seeing Sister Christopher next week. I tried, without success, to come up with an excuse to skip religious education the next Thursday. I couldn't tell my parents what had happened because I had certainly done something wrong, something to deserve the punishment inflicted by Sister Christopher, and if I shared the experience with my parents they would undoubtedly ask what I had done to deserve it. Not knowing why I had been shaken, I would not be able to explain why it had happened. My parents would take that as both a confession of guilt and an act of insubordination, which would lead them to add to my punishment in some way. So silence was golden, and I was glad that none of my classmates were riding home with us, and I hoped and prayed that none of them would tell their parents, who might then tell mine, leading to even further punishment for not saying anything in the first place.

We Catholic six-year-olds inhabited a complex moral universe, made even more so by the dark closet of confession. By the time we made our first real confession to Father Zeccarello, we had had a dry run in which we knelt in the church pews and waited our turn to enter the confessional, one of us on either side of the priest's door behind which Sister Christopher was playing the role of Father. Once inside we would listen to the muffled voice of the classmate confessing prior to us in the opposite closet, waiting nervously for the sound of the final "In the name of the father, and of the son, and of the holy ghost," a phrase recognizable by its rhythm despite closed doors and thick sound-absorbing curtains. Holding my breath, I heard the opening and closing of the other confessional door. I jumped a bit, startled, as the sliding door scraped open and I beheld the dark visage of Sister Christopher a mere twelve inches away, distorted by the screen that was all that separated us. Her glasses, teeth, and tip of her nose managed to catch and reflect bits of light that sneaked in from under the door, and as she inhaled a squeaking sound came from somewhere in her lungs or sinuses. Rattled, I bought a little time by clearing my throat.

"Bless me, Father, for I have sinned. This is my first confession," I said.

From there, somehow, I knocked my practice confession out of the park. I had planned a couple of serious but not mortal practice sins to confess: "I punched my brother because he wouldn't get off my bed." "Did you hurt him?" Sister asked. "Not really," I said. "He didn't cry, but he punched me back." "Hmmmm." I managed a perfect Act of Contrition, with perfect pronunciation throughout because I had been drilled by my older sister, Jeanine, who had made her first confession two years before and considered herself an expert. When Sister Christopher gave me my penance—three Hail Marys and two Our Fathers—we both crossed ourselves and I reached for the door knob as quickly as I could without seeming clumsy or rude, and when I opened the door of that closet I felt as though I had been liberated from prison like the Count of Monte Cristo in a movie I had seen recently on television. I went back to my pew and said my penance prayers and finally sat back and relaxed, hoping that it was okay to relax while sitting in a church pew.

The moral complexity became more acute when the day finally came to make my first real confession. While my sister and mother and I were getting ready to go to the church that Saturday afternoon, my mother asked, "So, what sins are you going to confess to Father Zeccarello this afternoon?"

I had not anticipated the question. One thing I understood from all of our training was that confession is private, between the confessor and the priest, or, really, God. Sister Christopher had told us that if a murderer confesses his crime to the priest, the priest cannot go to the police and turn him in, because that would break the seal of confession. So it didn't make any sense to me to reveal my sins prior to confession just because my mother was curious. I knew I didn't want to answer her, but I had to say something.

First I thought that perhaps I could make up a couple of little sins. But if I did that, I would have to add lying to my mother to the list of sins that I had planned for Father Zeccarello, and adding one now would probably confuse me and I might leave one of the other ones out, and then I wouldn't be really ready for my first communion the next day because my soul would not be cleansed. If I didn't answer her, though, I would be disobedient, and that would be *another* sin that I would need to add to my list. And because confession was private, and a sacrament, if I told my mother what I was going to say in the confessional, that was probably a sin too, and I would have to remember to tell Father Zeccarello that I had broken the seal of confession before I even made my confession, because my mother asked me what my sins were and I didn't want to lie or disobey.

My mother's question gave me no choice but to sin: lie, disobey, or break the seal of confession. I quickly reasoned that breaking the seal was the most likely to be a mortal sin, so I opted to tell a lie. But just as I was about to open my mouth, Jeanine jumped into the conversation.

"Sister Christopher says that confession is just between you and the priest. You're not allowed to talk about it anywhere else," she said.

My mother said, "I just thought Marty might want to practice."

"I don't think that's allowed," Jeanine said. This may have been the only time in my childhood that I welcomed Jeanine's know-it-all attitude, as it seemed to stop my mother cold.

I said, "I can practice the Act of Contrition, though. Okay?" I recited the prayer, letter-perfect, and we went out to the car for the final ride before the cleansing of my soul. I prayed all the way that we would not crash, leaving me dead before I could confess. I did not want to go to purgatory and have to deal with all the unbaptized babies Sister Christopher had told us would be there.

I can't remember the last time I had thought about Sister Christopher, but she is there, as frightening, large, and imposing as I perceived her when I was a little kid. I try to think of a way to banish these memories from my consciousness—not because they are bad or disturbing, but because I don't need them. I am no longer that person, I have put all of that behind me, and I gratefully acknowledge to myself that we never put our daughters in the position to experience similar fear and confusion. But then another stray thought puts an idea into my mind and I walk down the hallway to the third bedroom, the small one we've used as an office space for when Justine or I work at home. I'm thinking about a worn out briefcase that should be in the closet, and when I find it beneath some other bags and boxes I open it up and find what I'm looking for: an old Catholic missal with the Bible readings for Sunday mass all year round. I open to the first Sunday of Advent.

It starts with Isaiah: "He shall judge among the nations, and shall rebuke many people: and they shall beat their swords into plowshares, and their spears into pruning hooks: nation shall not lift up sword against nation, neither shall they learn war any more."

That was the kind of language that really got me going back in those days, the poetic and prophetic voice of an awe-inspiring God who commands his people to lay down arms and take up tools of creativity and productivity, tools that uphold the commonweal. The voice of this God rose like cream to the top of my vessel of religion and I was compelled to look for a Christian community that tried to live it out.

After I graduated from Montclair I moved to Manhattan, and after several false starts, I found a church that felt right. St. Luke's had a socially and theologically progressive pastor and a congregation that, by and large, bought into his perspective. The parish also had a strong sense of the aesthetic. Mass was serious business at St. Luke's. Celebrated at a deliberate pace, it lasted twice as long as mass at most other churches, and always featured a substantive homily that brought biblical and Catholic teaching to bear on contemporary issues: rampant homelessness, the growing divide between rich and poor, unseemly covert operations in Central America—all worthy targets for socially concerned Christians. There was also a family feeling among the parishioners, and many of them took their cue from the preaching and worked in the parish soup kitchen or collected clothing for the homeless or participated in other, similar initiatives.

The priest around whom it all revolved was Father Steve Rinaldo. He had been a priest for a dozen or so years and had a vigorous and inquisitive mind and a very large heart. He took a somewhat traditional, but not old-fashioned or archaic, approach to the liturgy. He liked incense and bells, good music, and he celebrated the mass with care and precision. Like an actor, he wanted to be present in every moment, even when he was not the focal point. When I was writing occasional articles for a Catholic magazine a few years later I interviewed him about it. "If I'm not actively listening when one of the lay readers is reading the Epistle, then I have no business being called the 'celebrant.' It doesn't matter that I've read that Epistle a thousand times, or that I was up till 3 o'clock the night before dissecting it to prepare my homily. I have to hear it again, anew, even at the risk of having to abandon my prepared sermon notes because a new insight, perhaps brought on by nothing more than a vocal inflection, has taken everything I figured out the night before and made it obsolete."

Even more important than that, though, was the demeanor he expected of a priest, and most especially of himself, while speaking the words of the mass. He told me that he never hesitated to walk out of a mass in which the celebrant mumbled through the Eucharistic Prayer and never took his eye off the script, the ornately bound book of rituals that was always in view on the altar. Off the record, he told me that he didn't care what the church officially said about the efficacy of the sacraments—that the sacraments are valid regardless of the merits or holiness or character of the priest who performs the ritual, or the manner in which it is performed. "Mumbling through a text with your eyes glued to the page does not produce a miracle," he said. "If you played Hamlet that way, you'd get fired."

My spiritual hunger back in those days was fed by these aesthetics and by the ethics of the Sermon on the Mount and Matthew 25 and parables like the Good Samaritan. Today, though, I look back and feel amused at my younger self. So serious and earnest, convinced that humanity's advancement was in some way dependent on a connection to something called "divine"—whether noun or adjective—which human beings have richly imagined for our entire history. We have given it all kinds of names and images. Lacking any evidence of its actual existence, we regard it with more certainty than we do the impermanence of our own physical existence. We have attached to it rules and regulations that exceed the worst kind of bureaucracy, and the penalties for breaking the rules have been radically inhumane and tragic.

At the same time, when it works, it can seem to be the sweetest thing you could ever envision. And when the time comes to give it up, it can be so hard to let it go.

I tuck the missal into the briefcase I take to the office. Our copy of the Sunday Times has been delivered—we've long since given up going out and picking up a copy on Saturday night—so I bring it inside, separate the wheat from the chaff and drop the latter into the recycling bin, and sit down at the kitchen table with coffee, toast, and the book review. I hear the radio come on upstairs in our bedroom and notice that it is eight o'clock. A minute or two later Justine goes into the bathroom and brushes her teeth before coming down to the kitchen. She kisses me on her way to the coffeepot, then sits beside me with her steaming cup.

"You cried the other night," she says. "That was a first."

"No big deal." I try to pretend that I'm willing to talk about it, even though we pointedly avoided the subject all day yesterday.

"It *is* a big deal." She says it in her "mama knows best" tone of voice. I had not merely cried, after all, I had wept, gaspingly, and had fallen asleep in Justine's arms.

"You okay now?" she asks. I hesitate, then shrug. "It's okay if you're not," Justine says. "But I promised you yesterday that I'd hold you to account, so I have to ask."

I acknowledge her by clasping her left hand between mine and kissing her fingers. "Thanks. I understand. There's nothing really to say right now. It was good, though. It was good." I don't need to be the stoic one anymore.

"Did you set the radio alarm last night?" I ask. I never use an alarm—I just wake up at six most mornings whether I want to or not. Justine always has the public radio station come on at eight in the morning. But she hasn't set the alarm since August, letting herself sleep a little longer, sometimes till almost nine, even on workdays. I've often had to wake her up to let her know

I was leaving for work, otherwise I'm not sure she would have gotten up.

"I'm trying to get back on track. Like I said the other day. It's practice for tomorrow morning."

Arise, shine; for thy light is come. More words of Isaiah flash through my mind, but they stop short of the part about the glory of the Lord. I'll stand in the light, I'll glimmer like a sonofagun, but I'll not attach it to the glory of an ancient fiction.

"That's my girl," I say.

"If you've got any more tears that you need to cry, you cry them, okay?"

I nod.

"Promise me."

"Promise you."

After some breakfast and paging through a few sections of the Times, Justine takes a shower and gets dressed. She goes into the spare room, as I had done earlier, and I hear her rummaging around. I can't see what she is carrying when she comes out, but a little while later I go out to the living room. Justine is sitting in her favorite chair, over by the large living room window. Despite a partially cloudy sky, the light is good, and she is sketching on a pad in her lap. A box holding what must be dozens of colored pencils rests on the small table beside her, and though her concentration is fierce she has an easygoing expression on her face.

She continues to draw as I sit across the room with a play script I need to read, but despite the script on my lap I am watching Justine, and she knows I am. Most of her work these days is done on computers, so it's rare to see her so intent on drawing. I can tell she is finished when she stops and puts her pencils back in the box, looks away from the picture and out the window for a few minutes, and then looks again at the drawing. She looks up at me, inviting me with her eyes to come and see.

In just a short time she has made a beautiful picture of Janet and Celia. As I have known since the day we met—it was in fact the first thing I ever knew about her—Justine is very good at likenesses, and this sketch is no exception. Janet and Celia appear in the sketch just as they did last August during our stay at the place we rent near Saratoga every summer. Justine has even indicated the setting by including a plant just like the one that hangs from the porch of the cottage, the leaves spilling over the side of the pot acting as a visual echo of Celia's long light red hair, unruly as Justine's has always been.

I can't find any words at first, but finally I say, "It's a keeper. Please." I can't look at it any longer, not right now, but I don't want Justine to destroy it. I take a few deep breaths, feeling almost like I'm about to hyperventilate, then a few tentative steps away from Justine and the drawing. I point to my wristwatch.

"It's time for me to go up and see Ned." Ned Flynn is more or less retired now, except for the occasional New York television job and summer theater adventures that get him and his wife, Molly, out of the city during the hottest months. Every weekend in the fall I have a standing appointment to go to his apartment and watch the New York Giants football game with him. "They play today at one," I remind Justine.

I go to the closet and take out my jacket, not sure how cold it is outside or whether I'll be warm enough, but it doesn't matter, I'll manage. I stand in the open door and tell Justine, "I'll be home right after the game. I promise." She straightens my jacket collar and we kiss, and I leave, and Justine closes the door behind me as I walk to the elevator, and I'm certain that an afternoon with my unusual old friend will bring everything back to normal.

I walk toward Central Park. From there it's a pleasant walk of about ten blocks up to Ned's place. I take my iPod from my pocket. Tiny as it is, it holds music I've been carrying around for at least thirty years. I put the buds in my ears and set the device to play at random. The first selection to come up is the finale of Bach's Mass in B Minor, "Dona Nobis Pacem." Give us peace. I don't know whether it is the music or the cold gusts of wind that brings tears to my eyes, but the tears have returned. Then the iPod makes an abrupt shift in genre, if not subject, by playing "Peace in the Valley," sung by Johnny Cash and the Carter family.

I know better than to wonder if the universe, much less my iPod, is trying to tell me something. With eight thousand or so songs to choose from, it is bound to occasionally play some religion-inspired music, but it'll be no surprise if Cash is followed by some very secular Led Zeppelin or George Carlin. But I am struck by how, although I gave up religion some twenty years ago, I never came close to letting go of its aesthetic. My life is better without gods and dogmas and institutional hierarchies built on shame and power. But my life is also improved by the artful presence of Bach's *Mass in B Minor* and Johnny Cash singing tunes from his mother's hymnbook. Memories of singing Randall Thompson's *Alleluia* and Vivaldi's *Gloria* in high school choir probably did as much to turn me back toward religion when I was a young man as any desire for community or structure. Whether I believe in the religious tenets that underlie those works of art is immaterial.

It struck me, at some moment in my early years with Justine, that religion is essentially about human yearning. Take away the rules and regulations, the personalities and saints and scriptures, and religion is about yearning to make sense of the world and our place in it. It's about finding one's own meaning—not one imposed from the outside—by finding answers to the questions, Who am I in this world, and how can I make it matter that I am here? Discussion of religiosity is necessarily limited by the religions that we know—to their outer trappings and beliefs rather than to the drive to find meaning. Take away

God and dogmas and rituals, get to the heart of it, and it comes down to being completely and radically human. And contrary to what is taught by the religion I have studied and practiced most, I don't think it's possible to be radically human if we are dependent for meaning on something we set apart as divine and transcendent.

I have only to think of Janet and Celia when they were babies. With just the rudiments of language, and certainly no understanding of concepts like God, they reached. And reached and reached, physically, relationally, conceptually. The answers to their reaching questions were baby answers, though. Eventually they had to get beyond their infant understandings of everything from how their bodies work to what happens when the sun sets and when people die.

That was the hardest question for Justine and me to answer—What happens when people die?—because by the time we started hearing that question I had joined Justine in rejecting the answers that religions give. We were almost willing to hedge our bets and give them a multiple-choice answer, but we opted to tell them straight how we saw it. Other parents, we were told by our daughters, had such *interesting* answers. "Death is the end, and we are left with our memories of those who have died" doesn't hold a candle to heaven or reincarnation, especially when embellished with angelic harp players or speculation about being Cleopatra in a previous life. Endlessness is very appealing. Janet used to get angry at the idea that anything had to die, but she was always a scientist and even when she was little would rather take a magnifying glass and study the bug—dead or alive—on the sidewalk than speculate on its ultimate fate. Celia just thought death was a stupid idea, but once she started drawing everything in sight she had nothing more to say about it.

Ned Flynn has always been a staunch but good-humored Irish Catholic—as consistent in his faith as in his acting career.

We started our tradition of football on Sundays not long after Stuart Spender died. The extra chair by the television in Ned's apartment had long been Stuart's on Sunday unless Ned was working or out of town. But as Stuart's final illness advanced, Ned and I found a common bond as we witnessed the death of the man who was his oldest and best friend and most valued business associate, and my friend and mentor. Their relationship was spiced by the fact that, in terms of New York sports, they were opposites—Ned is all about the football Giants and the baseball Yankees. Stuart was a Jets and Mets man.

Ned is an ebullient fan, but this season he has been subdued. I have no doubt that he is showing respect to me, allowing me to set the level of enthusiasm. He was doing summer theater in Grand Rapids, Michigan in July and August, fulfilling a promise to an old director friend to play Norman in *On Golden Pond*, and stayed on to play Erronius in *A Funny Thing Happened on the Way to the Forum*. When that ended, he and Molly went to the Upper Peninsula for a couple of weeks of fly-fishing at a remote fishing camp, so it was late September before we watched our first Giants game of the season together. By that time we hadn't seen each other since June, and had spoken only briefly to check in on business matters. By now, though, we are back to our usual easy, if not rowdy, way of watching football together.

Ned is a sharp observer, though, and I can tell by the way he looks at me that he sees something different about me, and that he has located it in the area around my eyes. He says nothing about it, but I suppose he has tucked the thought away and awaits the right moment, if it comes, to mention it.

Molly is in the kitchen. I can smell the gourmet pizza she is preparing, which she makes for us from scratch, crust and all. She hovers around the apartment while Ned and I watch the game. She is not interested in football, but she gets a kick out of watching Ned watch the game. They've known each other since they were teenagers in Boston, and Molly says that watching sports make Ned seem like a kid again.

At the end of the first half the Giants are ahead by a field goal. Ned gets up to go to the bathroom, and as he walks back to his chair he looks me straight in the eye. As he sits again he mutes the television and gazes at me.

"I hope you're all right," he says.

"Coping," I say.

"Is that enough? Coping?"

"It's what I've got. This stuff, you know—it comes and it goes."

"You're lucky, you know, like me," he says. "You've got a great gal to help you get through. How's she doing? You should bring her next week, I know she doesn't go for football at all, but I'd love to see her. It's been a while. Months. Not since that ballgame on Staten Island, you know?" The four of us had gone to a minor league baseball game together in June, before Ned and Molly left for Michigan. He continues, "I'm still so sorry Molly and I couldn't be here, in August, for you two. The circumstances—"

I breathe and nod and say, "You're here now. The last couple days have been lots of up and down. Thanksgiving, the holidays, all that. But Justine's a rock right now, like it's okay now for me to get shaky and pathetic."

"Pathetic. What a word. There's nothing pathetic in any of this."

We are silent for a while. Molly is back in the kitchen, and I guess she has stopped whatever she was doing so she could hear our conversation.

"Do you ever have doubts?" Ned asks.

"About what?"

"You know—doubts about giving up the faith. That could be the rock you need, the rock you and Justine both need. It's brought me, you know, a lot of comfort when I've needed it. A lot of peace. You know, like when Stuart died, when you lose a friend like that. Or a couple other actor friends who've passed over the years, and my parents years and years ago." He stares at the wall for minute. "God forbid I should outlive Molly, I don't know how I'd—but that's not what I'm talking about. You know, I do think, saying a prayer, offering it up, thinking about Jesus and his sacrifice on the cross—it can help, it's just, I don't know, intangible, but it can help."

In my peripheral vision I see Molly has poked her head out of the kitchen and into the living room, but then quickly pulled back. She is as likely to join in and support Ned's line of thought as she is to tell him to mind his own business. We have argued, jovially, about the Catholic church before, the three of us, never with any bad blood, but this is the first time it has come up in quite a while, and I'm not sure how to respond. I know that Ned's intentions are good and that he and Molly are sincere, but I'm uncomfortable with the direction of the conversation.

"It's been a long time, Ned, twenty years," I say, stating the obvious to avoid having to think or say anything substantive. "I've burned that bridge."

"It's not a bridge that can be burned. That's the kind of faith I have."

"Burned or not, it's a bridge I do not want to re-cross."

"It could help, though. You need to come to terms. God can help you come to terms."

"I don't think there are terms to come to. I'd have to wonder about myself if I could come to terms with the worst kind of loss. And you know, because I have told you before, that I'm not merely indifferent to God. I actively do not believe in, do not accept the reality of, such a being. I am an atheist. I'm not capable of believing. Not anymore. Maybe I never was, despite what I thought I believed."

I look at the TV and notice that the second half has started. "They're three minutes into the half already, and we're sitting here yapping."

Ned looks at me and reaches forward, putting his hand on mine. Though he is my father's age, he seems more like a grandfather at this moment. "This is important, Marty."

I take a deep breath and shrug as I exhale.

"You know, Marty, I remember something you said, way back when we first met. The first time we ever talked about the Catholic stuff." Ned pauses, perhaps for effect. "Stuart was there, in that old office of his, back before you re-did the whole place. You said that you had an abiding sense of God in your life. An abiding sense of God. I thought that was marvelous, a marvelous thing for a young man to say. What happened to that?"

I close my eyes for a moment and consider. "I would name it differently today. An abiding sense of love, creativity, yearning—these are human attributes, truly human, ineffably human, without the unverifiable 'divine' and all the baggage and institutional folderol that come with that. Whatever it is that's abiding, though, well, I'd say it *does* sustain me still. But it doesn't come from somewhere out there. It's not magic or grace or a sacrament. It's part of how we're made, as human beings."

Molly steps into the room, a glass of Guinness in each hand. "Ned," I say, "I'm not trying to come to terms with anything. Like I said—there just may not be terms to come to. No script, no contract or ritual that sets it right. I can only keep going, day after day, no matter what each day brings. That— *that* is what I've come to terms with."

Molly rests our glasses on the coffee table and takes the remote and unmutes the TV. "You gents get back to your game, huh?" Her voice is just above a whisper but her tone is authoritative. She knows that Ned and I will not get into a knock-down-drag-out argument over this, that neither of us would ever let our differences bring us to that. Still, she thinks the conversation has gone its limit. Molly is a blessed peacemaker, and the Guinness is good.

Ned re-mutes the sound, though, and takes a thoughtful sip from his pint. He says, "You must consider me nothing but a naïve old coot, still believing what I was taught as a child, seeking comfort in God, in Jesus and his mother." His tone is resigned, not confrontational, and his voice trails off. He stares down into the dark liquid in his glass before glancing over at a small but detailed crèche on the end table beside him—a traditional depiction of Mary, Joseph, and the infant Jesus, the Holy Family that is so dear to him, especially at this time of year.

I look at the space between Ned and the crèche and feel a sharp sudden twinge of heartbreak, unrelated to Ned's lifelong devotion, but I force my attention quickly back to what he has just said. If I were so inclined I would tell him that yes, he may be naïve, but that has not stopped him from maximizing the creative impulse that is at his core and transcends faith's artifice. In his life and work this impulse seems not to have been buried or suffocated by the institutions and dogmas that guard the tenets of his faith. I would have to say that he is lucky in this way—I can see now that when I was younger, and quite naïve, those artifices inhibited forward movement in my career and personal life.

That says more about me than about him, I would tell Ned, but I can see only from where I am now standing.

I would say to Ned that Jesus and his fatherly God are brilliant creations, made by humans just as Hamlet and Athena and Don Quixote were, and if we understood them in the same terms as these counterparts I would be willing to wager that our lives would become more vital. If I could, I would tell him that I deeply fear the manipulation of naïve populations by the worst kind of true believers, the ones who play games with others' credulity simply for their own gain. Televangelists. Politicians. Corrupt priests and bishops. I would remind him, You've played them all on TV or in the movies, you know who I'm talking about.

I would admit to him, if I could say it without it being hurtful to him, that on balance I think religion is malevolent and that humanity's prospects are diminished by its influence.

I would say, if I could form the words in my mouth, that I am enthralled with being a physical, temporary, infinitesimal blip on the radar of the universe, forced by circumstance to construct meaning in whatever way I am able, free of the constraints of alleged absolutes drawn from tenacious but flawed sources of understanding.

But I can't say any of this to Ned in this moment. Instead I say, "Ned, my whole life is centered on how people act, not on their beliefs. On stage or off, you've earned a standing ovation."

We focus on the game for the rest of the afternoon. Though it is exciting and is not decided until the final thirty seconds, my attention is as much inward as outward. Ned has opened a line of thought that had not really occurred to me before. I have never thought of the possibility of doubting my unbelief, of re-cloaking my temporal reality in webs of myths of everlastingness. How convenient that would be . . . and I am glad when the time comes to leave and I step outside into the cold. I try to focus on the sounds of the city as I walk the blocks to Justine and home, but Ned's idea nags like a pinched nerve in a vertebra. I am relieved when I open my front door to the aroma of baking bread and the offer of white wine, the glass held out to me by the pale skilled tender hand of my wife.

Wednesday

For anyone who has lived in New York City, or any city, for as long as I have, there is hardly a corner or block or neighborhood that fails to inhabit some piece of memory. I have been up and down this city, and across it and back, more times than I could begin to count. I have walked, driven, cabbed, bused, bicycled, and subwayed my way to shops, theatres, museums, rehearsal halls, and apartments all over this town for decades. No matter where I am, especially if I am alone, these memories find me—they peek out from behind park benches, jump out from dark doorways. They give off aromas, like the stale beer I smell as I walk past an upscale restaurant that was, before gentrification, a smoky dive in which camaraderie came easy and killing a thirst was cheap.

There is a street in the East Village that I avoid except for one day of the year—today. One day many years ago—I'm not sure how long, but Janet was little and Celia had not been born yet—I turned the corner onto this street and felt the presence, palpable and unmistakable, of a young actor I had worked with on my first acting job in New York. We were young idealistic actors, and he was good. The undiscovered real thing—that kind of good. His name was Daniel. Not Dan or Danny. Daniel. He had a dark and wild side that was tempered by a sweet vulnerability, and he made the character he played, in the forgettable two-man, one-act play in which we had both been cast, a multidimensional sympathetic being who was so much better than the words on the pages of the script could ever indicate on their own. Everyone—the director, the writer, me—was lifted and made better by Daniel's excellence. We performed the play six times over two weekends in September, in an empty East Village storefront temporarily converted into a theatre-like space, and after the cast party I never saw him again.

A half a year or so later I heard that he was dead, that he had been walking quietly down Broadway on a cold evening in December when a yellow cab's brakes failed. The car jumped the curb onto the sidewalk and hit him, and a couple of other pedestrians, from behind. The others survived, but Daniel was killed instantly. I did not hear about his death until a few months after the fact, when his name came up in a conversation with mutual acquaintances. I never knew the exact date, just that it was sometime in the middle of December. And then several years after that—my life had changed greatly since that first job, and I was a husband and father and a talent agent, no longer an actor—I was in the East Village on a December afternoon, running an errand that I don't even remember, walking along absent-mindedly, and I felt Daniel's presence. I can only describe the feeling as an actor's rush, the rush of being on stage and connecting on all cylinders, which was how I would describe my experience of working with Daniel. I stopped cold and looked around. I peered down the street toward the intersection and the street signs. I wasn't even sure how far I had walked since getting off the subway, but I realized then that the cigar and tobacco shop I was standing in front of was the store in which Daniel and I had done that play years before.

I couldn't move. I was stunned. I looked through the window of the tobacco shop and could vaguely see the figure of a man reaching up to a high shelf. As I slowly regained the ability to move, I stepped closer to the window and peered in. Then, gathering as many of my wits as I could find, I pulled the door open and walked in.

The man inside didn't say anything at first. I looked around, trying to disguise the fact that I had no interest in the merchandise. My only interest was to confirm that this was actually the place. The man—the owner of the shop, as it turned out—finally asked if I needed any help.

"No," I said, "I'm just looking—well, really, not looking, but I think, back when I was an actor, I did a play in here? Is that possible, say nine years ago?"

"That's before my time, but quite possible. When I bought the building the storefronts were mainly abandoned except for the newsstand on the corner. That's five years or so now. Before that the owners did lots of short-terms leases, so I wouldn't be surprised, I heard this shop was even an illicit strip club for a while. Part of the reason I got it so cheap, I guess."

"Can I—just take a look in the back?" I asked.

"Knock yourself out." He gestured toward the doorway behind the counter.

It didn't take long to confirm that this was the place—the double-rows of high windows with distinctive storm glass and a narrow stairway to the basement were the main giveaways. I went back out to the front of the store.

"It's definitely the same place," I said. "Thanks for letting me nose around."

"Well, it's a tobacco shop. Nosing around is standard operating procedure. Can I interest you in a sample? A nice cigar?"

"Thanks, no. It would be wasted on me. Sorry. I never developed the taste." I took a business card from a stack next to the cash register. "I have a few friends who are connoisseurs, though. I'll tell them you're here."

Back outside I noticed, across the street, a flower shop. I crossed slowly and went inside. I wasn't sure what I was looking for. The girl behind the counter asked if she could help me, and I heard myself say, "Petals? Rose petals? Any flower—to scatter, to mark a spot." She looked at me like I was potentially dangerous and went through the door to the back of the store. I shifted my position so I could see where she had gone. She was scooping loose petals from a workbench onto a sheet of waxed paper. Then she folded it carefully and came back out to the front and held it out toward me.

I took them. "Thank you. What do I owe you?" She just shook her head and didn't say anything. A phone rang in the back and she disappeared again, so I left a couple of dollars on the counter and went back across the street.

Trying to look as though there was nothing unusual about what I was doing, I scattered the petals on the sidewalk in front of the tobacco shop doorway and then leaned against a lamp post for few minutes watching the breeze catch them, watching other pedestrians walk through them. Finally I continued on my way, trying to cast away the feelings of the last several minutes the way a dog shakes off snowflakes.

Later, at home—Janet was asleep and Justine was heating up a late dinner for me—I told Justine about what had happened. She said, "Your body remembered. Even if you didn't consciously, your body did." She was more pragmatic than I was back then. It made sense that she would demystify the experience. I must have had a puzzled look on my face. Justine looked at me closely and said, "You don't want to believe it was a ghost, do you?" There are no such things as ghosts, I knew that, and such things had never been part of my own religiosity. But the idea that my *body* remembered was almost as strange as a ghost. As I thought about it, though, Justine's notion appealed to me much more than the idea of a ghost, or even some sort of "cosmic connection," ever could. It suggested a more elemental bond between two human beings than can be signified by something as trite as a ghost or as vague a purported spiritual intersection.

Daniel was dead, after all, and had been dead for a number of years, and my sole bond to him had been the very satisfying work we had done together behind the doors of what was now a nondescript tobacco shop in the East Village.

"Yes," I said to Justine. "That must be it. My body remembered."

Every year since, on this December day, I come again to this spot. I have never told anyone, not even Justine, about this little annual ritual. The tobacco shop and florist are long gone, and I barely notice from year to year what has taken their places. I pick up a bagful of flower petals at a shop in my neighborhood uptown, or near my office, and then make my way here by cab or subway. This afternoon I have taken the subway, and brace myself for the cold as I come up the steps from underground to walk the rest of the way.

Coming here every year has served as a *memento mori*, a reminder of the reality of death, of the necessity to grasp hold of each moment we have and make the most of it. If there is one thing I learned from—and sometimes in spite of—the theologians I read and studied, it is that the best thing we can do with death is to know it, own it, and let its reality and inevitability make more vital and essential human beings out of us.

Eight or ten months after Janet was born I audited a graduate course in theology at Fordham. It focused on the paschal mystery, the death and resurrection of Jesus, which is celebrated daily in the holy eucharist. When the professor, an engaging but tradition-minded priest in his sixties, broke down the mystery into its component parts I saw that the dynamic demonstrated by the story of Jesus' death and resurrection was universal. Stripped of its dogmatic associations—that it proves that Jesus was God, or that it was the ransom paid by God, to himself, to redeem humanity from the sin of Adam and Eve—I began to see this dynamic of new life through death everywhere. Almost, literally, on every street corner, in any place or situation in which loss is the precursor of growth, no matter how elaborate or mundane.

The religious and institutional ramifications of the Christian version of new life through death are significant. It is the basis for the establishment of the church and its traditions, its claims to authority, and its actions, for better and worse. But it is an everyday dynamic, not limited to Holy Week and Easter Sunday, try as the church might to corner the market. Whether a death is literal or figurative—some "little death" like loss or failure—this dynamic is working every day. We speak axiomatically of learning from our mistakes. Nietzsche said, "That which doesn't kill me, makes me stronger." Ernest Hemingway wrote of being stronger in the broken places. The characters in Shakespeare's comedies, like the runaway lovers in *A Midsummer Night's Dream* and the exiles is *As You Like It*, are always in peril and skirt the edges of death, only to come through it newly minted, reinvented. Shakespeare's tragedies tend to end in bloodbaths, but the resulting catharsis takes the viewer of the play back out into the world, in theory at least, with a new perspective on life.

The professor of theology who opened this all up to me wanted to make the point, through the paschal mystery, that Christ is unique and universal—his is a story that applies to all lives at all times and makes the Christian faith the supreme faith. Instead, it struck me that the Christ story is a great archetype but in no way is it the one and only, or even the superlative, expression of this dynamic. Something clicked one day, and in that moment I began to feel that the professor's claim of the supremacy of Christ's suffering, death, and resurrection had taken a turn toward the exclusion of any who chose not to believe in the Christ he described. I flashed back to my days in Georgia—the experience of being marginalized and manipulated—and raised my hand.

"What you're saying about Christ," I said, "if I'm following correctly, is that his experience of death and rebirth was unique, even supreme. But that's a common everyday experience—growing through loss."

"Coming back from the dead is a common everyday experience?" It wasn't the professor who had spoken, but a guy named Brian, a seminarian with a superiority complex and a taste for the literal. He was about my age.

"No, I'm talking about growing through loss—making something new, or renewed, out of circumstances of brokenness—that's the paschal mystery in everyday terms. I'd rather call it the paschal dynamic, though, it's a driving force, a universal reality. It's not mysterious at all, really, but it can be literally painful." I laughed, suddenly uncomfortable with the possibility that this conversation might start to center on me—not even enrolled as a graduate student, more of a curiosity seeker, sitting in this room with the help of connections from people I had met through Stuart. Everyone in the room was looking straight at me, though, so I dove in. "What I mean is that the story of Jesus is not about the suffering, this grand bloody experience that we sinful humans somehow caused. It's a picture of how life happens. Being fully human, incarnate, in the flesh, in the meat, which is what the word *incarnate* means, like *carnivore*, requires growth, and growth requires loss and pain. Every one of us is a product of pain, of death."

"Pain and death are the result of sin," someone said.

"That's arguable, but it's not what I'm talking about. Not sin. Loss. Pain. Death's best friend. Ten months ago I watched with a combination of awe and horror as my wife screamed and pushed our baby girl out of her body. That's the paschal mystery for you, and it happens a million times a day. Sexuality. Procreation. The paschal mystery resides there, too. It's probably where we're the most human—vulnerable, creative, alive."

I was formulating my thinking as I spoke and wasn't sure if I was making any sense. The seminarian spoke again, aghast. "You're comparing the suffering of Christ to a woman giving birth?"

"Sure. Jesus does, so I guess I can, too. In the gospel of John, Jesus says, 'A woman, when she is in labor, has sorrow because her hour has come; but as soon as she has given birth to the child, she no longer remembers the anguish, for joy that a human being has been born into the world.' That's Jesus himself making the comparison, or at least someone writing about Jesus and putting words in his mouth. He's describing a clear example of what I've been calling the paschal dynamic."

"Jesus was innocent, sinless. He suffered horrendously for our sake. We should never forget that."

There was an awkward silence, but I said, "What's this pre-occupation with sin all about? And Jesus, innocent? Really? He spent his ministry flipping the bird at the established leaders of his time, religious and civil. If he wasn't aware that there might be consequences, he was worse than innocent, he was painfully naïve."

Brian, the seminarian, seemed fixated on the suffering of Jesus. "A death on the cross, crucifixion, was a brutal punishment. The pain, the blood he spilled, to atone for our sins—"

I couldn't let him finish. "A few hours—whipped, tortured, an awful death, yes. But did you ever notice how *little* the gospel writers say about that? Hardly anything. Statements of fact, but nothing that by itself could have inspired the pornographic violence depicted on crosses like that one." I pointed to the crucifix front and center in the classroom, above the chalkboard, its body of Christ both erotic—buff physique and smooth skin— and gruesomely dead. I noticed as a few students reached for the same symbol dangling around their necks. "Where does all that grisly imagery come from? I don't know, but I don't see it in the gospels. I don't think that was the most important thing for the communities that wrote those books. Yeah, an awful death, crucifixion. What about a child born in a third-world county, malnourished, life-expectancy four years, the whole time hungry and in pain, and never even learned enough language to say the names of the authorities that kept the food from its mouth? Thousands upon thousands of children die that death every day around the world."

"The expiation of our sins required that Jesus suffer and die for us so that God could raise him up. And we must believe if we are to be redeemed."

There was another silence. The professor looked around the room as if to see if anyone else had anything to add, then he looked at me. I said, "Well, Brian, the whole atonement thing is starting to look pretty shaky to me the more you say about it. I guess Jesus speaks to me more effectively when his life, death, and resurrection serve as a metaphor that demonstrates how to deal with our mortality and losses. I don't think *Jesus* saves us so much as the *story* of Jesus saves us. It's a redemptive, cathartic story. But if you demand that I believe the story is literally true then you're telling me to believe in a freak of nature."

"A freak of nature?" Brian nearly shrieked.

"I don't believe in magic. People don't come back to life, fully human or otherwise."

"And fully divine. The risen Christ was a transformed being, not a walking corpse." Brian stood up as he spoke and gestured emphatically. "His disciples saw him, spoke to him, touched him. God is capable of miracles, and this is the highest of them all."

"That's what the stories say, yes," I said.

The professor suggested that Brian sit back down, then said, "There are obviously many ways to view the death and resurrection of Jesus Christ."

"And some are heretical," Brian said.

"And some," I said, "are so fanciful and highfalutin as to have nothing to do with life as we know it."

"Well," the professor said, "perhaps we can use this discussion as an invitation to look at some high and low Christological ideas." The final ten minutes of class were taken up by his preview of the chapters we were expected to read before the next class.

I am thinking about all of this as I walk west along the Seventh Street side of Tompkins Square Park. New life through death, the paschal dynamic. Jesus saves. No, not Jesus, but the story of Jesus, saves. Not even that, but the dynamic that the story of Jesus shows us is the trajectory of energy we need to embrace if we are to stay vital and sane in a crazy fragile here-one-minute gone-the-next kind of world in which very little is under our control—tectonic plates, the weather, the orbits of asteroids, the growth of cancer cells—and most of what we have learned to control, through reason or technology, is one breakdown away from potential madness.

And death, death. *Memento mori*. Without death there is no life. It doesn't take high science or math to figure out that once there is a plant, the seed is no more. The babies that we once were exist now only in our parents' memories. I have guided careers of actors for decades now, have seen dreams dry up and die knowing that the only thing I could hold out to those clients was the hope that something new was inevitable and that I would do what I could to enable them to discover and manage what that would be.

But death, real human death, the death of a loved one, a dear one—the promise of most religions, that there will be something after death, a heaven or a transmigration to a new body, do nothing but agitate me. I find them, at least, trite and blindly hopeful, the inventions of people who somehow had not grasped the very trajectory that, in Christianity at least, is demonstrated by the narrative of the death and resurrection of Jesus. Today as I walk I hear myself breathing hard, aggressively, at the thought of these fancies being promoted by the very churches that claim ownership of texts that reveal, once the archaic rhetoric is put aside, that we have this life and this life only. My anger rises at a culture so imbued, so entrenched, with the false promises that, although I have rejected them, still gnaw at me, tempting me to give in to the counterfeit ease they offer in the face of unimaginable tragedy.

I have been walking with tunnel vision, or not even that, because I don't remember anything that I passed as I walked, I don't remember waiting for traffic to break before crossing streets, but I see that I am at Astor Place, the corner of Lafayette Street, so I stop to look around. I don't need to get my bearings, but I do need to figure out where I am going. My gaze feels pulled toward the south, toward Soho, and I turn and walk down Lafayette. When I reach Third Street I realize where it is my feet are taking me. It was called The Mercer Stage back then. It seated about two hundred and fifty audience members and had a quirky thrust stage and ancient wiring that drove master electricians crazy. But it was a respected venue artistically, even if its structural imperfections made every production even more of an adventure than it already was.

A client or two had worked there ten years or so ago, and that is the last time I can remember being there. It was still called Mercer then, and may still be now, and I shake my head at this lapse in my knowledge—which I take as a sure sign that I need to get closer to the ground in my work, that being the boss to so many associate agents has put me at too far a distance from the actual theatre life in New York. I curse this as I walk, adding it to religion, theologians and their obsolete discipline, and promises of life after death, as objects of my present anger. I look carefully to the left and right as I cross Houston Street into Soho and halfway across the intersection I begin to wonder why I am walking in the cold as dusk falls toward The Mercer Stage, in the opposite direction of office or home, and then it comes to me.

The Mercer Stage is where I met the decidedly non-theatrical and irreligious Justine Damont, and on this dark day I'm feeling the need to encounter a happy place on memory lane.

It was a Monday evening, in that small theatre in Soho, where I was rehearsing for one of my rare acting jobs. I had been working for Stuart for nearly three years as associate agent. A buddy of mine from Montclair, Hal Mooney, had been hired to direct an off-off-Broadway production of Kurt Vonnegut's play *Happy Birthday, Wanda June*. Hal had been working with a comedy troupe in Chicago but decided to take a break from that and come back to New York when a quirky theatre company in New York made him the offer. Hal and I had always been big fans of Vonnegut, so when the time came to cast the show he asked me if I had any clients I would like to pitch to him. I did, and two of our actors were eventually offered roles. When I attended the last of the audition sessions, Hal took me aside during a break.

"Marty, I'm not coming up with anyone I like for Herb Shuttle." Shuttle is a thirty-five year-old vacuum cleaner salesman and a somewhat inept suitor to the leading lady, Penelope Ryan, whose ultra-macho husband, Harold, has been missing for several years.

It was short notice, but I thought I might be able to get another actor over to audition for Hal. "Let me call in to the office—I've got a couple of ideas. We'll see what we can do."

"No," Hal said. "Why don't you read it?"

I would normally have said no, no way, not today or ever, I am done with acting, but I had vivid memories of the times I had worked with Hal, whether in acting classes or actual productions, and what a it blast it had been.

"Give me the script," I said.

Wanda June was a part-time job. Three weeks of rehearsal at odd hours in out-of-the-way studios, until the final week when, starting on Sunday afternoon, we worked on the actual stage while the set—a contemporary apartment worthy of a wealthy man—was maneuvered into place around us. I was sitting with Hal when we broke for lunch the Sunday before opening night. The set designer, a guy named James de Grasse, walked by. Hal called to him and he came over.

"What about the portrait of Harold?" The set includes a large portrait of Harold Ryan, the leading male character. Two weeks before, James had taken a couple of Polaroid pictures of Kevin, the actor playing Harold, to use to create the portrait.

"Tomorrow night," James said. "It took longer than I expected, but I found this chick over at SVA to do it for the pittance we could pay. She'll be here tomorrow at four or so. Wants to put the finishing touches on with the actual model in the room, not just the Polaroids. I asked Kevin, he said he could be here."

Hal looked thoughtful. "So is it any good?"

"I'll tell you tomorrow night. But I saw the chick's portfolio. She's talented." James ran backstage, where it sounded as though an argument among crew members had broken out. Hal rolled his eyes.

"Last minute. What would a show be without every goddam thing coming down to the last minute?"

Hal had a case of the jitters, so I mentioned that I thought everything was going quite well. "The cast is gelling, the set is coming along—by Thursday night I think everything will be shipshape for opening night. Stop being so anxious."

"Okay, Pollyanna," Hal said. "You've been behind the scenes for a few years now. Wait till opening night and we'll see which of us makes the most trips to the bathroom."

He was right—being on stage stressed me like nothing else in the world, and though I was confident I would make it through the eight performances of *Wanda June*, the experience would probably confirm that my calling was not to be in shows but to put far better actors than me into the position to excel at what they do.

The next day I arrived at the theatre just before five o'clock for rehearsal. In the lobby, where bright daylight streamed through the floor-to-ceiling entry doors and windows, Kevin, the actor who was playing Harold, was posing for a young woman standing at an easel that held a painting that must have been about four feet high. The image was not so much a likeness of the actor as it was of Harold—the painter had captured his menacing swagger along with the pretension that fed it. I stood behind the painter, at a respectful distance, I hoped, so as not to distract her, and watched.

I hadn't seen the painter's face yet, but her long, unruly, strawberry-blonde hair cascaded over her shoulders and half-way down her back. It had been an unseasonably cool day for May, and she was wearing a loose-fitting grey sweatshirt and a pair of jeans that fit snugly but not too tight and accentuated the very nice shape of her hips and bottom. She turned her head to look at Kevin, and I caught a brief glimpse of her pro-file, then she turned back to the painting and made a couple of subtle adjustments around Harold's eyes. She took a wider brush and played with the colors on her palette for a moment before applying a wash to the background around Harold's head. After several strokes she took a narrow brush and cor-rected the color closer to the outline of Harold's face. The new background brought greater contrast to Harold's facial features and made it almost seem as though he was about to walk out of the painting.

Fascinated, I stepped a little closer just as the painter took a step or two back. Her heel landed on my toe and as we both jumped she turned toward me and her bright hazel eyes, star-tled by the sudden contact, flashed in my direction and then she smiled. "Sorry," she said.

"My fault," I said, catching my breath. Standing beside and slightly behind her now, I gestured toward the painting. "It's great," I said. "It's Harold." If you had told me then that this was the first of countless times I would look over this woman's shoulder and comment on her art, or that I would look over the shoulder of our daughter Celia for the same reason, I would not have believed you, I could not have imagined it possible.

"Well, I think it's done," she said.

"Not a moment too soon for Hal," I said.

"The director?" she asked.

"Yeah."

"I figured you were him."

"No, I'm in the cast," I said.

We were interrupted by Kevin, who had walked away from his pose to look at the painting. After a glance, he said to the painter, "Am I done?" She nodded and thanked him and he left to get ready for rehearsal.

She started cleaning up and putting away her paints and brushes. I should have gone into the theatre but I lingered. "So who do you play?" she asked.

"Herb Shuttle."

She laughed, suddenly and boisterously, at the name. "He told me to take a flying fuck at the moon," she said, reciting Shuttle's best line from the play. "Vonnegut. I just love Vonnegut," she said. "I sure as hell didn't paint this for the money."

"Well," I said, "I hear you on that. My name is Martin Halsey." I extended my hand a little awkwardly.

She took my hand and shook it firmly. "Justine Damont. Nice to meet you."

Her smile was disarming as her eyes and lightly glossed lips seemed to catch and throw back the late afternoon sunlight that shone through the high windows of the lobby. I stumbled over an attempt to say something, then found my tongue again and said, "Do you—need help getting this inside?" I pointed uncertainly at the painting.

"Great. Yeah. Thanks." I started to gather up paint tubes. She said, "I'll get the easel and the rest of that stuff on my way out. Maybe you could just—carry the painting into the theatre." It was not so big that we needed both of us to move it, so I carried it while Justine made sure I didn't bump into anything.

Inside, Hal and James and the other cast and crew members who were already there gathered around. Hal was relieved and nearly ecstatic when he saw the painting, while James looked at him as if Hal's doubt was both a personal and professional affront to him. "It's not quite dry," Justine said, "so be careful. It's acrylic. It won't take long." James insisted on taking the painting somewhere away from dust and other potential hazards. "We'll hang it in its place tomorrow," he said.

I had lost contact with Justine in the crowd of actors and crew, so I stepped apart in order to get a sense of where she might go next so that I could get there first. As she headed toward the door to the lobby I got into her path and suggested I give her a hand with her easel and paints. Hal Mooney called out for everyone to hear, "Let's get started, people, find your places and let's get going. Our goal tonight is a full run-through, no stops."

I acted as though I was not among those being addressed. As I folded the easel I said, "Are you going to stay and catch the rehearsal? The show is really looking good."

"I can't," she said. "But they gave me a pass for opening night. I've got a school project to finish tonight if I want to graduate."

"School of Visual Arts, right?"

"Yup."

Hal Mooney stepped into the lobby and looked around. When he saw me talking to Justine he turned around and went back in. "Just a couple more minutes and we'll get this show on the road, people," he said, purposely loud enough for me to hear him.

"I guess you better get to work," Justine said.

"Yeah. I guess. But, listen, my office is not far from SVA, just a few of those long blocks to the east—maybe we could meet for lunch? Tomorrow?" I surprised myself by being so forward and direct—it was out of character for me, but this girl was compelling.

"Umm. Okay. You have an office? Sure. What time?"

I had no set schedule, and I was ready to shape my day to fit hers, but I decided to sound as though my window of opportunity was narrow. "One-thirty would be best."

"Sure. Do you know the Primrose Coffee Shop? Twenty-third and Sixth?"

I fished a business card out of my wallet and handed it to her. "Primrose. One o'clock."

She read the card. "I'll be there. You're a talent agent, huh?"

"That's my real job. Here I'm just having fun working with my friend Hal again."

"Break a leg, Martin." Laden with the easel and a tackle box of brushes and paint, she headed toward the door.

"See you tomorrow, Justine. Good luck with your project."

Hal bellowed, "Places, *now*, people." I bolted into the theatre without another word.

When we stopped for the first intermission Hal gave us notes and an extra five-minute break. With a Groucho-style leer accompanied by rapid movement of his eyebrows, he pulled me aside and said, "Marty likey the painter-girl, huh?"

"I'm meeting her for lunch tomorrow."

"Smooth."

"Yeah, you know me. A regular Casanova."

"Break a leg. Places!"

Lunch started with coffee. "The strongest you've got please, Tildy," Justine said to the waitress.

"I'll pour yours from the special pot," Tildy said, winking.

Justine laughed, and I did too. "Tildy's my favorite waitress anywhere," Justine said. "It's like having a special aunt right here in New York for me."

Justine told me she had been up past three o'clock finishing her design project. "It's not as though I left it till the last minute," she said, "it's just that I get all my best ideas at the eleventh hour. If I'm going to make a living doing stuff like this I'm going to have to be more practical than that. Or learn to live without sleep."

I said, "Well, we finished at about two, after some last-minute costume fittings and running through some scenes extra times for the tech crews. I passed on the option of going out for a late dinner. I knew I had leftovers in my fridge if I really needed something to eat."

"And you have a real job."

I half-nodded, half-shrugged. "Yeah, real enough. Not exactly nine to five, I do spend a lot of evenings out at shows, and auditions often happen at odd hours, so I'm not always at the office bright and early. I write theatre and film reviews now and then too."

"For a magazine?"

"Well, yeah," I said, "for this little Catholic magazine that comes out every two weeks. Reviews written from a Catholic perspective." I had picked up a few assignments by way of a professor at Fordham University, where I audited theology and religious studies classes from time to time.

Justine didn't say anything so I asked her where she was from. She named a small town I had never heard of out in the Finger Lakes region of New York. "It's a place to get away from. I am not motivated to go back." She didn't offer a lot of details, but readily admitted to having come from broken family. "My brother and sister and I all have different fathers," she said, "none of whom ever really stuck around. Except the last one, my younger sister's dad, who was no prize but at least paid his share of the bills. My mother doesn't seem to have particularly wise taste in men." Justine was the middle child, and was convinced that her siblings would never follow her out. "My art teacher in high school inspired me to get out of there. Pushed me, really. She knew something about my family life." She laughed. "It was all kind of out there in my artwork, for anyone to see."

Hoping not to sound apologetic for the relative normalcy of my upbringing, I gave Justine a short version of my back-story.

Something about the situation and the conversation almost made me wish I could admit to some major abnormality. My mother's a convicted felon on parole, or we had seventy-eight cats, or our family tree includes several known ax-murderers. "Just your basic middle-class working family," I said.

"Well, you seem to be fairly well adjusted in spite of that," Justine said. She smiled slyly. "*Catholic* middle-class working family, to boot."

"Half Catholic, actually. My mother's side. It was only an average part of growing up. It was important at times, of course—first communion and times like that. And confirmation—that was a huge deal for my grandfather. I've become more interested in other aspects of it in recent years. Social justice, and the aesthetics and symbolism. Like some of the great music we sang in high school choir. Vivaldi. Mozart. The theatrics of it all, in a way."

Our waitress, Tildy, returned with more coffee and the sandwiches we had ordered. She winked at Justine again and said, "You let me know if you need anything else, girl." Justine told her "Everything's good," and Tildy walked down the line to another table.

I said, "She's very attentive."

"She watches out for me when I'm here. She's very suspicious of college boys, and doesn't like it when they start getting a little grabby." She laughed quietly. "My mother had a few grabby boyfriends." She clenched a fist and smiled broadly. "I learned how to use this on my own behalf." Her left front tooth was slightly crooked—one of many points of interest on her unconventionally pretty face.

"God, I should shut up," she said. "I'm saying things that must make me seem like a twit, a bitch, or a swindler."

"No, everybody has their things, you know?"

For a few moments we ate silently. I took a long pull of the water Tildy had poured for me when we first sat down. We talked about other things, New York things and art and theatre things, riffing from topic to topic like a couple of old jazz musicians. Finally, as we were finishing our meals, I said, "Justine, I'd like to see you again." I didn't want to tell her she was intriguing. That seemed like too strange a word choice. "You'll be at the opening on Thursday?"

"Yes. *Wanda June*. Can't wait to see it."

"I'll see you then, sure. And there'll be a party afterward, I don't know the details yet, or if you plan to go—"

"No," she said, "I can't have a late night. Friday morning at eight I have to face the faculty judges on my final project and I really need to be rested and ready. There's a potential job, a staff job at a design firm, tied up in it all, so I need to make my best impression, and early mornings after late nights are not my strong suit."

"But come backstage, after the show, for a minute anyway," I said. "I'd love to know how you liked it. One Vonnegut enthusiast to another, you know—okay?"

Justine nodded. "Yes. Absolutely. On Saturday I'm planning to see an exhibit, though—up at the Whitney—I've been meaning to get up there, but school has just been, you know, too much. I don't know if you'd be interested?"

Wanda June wasn't till eight o'clock on Saturday night, so my day was wide open until seven. I had no idea what was on display at the Whitney, but it didn't matter. "What time? I'll pick you up."

She named the time and then reached into her shoulder bag. "I was inspired by your business card, so I made one for myself. I was up so late anyway, it was just one more thing. I dashed it off."

She handed me the card—her name, address, and phone number artfully lettered amid a geometric design—and said, laughter in her voice, "Don't lose that. It's one of a kind."

I paid the bill and tipped Tildy generously. Tildy, for her part, gave me a secretive thumbs-up sign even before she saw the tip. If I felt confident because Justine had suggested a Saturday date, it was boosted even more by Tildy's show of support. I walked Justine to SVA and continued back to my office, stopping two or three times to stand in doorways and read her business card until I'd memorized it.

I have that card still. Justine's cards ever since have been variations of the first, but it remains one of a kind.

Justine and I talked briefly at the opening of *Wanda June*, but she seemed distracted by the crowd and volume of noise in the small backstage area. True to her word she did not stay long. On Saturday I met her in front of her building at eleven in the morning—she didn't ask me in, saying that her roommates were still asleep—and we took a cab to the Whitney. I had run up there on the subway the day before and taken brochures about the current exhibits, hoping to glean a little knowledge about the art. But she never mentioned which of the exhibits she specifically had wanted to see.

Justine told me she had job interviews on Monday and Wednesday and was working all day Sunday and Tuesday night at her part-time job cleaning offices in a building on Park Avenue. She said it would be nice to get her mind off all of that by looking at art, but as we toured the museum Justine was much more concerned with the job interviews than with the exhibits. "I've got to land something substantial here and get started," she said. "I don't want to have to go back upstate."

I asked, "Do you go up there often?"

"It's been about two-and-a-half years since I've been."

"Really?"

She was about to say more, but stopped herself. "I really shouldn't talk about all that."

"I—I don't mean to be nosy," I said. I stopped to look at the nearest painting, a multimedia abstract, and studied it intently. Justine stood beside me, our shoulders nearly touching. "I like how this one catches and keeps my attention. But I'd need to stand here a couple of hours in order to really grasp it. Like going to a play." We moved on. I asked Justine about her job interviews.

"One is a design studio, the other is a design department for a big company, you know, department stores. My faculty advisors helped connect me. And I'll be cleaning offices and bathrooms in between. I took whatever extra hours I could get now that I have time because I need the money. And then graduation day."

"When is that?"

"Next Saturday. I tried to get my sister to come down—she's a couple years younger than me. Hoping, maybe, getting her on the bus and into to the big city might inspire her to leave home."

"How you gonna keep them down on the farm now that they've seen Paree, eh?"

She nodded. "That's what I hope for. In vain. Maybe she'll make it as far away as Buffalo someday. But she won't leave town without her boyfriend, and he won't come. I've never met him, but I think I've got a pretty accurate picture. Highly dependent and undependable."

"And your mother?"

"I can last a few more years without seeing her." She scowled. "That sounds awful, I know, but I'm being honest. Sorry."

"Reality is reality. You don't need to apologize to me." I hoped my tone was as light as I intended it to be.

A little while later we had left the museum and were walking along Central Park. Justine had changed the subject by asking me about my job, and Stuart Spender, and how it had all come about. "And you like it? Really like it?" she asked. I told her that I did, that no day was ever the same as any other, and that I was learning the trade from one of the great old hands in the business.

"Nothing is perfect, though," I said. "There are always issues and pressures and frustrations, but I could imagine a lot worse."

"Yeah, like cleaning toilets on Park Avenue."

"No, I think cleaning toilets in Alphabet City or the Port Authority would be even worse."

"Clearly you have not seen the so-called high-class bathrooms of Park Avenue," Justine laughed.

"But that's just temporary work," I said. You've got some of your teachers in your corner, trying to help you out. If they have that kind of confidence in you, then you should too. I mean, I've seen very little of your work, a portrait and a business card, but it's enough to know that someone should take you seriously."

"You're flattering me, Mister Martin Halsey, theatrical agent," Justine said, obviously enjoying it. "Do you mind if we sit down for a bit?"

We sat on an empty bench near an entrance to the park. The day had warmed up but we were shaded by a row of trees. "I'm just—I don't know," Justine said. "Scared? Nervous? For the first time in four years I don't know what's happening next in my life. I love 'being an artist,' you know, but I have no idea how to get along in the world as an artist. So I'm scared. And now you come along, and I step on your foot while I'm painting and all of a sudden we're having lunch and going to a museum together. You're the first *normal* boy—guy, man, I mean, hell, I'm a college graduate almost, and you have an actual career— to be interested in me in a long time, maybe ever. Normal's a good thing, don't get me wrong—I've had it with all these angst-ridden artists who either take their own talent for granted or expect the world to bow down and worship them. And I'm sure I'll scare you away because I come from this messed up family, I mean the only real thing I know about my own father is that his last name was Damont because he stuck around long enough to get his name on my birth certificate. And I'm scared about religion, and, I'm sorry, I know you're kind of religious, but—my stepfather, my sister's dad, the man who stuck around, became some sort of crazy-ass fundamentalist Christian back when I was about fourteen, and when he wasn't trying to convince me that I would go to hell if he didn't save me he was trying to reach up under my shirt or into my pants, so that's what I know about religion. But I like you and I don't want to be scared about this, and my future, and my past, and—"

She trailed off, spent, and slouched back onto the bench. After staring at the sidewalk for a long moment she glanced up at me, then quickly away, which I took as an invitation to say something.

"Okay. Well. First, I've been around those kinds of Christians before, the hellfire ones—but without the molestation—and that is not where I'm coming from. I guess you just have to trust me on that. I'm not scared of your past, or your family, and I can understand, just by the little you've told me, why you don't want to return to that. And—I like you too, and I was very relieved when you stepped on my foot because I might have been too shy and nervous to say anything to you otherwise."

We stared at each other, our faces about two feet apart, but remained silent for at least a couple of minutes. Finally I said, "Look, this is a crazy couple of weeks for both of us. My show, your job interviews and graduation, all that. Let's just go about our business, pace ourselves, maybe touch base once or twice on the phone, and let things settle down."

"This isn't just a way to let yourself fade away, is it?"

"No. Of course not," I said. I was a little surprised at her show of low self-confidence—that had always been *my* strong suit in relationships and I was more accustomed to kicking my-self in retrospect than in having to bolster someone else. And fading away was the last thing on my mind. I turned and faced her directly. "Let's make a plan. Dinner a week from Tuesday or a Mets game or something like that."

She fished an envelope out of her purse and handed it to me. "Will you come to my graduation? It's at one in the after-noon next Saturday, so it won't interfere with *Wanda June*. It would be nice to have someone there since my sister won't come."

I accepted the invitation and promised her I would be there.

"I must seem pathetic," Justine said. "I mean, I won't be all alone or anything, so you don't have to."

"I want to. I'm glad you asked. That's *Wanda June*'s closing night. Will you come to the cast party? It'll be a late night."

"Can you get me another ticket to the show? I'd like to see it again," she said.

"It's a deal."

With that understanding reached we walked toward mid-town along Fifth Avenue, our conversation flowing now without inhibition, the city our stage and backdrop. We shifted away from the subjects of our work to talk about some of the rest of the world, everyday things like rush-hour traffic and baseball (Mets or Yanks?) and cars (manual or automatic?), settling into a comfort zone that was commonplace and electrifying at the same time. I felt light on my feet and reveled in the fact that as we walked along, other people—strangers, whatever—saw us, Justine and me, together.

By the time we reached the point where we had to part company—I to my apartment for a quick shower before going to the Mercer Stage, and Justine to babysit the kids of one of her professors, in Brooklyn—I was loaded, almost overloaded, with sensory data, images, sounds, and smells. Justine's eyes lit by excitement with every little thing, her hair caught by the breeze, her laugh emerging from deep in her gut, a remnant dab of perfume escaping her orbit and reaching me.

Three senses of five, anyway. Since our initial handshake we had not touched, much less experienced a taste. We had set the pace, though, and I would abide by it.

Just about every friend or acquaintance I had in Manhattan back in those days met with a therapist once a week. I did not see one, but I did have a priest, though I had never thought of him as a substitute for a therapist, and never intended to approach him with that idea in mind. But the next morning, after Sunday mass, I loitered a while after the coffee hour. I intended to help clean up, but as the room cleared out I found myself talking alone with Father Steve. It was usually difficult to get one-to-one with him without an appointment.

I was an anomaly in this parish—a single man, almost thirty, in a group comprising mainly families with children ranging from infants to teens and sometimes twenty-somethings in transition after college. I had no interest in becoming a priest—people asked me about that from time to time—and there turned out to be few opportunities at church to meet single women in my age range. In the context of the parish I was a man without a peer group, there for the artful liturgy and some sense of belonging to something larger than myself. Although I would have welcomed any opportunity to meet a woman who was a kindred spirit, it was looking more and more as though that would never happen at church.

Father Steve asked how things were going at work. Steve loved theatre and drama and was always interested in hearing about my work as an agent. I hadn't told him before about *Wanda June*, but when I did he immediately opened his pocket schedule book and marked it down for Wednesday's performance. The conversation eventually meandered around to my social life, and that led to Justine.

I told him I had met this fascinating woman, but had to admit that I had concerns about what was going on with her. Most of the time I had spent with Justine, I told Steve, had been remarkable—easy conversations, laughing and joking and common interests, and a great feeling that there was a whole lot more to discover about each other as our comfort and familiarity increased. I said all this to Father Steve, almost breathless as I spoke, but then confided where my doubts came in.

"We're from very different backgrounds, you might even say different sides of the tracks," I said. I told him the basics of her story, as far as I knew it. When I mentioned our differences about religion and her experience with her mother's fundamentalist boyfriend, Steve surprised me.

"Tread carefully, Martin. Religion is tricky. There's a lot of bad religion out there, including bad Catholic religion. People have good reasons to suspect it or reject it. The hardest thing sometimes is to figure out what matters more—what you believe, or who you love. I don't mean to jump to conclusions, but I want to put that out there."

I said, "Well, you know, you're always hoping to meet someone who is a kindred spirit at least, or who shares what you believe in—"

Steve held up his hand like a cop at cross street directing traffic. "There's more to it than that. I've seen some ugly Catholic marriages, believe me. Don't be afraid to see where it goes," he said. "You're a theatre guy. Listen for your cues. You don't want to wake up in ten years and realize that you missed your entrance, you know? Don't tell the pope I said this, but if I were faced with making a choice about a relationship, religion wouldn't be the litmus test. No, love trumps religion. Love is more important. If love is happening and religion gets in the way, well, I know which one I would follow. But, you know, I'm just a celibate priest, approaching middle age, who happens also to be a bit of a romantic, so take my advice with a grain of salt."

"Love trumps religion," I said, grinning. "I'll do some thinking about that."

"When you do, think of the two great commandments. Love God, and love your neighbor as yourself. But I think if you find a great neighbor to love, well, if 'love is of God,' as the saying goes in John's letter, then he's involved whether you know it or not. Or care or not."

On my walk home I detoured over to Twelfth Avenue to watch the Hudson River flow by the piers where the sightseeing boats come and go. Sunlight flashed off the plate-glass windows of sundry storefronts, my own reflection there too, peripheral, as I watched a memory parade of the women in my life during the past few years. I had passed half a year with Cheryl, devoted to God in Nature and the Power of Herbal Tea. There was Judith, several years older than me, an avid follower of Mary Baker Eddy and G. I. Gurdjieff, with a splash of Madame Blavatsky thrown in. After a bad and impoverished marriage she felt that the world owed her material wealth to go with her accrued spiritual wisdom, and strung me along as a sideshow while she slept her way up the ladder of a property management business, eventually settling with an Episcopalian sugar daddy in real estate.

I recalled the otherworldly gaze of a quirky centering prayer enthusiast who, it turned out, was as firmly committed to chastity as she was to prayer—and probably so afraid of intimacy that in the unlikely event of a breakthrough the upshot would be either unbearably bad or unbearably good, with no inbetween. So I opened the door to a dancer who thought that God was talking to her through a matronly Italian woman who for twenty-five cash dollars would look at your hand, ask leading questions, and then declaim inane insights about you.

When the psychic didn't see our names in each other's tea leaves she danced away into the twilight and stopped returning my phone calls.

Father Steve had a point. Maybe I had been looking for love, if not, as the song says, in all the wrong places, then with the wrong priorities. I had it in my head that I needed to be with someone on some sort of spiritual wavelength. The godless or indifferent need not apply, but a girl with a tenuous hold on reality coupled with some irrational dogma or spirituality could fascinate me for weeks at a time. I had been applying what I could now see was a very strange and misguided standard in the way I thought about love and relationships, and I had been ignoring my gut.

Until, perhaps, now. And maybe not a moment too soon. Considering my history of relationship choices I was almost surprised I had given Justine a second look.

It also suddenly struck me that I had never even been terribly comfortable inhabiting my own skin. A high inventory of self-consciousness, together with questionable self-esteem, seemed like plenty to overcome in creating and building relationships without adding divine expectations. But the doses of self-doubt that usually accompanied my dealings with women seemed to be absent with Justine. I hadn't noticed that before. It was too important to ignore.

Love trumps religion. Okay. And maybe love starts with a jolt, not with a common interest in rules for a spiritual road. Justine had jolted me. No doubt about that. We had met in a theatre—my real home turf, more so than any church—and we had made many points of contact. We shared literary heroes and favorite movies, and her artistic ability enthralled me. I was fascinated by the way she stood in front of that painting for *Wanda June* and the ease with which she applied paint in detailed and broad strokes, and I re-ran the image of her working on that canvas over and over in my mind.

She had an eccentric and addicting beauty. I had memorized every detail of her face, the way it was framed by her hair, the way she gestured when she got excited about something. The rhythm of her walk invited me to match it step for step like a dance. Hesitation, I saw, should have no place in my approach to Justine.

A Circle Line boat loaded with families and sightseers pulled away from the pier, headed, I supposed, for the Statue of Liberty and Ellis Island. I watched those families wave to people on shore and wondered, based on my own inept experience, why it seemed so easy for most people to establish these relationships and build their entire lives around them. I had wasted too much time on bad connections, hanging around and trying to force it, afraid to admit my mistake and move on.

"Fear." I heard myself say out loud. Here I was, alone on a beautiful Sunday morning talking to myself and watching other peoples' families go about their daily lives while a woman who had ignited me was cleaning offices somewhere up on Park Avenue. I was standing here alone thinking about overcoming fear. Just a few years earlier, Stuart Spender told me I could be a great agent, but just an okay actor. "You're gun shy as an actor," he told me then. "You're at sixes and sevens with yourself." Stuart was right—I could not handle an actor's fear as part and parcel of my daily life. It was no insult that Stuart believed it was a fear that I would not be able to get over, and that I should make a change before it damaged me.

And I was damn glad that Stuart had spoken when he did.

Now Father Steve had offered his own startling advice. Love trumps religion. Listen for your cues, don't miss your entrance. And the very biblical Be Not Afraid.

I took Justine's handmade business card out of my wallet and studied it as the Circle Liner sounded its horn out on the river. I felt a smile spread across my face. There's no way I'm missing this cue, I thought, and I tucked the card neatly back into my wallet. I walked to where I had the best panoramic view of the river and watched the current flow south to the bay. I let my fear go with it.

3

Second Sunday

Today is the Sunday of Ned and Molly Flynn's annual Family and Friends Christmas Pageant, which preempts our normal football-watching schedule. The tradition started back in the mid-sixties when their kids, who are about my age, were little. As the story goes, the Flynns invited friends and their children to a festival at their apartment, in which they sang carols, recited poetry, and feasted on a potluck of desserts and beverages, fermented and otherwise, and staged the Nativity story. They had such a memorable time that they did it again the next year. Various adults and children played the roles of Mary and Joseph and shepherds and sheep. Wise men were played by women and girls as often as by men and boys. Almost every year there seemed to be a new baby to play the infant Jesus. In the absence of an appropriate baby the role would be taken by a suitable prop from someone's toy box.

By the time I started working for Stuart Spender, Ned and Molly had been hosting the pageant for almost twenty years. As soon as I walked in the door the first year I attended, Ned assigned me the role of Herod. It was the first of many memories of this event. Two years later I brought Justine with me, and though neither of us played a role in the pageant that time we sang together in public for the first time, a rendition of "Winter

Wonderland" with impromptu accompaniment from a fabulous guitar player I had never seen before and have not seen since. The next year I played a cow and Justine played a lamb, mainly so that we could be near the cradle in which Janet, not quite two months old, played the role of the baby Jesus.

The only rule Ned and Molly applied to the pageant was that the Nativity story was never to be rehearsed. As the guests gathered, Ned circulated around the apartment and assigned roles, and when the moment came he bellowed a very theatrical "Places!" and the improvisation began.

Ned prefers the story as it is told in the gospel of Luke, with a little bit of Matthew thrown in. Though no animals are mentioned in the gospel accounts of the baby in the manger, Ned honors the Nativity story tradition by including them anyway. Among his family and friends are plenty of singers to enact the roles of choirs of angels, and over the years we have heard a huge variety of Glories to God in the Highest, from classical and jazz to bebop and bluegrass. Like any improvisation, it is always on the brink of disaster, and sometimes can only be saved by the audience's willing suspension of disbelief.

The pageant represented, in an unconventional way, what I most valued about Christianity. I was always aware that the Bible contained many ideas worthy of rejection, many characters and rules that repelled me, from Leviticus to the letters of Paul. I could not believe it in its entirety, and certainly not literally. I had read and studied it too much for that, and like every Christian, whether they all admit it or not, I picked and chose and created a version of the faith that worked for me and played out in the world the way I thought a faith should—it promoted equality and justice at the least, seeking to make the Kingdom of God a present reality. Peace on Earth.

I gave little thought to salvation, a relationship with Jesus, the afterlife, virgin birth, bodily resurrection, and the second coming. I was a product of public schools, and though science was never my best subject I understood, at least, that facts and evidence lead to conclusions about the world. I had read a broad range of literature, too, and understood how poems and stories convey meaning without the necessity of facts—that literature is a trickster and should always be regarded with a combination of respect and suspicion. And the Bible is nothing if not literature.

A few weeks before the pageant one year, in the late 1980s, I discussed this with Ned. I was on the edge then, one step away from rejecting the God I believed in and the church in which I claimed membership, and declaring myself, inwardly at least, an atheist. I suggested that the improvised variations on the nativity story at his pageants were similar to variations in the stories in the gospels. I said that none of these stories could be literally true, that the underlying symbolism of Jesus as Son of God was expressed in multiple ways by assorted communities. Ned was with me until I said, "So people find their way to God's love through the stories they tell. All the creeds and dogmas, clergies and hierarchies—all of that just stands in the way. It's an obstacle."

We were sitting in my office. I was already a partner in the agency, and because Stuart had been ill I had taken over Ned's affairs rather than delegate them to an associate. Ned asked, "Is that what they teach in those theology courses you take up at Fordham? That the church is an obstacle to the church?" It had actually been about two years since I had taken a course, but I didn't say anything about that.

"No," I said. "This is just me thinking about it, trying to make sense of it. I think the Nativity story is more about radical, revolutionary love than about what to believe about God, or Jesus, or any of that. I think it's about the way humanity needs to love humanity. There's no proof that God even exists, but we walk among human beings all day long. It's how we deal with one another that matters most, not how we deal with a deity that may or may not exist. Institutions created by humans can help or hinder that. More and more I think the church is a hindrance."

Ned sat with that for a few moments. Finally he said, "The church comes from God, to do his work. Human rules don't always apply."

"'The church comes from God' is a statement of faith, not of fact. And deciding what is God's work—whose job is that?"

The Catholic church had recently made it official that it forbade the use of condoms to prevent the spread of AIDS. As people working in the New York theatrical community in the early days of the AIDS epidemic, Ned and I were not strangers to the suffering and loss brought on by the disease. The continuing spread of the epidemic in Africa was also much in the news. Ned and I had talked about all of this before, especially as it related to people we knew in show business, our colleagues and friends, but now I put the subject in a different light. "What piece of God's work is served by that church teaching?" I asked.

Ned hesitated. I knew he was thinking about an actor he had worked with often in the sixties and seventies, one of his best friends, who died in an early wave of AIDS deaths. Hardly anyone even knew the acronym had been invented at the time. He said, "It serves bullshit. Okay, I admit that. But I won't throw away the whole thing, a lifetime of being part of the church, over something like this."

"I'm not suggesting you should," I said.

"You think about things too much," Ned said. "That's your problem. I just have the simple faith my mother raised me in, I don't need more than that."

I shuffled some of the papers he had signed just before our conversation had taken its current turn. "I hope you're happy with these contracts," I said.

"They'll keep me out of trouble for a while. Molly loves it when you swing me a January gig in San Diego." His smile was back.

"Anyway," I said, "I'm looking forward to the pageant. It's been a long year since the last one."

"I love December in New York. Your little Celia may have to play Jesus for the second year in a row. There are no new babies this year—she's still the youngest."

Celia was eighteen months old. "You can try. She's a live wire and loves to wear pink."

Ned chuckled. "I'll consult the wardrobe department."

We were quiet for a moment.

"Listen, Ned, we're friends. I'm not trying to mess with your world, but I need to figure out some things in mine. I hope talking about that is not off limits, but if it is, say the word. I understand."

Ned picked up a picture from my desk, the latest Halsey family portrait, taken just a few weeks earlier. "You are surrounded by beautiful women, my friend, a fortunate man. I'll let you know if you cross a line. On such topics I honestly do not know where my comfort zone ends. As an actor over the age of fifty, of course, I know my limits—my days of full frontal nudity are over—but when it comes to the holy Catholic church, well, I just don't know."

We laughed—there had never been a demand for nudity in Ned's career. "You know," I said, "Janet is going on five, and so we've got to be thinking about religious education and all—do we, or don't we, and where—and, you know, Justine comes from very different place on all of this than I do, so there's that—this whole issue is a bit loaded in our house right now, so when I'm having doubts of my own—"

"It was much simpler in my day," Ned said as my voice trailed off. "Educate the bejesus out of them at church, then let them reject it on their own when they grow up, as long as they keep it secret. But God forbid that they reject it, it would break my heart." It was time for him to leave for the theatre where he was rehearsing *A Christmas Carol*, but he couldn't leave without a parting shot. "Don't be surprised, son, to be assigned the role of Herod again this year." He exited with a wicked grin and was out the door before I could even consider thinking about a comeback.

We have never missed a Flynn pageant. Neither have Ned's kids—Ned and Molly have two daughters and two sons, all of whom still live in the New York area and have kids and grandkids of their own. The Flynn clan alone could fill Ned and Molly's roomy apartment, so the non-family invitations have diminished over the years, and we are honored to be included. This year, though, receiving the invitation spurs a cavalcade of emotions and memories of Christmases past. Despite the inevitable temptations to pass just this once, Justine and I attend as usual. Like Thanksgiving, this is our first Flynn pageant without our daughters.

It is around two in the afternoon when Justine and I arrive. Ned crosses the room as soon as he sees us and sweeps Justine into a long embrace. He has not seen Justine since June, before Ned and Molly flew out to Michigan for Ned's summer of appearing in the roles of elderly men. There just never seemed a right time for us all to get together.

"My dear, dear, Justine," he says, still holding her. He is a full head taller than Justine, and she easily rests against his shoulder and his trademark Irish wool sweater. "Dear girl, I am so thankful that you are here, so pleased." He loosens his grip and steps back slightly to look at Justine's face. His eyes are rimmed with tears that I know are not staged, and he moves his hands from her shoulders to her face, gently cradling her chin and cheeks as he places a long kiss on her forehead. "I am honored to welcome you to my home once again." He reaches to put an arm around me as well and says, "I've seen a good deal of Martin this fall, but I have missed you, Justine. And you must catch Molly and sit with her for a while today."

Justine says, "I will, yes, I would like that."

Ned's youngest son, Daniel, comes over to greet us. There are more hugs. Ned says, "I was so thankful that Daniel could represent Molly and me last summer when we were unable to be with you." He leaves me and Justine to chat with Daniel while he goes to get us something to drink.

"It's good to see you both," Daniel says. "I know it's been a hard year, but I can promise you it means a lot to Dad to have you here."

Neither Justine nor I encourage conversation about the hard year. "We wouldn't miss it," I say. "I counted this morning—this is my thirtieth pageant."

Daniel says, "I don't know what'll happen with this tradition once the folks are—gone." He stops as if he has taken a wrong turn in a maze.

"Still a lot of vim and vigor in Ned and Molly," Justine says brightly. I am happy, if a little surprised, that she is so animated. Ned arrives with our drinks, mismatched glasses of white wine, and gives the larger one to Justine. She says, flirtatiously, "I hope you're not trying to get me drunk, Mr. Flynn," eyelashes batting.

"Oh, my darling, don't give me any ideas I might not be able to follow through on," he says, and then stage whispers an aside, "Or might kill me!" Daniel rolls his eyes and reminds Ned to start assigning the Nativity roles, and Ned goes off and begins whispering in the ears of various guests.

Ned graciously avoids giving roles to Justine and me. But as the afternoon progresses I find my attention shifting from the performances in front of me to their counterparts in memory, memories of Janet and Celia. Both had played the infant Jesus, of course, but it is the contributions they made as they got older that flash before me now. Like Janet, at fifteen, assigned the role of the Blessed Virgin Mary. A scientist from the start, Janet brought a natural and exuberant skepticism to the role, pushing the character of the angel Gabriel for an explanation of the sudden urgent need for her to become pregnant:

MARY: How can this be, angel, I have not lain with a man.

GABRIEL: It's the holy spirit that will come upon you, and you will conceive.

MARY: No no no no, Gabriel, you don't seem to understand. A woman cannot conceive unless she has lain with a man. They have to have sexual intercourse, or make love, or [*she cups her hands and whispers a word in Gabriel's ear that raises his eyebrows*]—that's what it means when I say she has to have lain with a man, it's just language that's a little more delicate and Elizabethan.

GABRIEL: Well, well, you see, with God anything is possible. He can circumvent—

MARY: God, who created and ordered the universe such that a woman and a man need to make love, which from everything I hear—because I *am* a virgin—is widely considered to be a pleasurable experience, would circumvent his own rules?

GABRIEL: Yeah, well, you see, sweetheart, he wants to make a point—

MARY: A pretty Nixonesque point if you ask me. [*Mimicking President Nixon*] It's not a crime if the president does it.

GABRIEL: Well, honey, I just need to know if you'll go along with this, just this once. God wants his son to come into the world, and he prefers that his son be born of a virgin. Something to do with the prophet Isaiah, long story. He didn't give me all the details. "It's a long story," he said. "A *very* long story."

MARY [*She is really getting going now*]: So you're telling me that God wants me to let myself be magically impregnated at the age of fifteen, put on weight growing this big belly, have my breasts get all stretched out with milk, go through the excruciating pain of childbirth, I mean we only have one midwife in this podunk town, and she's a little, you know, [*mimes drinking*] glug, glug, glug, and then I'm going to have this baby to cart around, this baby that's God's son, and I don't even get to enjoy a little sex before all this happens? God can't manage to lay with me? What, I'm not pretty enough for God? He's gotta send somebody else? Plus, nine months from now is Christmas, Gabe, and I'm always very busy that time of year. And you want me to have this baby all by myself, an unwed mother, an unwed *teenage* mother? The fanatics in this little burg will stone me before the brat turns a month old and have him raised by some crazy priest in the temple—

GABRIEL: No, no, listen, sweetheart, he's thought of all that, you won't be alone. You know Joseph, the carpenter, over on Deuteronomy Boulevard? Well, God knows, because God knows everything, that Joe's a bit sweet on you, and we'll talk to him, get him up to speed on what's happening with God's little plan—Joe will understand, he loves God quite a bit and all—and the two of you will get married and he'll be the dad, and take care of you and the baby, and life will go on quite, you know, normally. For now.

MARY: There's still a lot that's kind of weird here, Gabe. I mean, Joseph, he seems nice enough but he's a little old for me, he must be at least twenty-seven, I'm still in high school, what'll the nuns think?

GABRIEL: We'll take care of all of that, honey, don't worry yourself about it one bit. You'll grow to love each other. But here's the thing: I gotta get back and let God know your answer. Because he's not *telling* you to do this. He's *asking*. And he's asking very nicely, and he thought of you first because, you know, you're a very special girl to him.

MARY: So, all I have to do is say no and that's the end of it? No consequences? God's not mad, no punishment?

GABRIEL: It's your decision. It's completely up to you.

MARY: Completely up to me.

GABRIEL: Your decision.

MARY [*girlish and off-hand*]: Okay. I'm in. Yes.

GABRIEL [*relieved*]: Thank you. Bless you!

MARY [*to the audience*]: And so Mary conceived after God used the lines—"Only if you want it, honey; it's up to you; you're so special"—spoken forever after in parked cars and darkened movie theatres all over the world.

"You're a wise-ass," Ned said later to Janet, "but a very funny and smart wise-ass. And you gave your old man a run for his money. He was lucky to keep up with you."

Yes, I had played Gabriel, and Ned knew what he was talking about. I had no idea what would happen when Janet opened her mouth. My legs were like jelly when the scene ended and I was grateful when Justine leaned into me and guided me to a shot glass of Irish whiskey.

Justine and I wondered sometimes, but were never sure, when Celia became aware of herself as an artist. "When did *you* know that, about yourself?" I asked Justine around the time Celia had gone to Vassar for her freshman year. "There must have been some point that you realized art was something your life would be about."

Justine's faced turned melancholy for a moment, her eyes going briefly dark as her brow furrowed. "Did you have that kind of moment?" she asked, "An 'I am actor' moment?"

Now it was my turn to balk at the question. "I can't really say. But it would have been wrong, because my career took a different turn. I never had an 'I'm going to be a talent agent' moment, that's for sure."

"That's just a technicality." Justine twirled a lock of hair around her left index finger, a gesture I often saw when she was concentrating on work in front of her. "High school," she said. "I had this great art teacher. She made me aware that I was good. Miss D, we called her, short for DeAngelis, and she was married, not a 'miss,' and pretty old, at least that's how I perceived her at the time. I knew I was good at drawing, even as a kid in grade school, but I thought nothing of it. My family, my mother, they sure were not impressed, but Miss D saw it and pushed me to work at it. Without her I would never have come to New York to study art. We wouldn't be having this conversation."

I hadn't intended my question to lead to hard memories, but I should not have been surprised. Mention of Justine's childhood always led to glum thoughts of her mother and Justine's halting attempts to fully reconcile with her, starting before Janet's birth and continuing, on and off, over the years.

"Well," I said, "Celia's been surrounded by it all her life. There was probably never a particular moment. Janet's the wonder—that a scientist came out of this household, this gene pool—"

"Celia *did* have a moment, though. I think I know when it was. It was that time she brought pencils and sketchbook to Ned Flynn's pageant. She was, what, twelve, thirteen?"

Justine was right. Celia spent the whole afternoon of the pageant sketching portraits upon demand. Each picture contained a person at the party and one or more members of the holy family. Ned still has his, in a nice frame in his foyer—Celia sketched him wearing waders and a fishing hat because of his love of fly-fishing, posed beside a river with his arm draped respectfully around the Blessed Virgin Mary. And Mary, though dressed more for a Palestinian desert and looking like a traditional Madonna, does not seem out of place.

Celia never told us whether she had planned to offer sketches, or had just brought a sketch pad in case of boredom. Either way, the next year Molly Flynn called just before bedtime a few weeks before the pageant and asked to speak to Celia. She told Justine afterward that Molly wanted her to bring her sketchbook again. "She said they'd set up a spot in the big room, but I said I'd rather wander around and draw all over the place."

"Were you planning to do it again anyway?" Justine asked.

Celia said, "I haven't even thought about it. I probably would've remembered that day. Now I'll probably forget!"

"I won't let you forget," Justine said. "The sketches last year were beautiful. Everybody loved them."

"I'm nowhere near as good as you, though, Mom. Maybe you should do pageant sketches."

Justine smiled and shook her head. "No, honey, this is your thing. You have the knack, you created it. And people love it. You've got a future with this stuff."

Celia yawned. Her homework was done and she was ready for bed. "You seem to enjoy it—art as a job. Do you? Right now it's just a hobby for me. I don't know what it would be like as a job."

"I do, Celia, I do like it. I hope I never lose *that*, because then it would be *just* a job."

Celia climbed into her bed and Justine tucked the blankets and kissed her forehead.

"Can I ask you something, Mom?"

"Sure."

Celia pursed her lips and thought for moment, trying to form the question. "Do all those people, the ones who come to the Flynn's, do they all believe all that stuff is real? The virgin Mary? I mean, I know where babies come from, you told me all about that. And angels singing in the sky, and other angels telling Joseph to go to Egypt and all that?"

"Well, I suppose different people believe different thi—"

"Because I think it's just a story. A really *cool* story, but just a story that people tell. That doesn't make it real. Just being in a book doesn't make it real. Ebenezer Scrooge is in a book, but I don't think he's real just because he's in a book." She stopped and thought some more. "It's just confusing."

Justine reached over and turned off the bedside lamp. "You're just too tired to think about all this right now. You get some sleep and we can talk about it tomorrow."

"Okay. Tell Daddy that I want to ask him about this too."

"Good idea. He's helping Janet with some homework now."

"Tell him to come in and kiss me goodnight, even if I'm already asleep."

"Okay."

Celia was asleep by the time Justine closed the door behind her.

Memories associated with Ned and Molly, and especially the pageant, keep coming at me. Another one flies in like scenery from above a Broadway stage: the time I bought a ukulele from a young actor who had recently become a client and was struggling to get his acting career moving forward. A couple of twenty-dollar bills would go a long way for the kid, and he was too proud to accept a loan or an advance on future employment. "I haven't played the thing in years," he told me. "Not since a vaudeville-style revue I did in college. I'm sure your little girls will enjoy plunking away on it." He even had the instructional pamphlet that had come with the uke when he bought it and made sure I took that as well to help the girls get started.

I hadn't thought until then about what I would do with the ukulele. Janet was nine at the time, and Celia was six going on seven. They alternated between being boon companions and fierce rivals. On the way home I took a side trip to Manny's Music and bought a second uke, hoping that the extra expense would give companionship an advantage over rivalry. The girls' initial response was indifference, but during the next weekend Justine and I heard occasional strumming and plucking as they worked the frets and followed the lessons in the manual behind the closed door of their bedroom.

The ukuleles provided occasional distraction for the girls, or an alternate outlet for their creativity, but didn't garner much attention until several years later when Janet was a junior in high school and Celia was in eighth grade. As we prepared to leave for that year's Flynn pageant, the girls quietly gathered their ukes and, with no explanation, carried them unobtrusively to the subway. At the Flynn's, Janet whispered something to Ned, who listened carefully and acknowledged her, and the day proceeded as usual with conversation, eating and drinking, Christmas carols, and the nativity story. While we were all singing carols, Ned emerged from the kitchen carrying the two ukuleles.

"It was brought to my attention earlier," he said, "that the young Halsey women, Janet and Celia, have prepared for us their own version of what is perhaps the greatest of all the Christmas carols, 'Silent Night'."

I would have to agree with Ned, that nothing says "Christmas" like a well-done "Silent Night," but I would never have put it together with ukuleles. I whispered to Justine, "Did you know about this?" She smiled and shrugged. "No idea. The Halsey girls—what do you expect?"

Janet and Celia took the ukuleles from Ned, checked their tuning, and played a sublime version in which they traded off between strumming the chords and picking the melody. After going through the verse twice they added their voices, reducing the accompaniment to a minimum and expertly weaving the melody and harmony. Janet had been singing in her high school choir and madrigal group for three years and had obviously learned something. Celia's voice was thinner than Janet's but they complemented each other and shifted the lead and harmony back and forth with each verse. They finished by returning to the instruments alone, but invited everyone to sing the first verse again, and the entire room was lifted by the melody as thirty or forty voices followed the girls' example of singing with exuberant restraint.

As the last words were sung the room fell silent, a silence that no one would dare break with applause. Applause was not needed. Silence was the best expression of appreciation. After a full two minutes of quiet, Ned finally rose to his feet and said, "I think, folks, that we have just heard the right note upon which to end our pageant. Thank you one and all." He swept his arm in a grand gesture toward the tables still covered with potluck dishes and desserts. "Please, eat as much as you wish, there is still plenty for everyone."

Wednesday

New York City takes on a new life in December. December brings out the best and the worst about the big town. New York is the capital of capitalism, and every way, shape, and form of moving dollars from one owner to another is active at full power. The bright lights and commotion at FAO Schwarz approach a level that I would find unbearable if this were a year that I had to go there. And on a nearby cross street a man who appears to be a transient also attracts attention with his own sale items—dolls, cheap toys, knickknacks, an inventory with no rhyme or reason. It is a rare block that shows no sign of commerce.

Another side of December in New York is piney and green, seen in the windows of ground floor apartments and on the entry doors of brownstones and offices. It is the wreaths and small trees and the manger scenes that are stored away for ten or so months of the year but become the focal point of people's homes for the twelfth. I am walking up to Times Square from my office on 23rd Street, just after five in the afternoon. I try to put on blinders to the commerce—there is nothing I need to buy tonight, in any case—and focus on the wreaths and mangers. I have no sense of devotion about them but they are at least an indication in this season that there may well be something that is not negotiable within the bonds of human love. And when all is said and done, I still maintain hope that love can in fact bind and heal wounds that I, that everyone I have ever known, inevitably suffer.

My walk to Times Square is occasioned by a happy turn of events for one of my clients. She is the understudy for the leading lady in the Broadway musical *Mary Poppins*, and is stepping into the role full-time until just after the new year. A pair of tickets waits for me at the box office on 42nd Street and I'm meeting Justine at a restaurant around the corner for drinks and a light dinner before the show. Despite the buzz of the world around me and my genuine happiness for my client, I feel as though I'm walking through ankle-deep mud in water-logged boots.

As I wait for the light to change at the last corner before the restaurant I see Justine standing by a storefront across the way. She is wearing her dressy winter coat with one of her long wool scarves wrapped snugly against the cold, and a matching hat. She sees me before the light changes and waves broadly as a knock-your-socks-off grin dances upon her face. I feel the weight lift a bit as I cross the street. Justine waits for me in the doorway of an electronics store, one of those entryways that is like an alcove, out of the wind, and when I get there she pulls me close to her by the lapels of my coat. She looks up at me, her smile like I haven't seen it for months, and lifts her face to be kissed.

I am restrained at first but Justine says "Don't be shy" and catches me with an open-mouthed kiss that both surprises me, out here in this doorway, and energizes me. Some of the weight I was dragging up Eighth Avenue drops away, and Justine, her voice rising from her core, not merely her throat, says "I feel *good* today," as if to explain herself and invite me to join her in uplift. I have heard the sound of that voice before: full, rich, and in control. I have heard its opposite, too: light, vulnerable, uncertain. Those voices, those Justines, have marked much of our life together for the past twenty-five years.

"I missed my period." Justine spoke, her voice measured and firm. Almost confrontational.

Justine had sat me down at the kitchen table in my apartment after pouring us each a cup of tea. It was the first Saturday in March. She had just come over from her place. We were all but living together at this point, seven or eight months since we met. Justine continued to pay rent on the apartment she shared with two friends from art school, but she spent the weekends with me, at the start, and then the weekend began to start earlier and end later, to the point where she slept at her place only a couple of nights each week. Last night, though, she had called me from her apartment right after work and said she wasn't feeling well and just wanted to crash early. She would call me in the morning, she said.

I thought nothing of it. Her place was closer to her job, so it made sense if she wasn't feeling well that she would stop there, and maybe just go to bed.

"It should have been three weeks ago," Justine said. Her body worked like a clock in that department.

"So I waited, and waited, and finally couldn't stand it so I went to the doctor on Tuesday." Her face was tense, her eyes showed traces of tears. "They called me yesterday afternoon at the studio. I'm pregnant."

I didn't say anything right away. I wanted to smile and tell her how great that was, but her eyes told me that was not what she wanted to hear. "Justine, I, I don't know what to say. I'm hoping this might be good news?"

She exhaled noisily, a breathy grunt, and said, "Of course you want it to be good news. That's the way you're wired. I'm only twenty-three. I'm not ready for this. I've got other things to—" Her voice trailed off into sobs but her body signaled that I should not come near her or try to hug her, so I reached across the small table and barely touched her hand. She didn't pull it away, so I wrapped mine around hers and held it.

Her sobbing subsided after a few moments and she took some deep breaths. I continued to look at her, trying not to give in to any emotion while hers was so large and complex. I remembered my father telling me, years ago, about how it drove him crazy, the whole getting pregnant thing. "Her period would be late," he told me, "and she'd cry and cry, 'Oh, no, I don't want to be pregnant again, wah wah wah.' And then she'd start to bleed and she'd cry and cry about that because it was a false alarm." He could laugh at it all these years later, but at the time he was a young husband and father with toddlers underfoot, and I can only imagine how perplexed he must have been.

Justine finally looked me in the eye and calmly said, "What if I don't want this baby?"

I didn't answer. It was not the question I wanted to hear.

"What if I don't. Want. This baby?"

I started to speak, then stopped, and eventually said, "You're saying 'what if,' so maybe it's too early to answer that question." I leaned closer and asked, "Do you want this baby?"

Now she hesitated. She stopped short of speaking, removed her hand from my grasp, and stood up and went into the living room. I stayed where I was, thinking maybe she was leaving, but I didn't hear the door open, so after a couple of minutes I followed her. She was on the couch, leaning against the arm-rest. I couldn't read her face now. She seemed for a moment angry, another moment confused, the next moment relieved. When I sat down next to her and put my arm around her, she didn't resist or push me away.

"I love you," I said.

"I love you too."

This was not news. We had said it plenty to each other, at first with delighted trepidation, then with enthusiastic confidence.

"What if—I hate that, 'what if'—but what if I said I wanted an abortion? I'm not ready, this is not the time, and I want an abortion? What if I said that?"

"I would want to know that you're very sure of that."

She considered that for a moment. "But—you're Catholic, you go to church every week, sometimes even on weekdays— you wouldn't try to talk me out of it, forbid it?"

I suppose I had never really thought about the associations and images that others, even Justine, might conjure in their minds when they put me and the word *Catholic* in the same sentence. *Forbid*—it was not a commonly used word in my vo-cabulary, but I shouldn't be surprised that it had come up in this moment.

"Even if I thought I could 'forbid' it," I said, shaping my words so that Justine would hear the quotes around *forbid*, "that doesn't mean I would." I paused, looking for the next thing to say. "We're adults. I don't presume that I can tell you what you must or must not do—and I would be afraid that if I did, I would lose you."

My mouth had gone dry and I swallowed hard.

"And I'm not going to do anything that would risk losing you."

The rest of the day we were tentative and sometimes tense. We didn't talk about the pregnancy. It was cold and rainy out, so we spent most of the day lazing on the couch watching whatever crappy old movies were on TV. At least, I thought, we're lazing together, making physical contact despite the silent gap between us. I thought a lot about the Catholic aspect of this, how Justine automatically supposed that my reaction to her pregnancy would be somehow dictated by religious doctrine. I wondered about self-identity, and whether I was comfortable with the characteristics and qualities attached to me by connecting my worldview to that of a largely conservative institution, even though I obviously approached it from a more progressive angle. I asked myself, Is my attachment to all that— the gospels and liturgy especially—more important than the here and now of this relationship and all that it could be in my life?

Justine fell asleep around mid-afternoon. I got up gently from the couch and arranged a pillow beneath her head and covered her with a blanket—the heat in the apartment was inadequate, as usual, but I'd gotten used to making do in the couple of years that I'd lived here. I knelt beside the couch and watched her sleep and listened to her breathe. Some black-and-white movie from the fifties played quietly in the background, the hushed tones of the actors devious and conspiratorial regardless of the actual plot. I kissed Justine's forehead, then her cheeks and lips, and she responded in her sleep with a slight smile, the first I had seen on her face all day.

I went into the kitchen to see if I had anything I could make for dinner. With a few more ingredients I'd be able to put together a nice stir-fry, the way Justine had taught me, so I put on my coat and ran out to the Korean grocer around the corner. Justine was still asleep when I got back ten minutes later. I boiled water for rice and sliced vegetables and chicken, measured out spices and oil. With the rice simmering I stood in the kitchen doorway and watched Justine as she continued to sleep. Whenever she woke up I would be ready to serve her dinner, ready to take care of her.

Maybe this is all the sacrament I need, I thought. Justine and me, and who we are together, taking care of each other, going through the world together, come ever what may.

By Sunday morning the sky had cleared and even though it would be chilly I could see it was going to be a nice day. Justine was asleep. She had eaten a small helping of dinner the evening before and had gone back to sleep in the bedroom. I had decided not to go to church, and was waiting to find out if Justine wanted to go out for breakfast or just stay in and eat whatever cereal I had in the cupboard. She woke up and noticed the time, and saw that I was not dressed.

"Isn't church in a little while?" she asked.

"I'll skip it today. What do you want to do for breakfast? You must be hungry."

"Don't skip church on my account."

Justine would attend mass once in a while, but this did not seem like a time to ask her to come with me.

"I'll be here when you get back. So go. Breakfast will be ready when you get home. It's my turn to cook."

"I really don't think—"

"Go. Go. You told me once how it gives you a space in your life that's not work, not home, not everyday stuff. If I had something like that I'd want it now."

I wondered for a moment if she was asking me to invite her, but she said "I'll stay here and play house."

"Okay." As I got dressed and ready to leave I looked around the apartment. It was much better than the one-room place I had when I started to work for Stuart Spender, but hardly adequate for a couple, much less a couple and a baby. Maybe the time wasn't right, plain and simple, maybe I was getting ahead of the game for us as a couple. Justine was waiting for me by the door. "I'll see you in about an hour, hour-and-a-half, okay? Pancakes and bacon and all that bad stuff ready to go as soon as you come home."

"Okay."

"Give me a kiss." I did, and she did, and it was so nice that I nearly started to drag her back to bed, but before I could act on the impulse she had pulled back and was ushering me out the door. I was quickly down the front steps and on the street, and had to pause and think for a minute to get my bearings and remember which way to turn to get to the subway.

I arrived at mass with just a couple of minutes to spare and said hello to Father Steve as he was preparing to process down the aisle with the opening music. As I shook his hand, his grasp lingered and he took a purposeful look at me. "Are you okay?"

"Far as I can tell," I said with a forced laugh. "Tough night sleeping, I guess." That much was true—I had tossed and turned for hours while Justine slept soundly.

I took a seat. The mass usually provided a feeling of an oasis—an aesthetic or intellectual space above or at least apart from everyday life. But today I was distracted by thoughts of Justine and the pregnancy. I ran through all of our interaction, from yesterday morning when she came to my apartment to the kiss goodbye as I left a short while ago. I thought about our months of intimacy and sharing. I had never felt more comfortable and excited about a woman before Justine, I had never been happier. Then I looked around the church. I shared common ground with some of the people here, but nothing approaching the quality of my relationship with Justine. I thought about the radical, prophetic narrative of the figure on the cross—one that I chose to understand as poetry, not doctrine, which put me at odds with the institution to which this little church belonged.

I stood or knelt along with the actions of the people around me in the church, hardly paying attention. I tried to focus, to get my mind off Justine for at least a moment, but as I mouthed the words of the liturgy my thoughts went off on a rant about the institutional church. The hierarchy of the church cut against my grain, and the grain of the New Testament. I wanted authority figures characterized by authenticity, who command respect rather than demand it, and the Vatican did not fulfill that, not even the pop-star pope who had been in office since 1978. The glitter and rhetoric of the Vatican never jibed with the peasant-hero of the gospels, and the church's reliance on literally miraculous occurrences to justify its doctrines and create its saints just seemed plain silly. Simplistic justification—Jesus is the son of God because he says so in the Bible—always left me shaking my head.

In this parish, though, I had a group of people and a leader who seemed to understand these things in a similar way. We didn't idolize the pope the way some Catholics do. We focused on effective aesthetics and sound intellectual discourse about God, Jesus, and his teachings. I could say out loud in this church that I would prefer to live without the epistles of Paul (whom I would not call "Saint"). I could say out loud in this church that the riches of the Vatican were shameful, as were the priests in communities all over the world who took advantage of their congregants by behaving as if they were "lords" and not servants, the worst of whom, as we all now know, were rapists of children while being protected by the larger power structure.

When I think about it years later, though, I can see that very early on I already had within me the seeds of the cognitive dissonance that would ultimately separate me from the church, Christianity, and the idea of God, uppercase or lower, itself.

For now, though, I was in church, mass was ending, and when my interior rant ended I went straight back to thinking about my pregnant girlfriend at home in my apartment getting ready to serve me breakfast.

Father Steve caught me at the door of the church and said hello again, then asked me to step into the stairwell adjacent to the foyer.

"I just want to talk privately for minute," he said. "I know I asked before, but are you okay? You seem very preoccupied."

"Oh, so you're a mind reader, are you?" I said, trying deflect him with lame humor.

"No, I'm a body-language reader and a face reader. Your body was here for the past hour, but judging by the look in your eyes that was all. When you didn't come up to receive communion, though, I absolutely knew something was up. You're not the penitent type." He said it with a smile, and Father Steve had a smile that invited you to take him into your confidence.

"I didn't receive communion?" I asked. "I must have been completely zoned out."

"So let's talk."

"Okay," I said. "But just between us, of course."

"Absolutely."

"Justine is pregnant. She just found out on Friday."

Steve waited for me to say more.

"She's not sure she wants to keep it."

"So, are we talking adoption?"

I knew he knew otherwise, but I answered, "No."

"Has she made up her mind?"

"No," I said, "I think she's really trying to honestly figure it out. She says maybe she's too young, not ready, all that."

"And you?"

"I'm ready. Or ready as anyone can ever be, anyway. I don't think you can really be ready to be a parent, but it probably helps to *want* to be one. She's afraid I'll try to forbid her from having an abortion—you know, because I'm Catholic."

"Would you?"

132

"No. I think trying to assert myself that way would kill our relationship. And besides, to be completely honest, when it comes to abortion I'm more in line with the Supreme Court than with the Catholic catechism. You can kick me out of here if that's a problem."

"It's very different, though, I would guess, when it's your baby too," Steve said.

I thought about it for a minute. He was right, of course. But I said, "It's not just that. This is not a casual relationship. This is Justine. Justine Damont, Steve. A week after I met her, before I had so much as kissed her, I knew. And I thought she did, too."

"But she's afraid she's not ready."

"You know, she hardly knew her own father, and what she did know of him wasn't good. I've told you—she's one of three siblings, each with a different father. She doesn't have a lot a confidence in mothers *or* fathers."

Father Steve sat down on the steps, vestments and all. He sighed and said, "She doesn't have to make an immediate decision, right? She's not that far along. Just make sure she's aware of that. And that you don't force anything."

"Yeah, I hear you."

"And I want you to know—I'm not interested in manipulating the situation so that an abortion doesn't happen. If you feel that I'm trying to pull something over on you, you be sure to tell me to fuck off. I know and understand and respect the church's position—that's part of my job description—but I also know that real life is real life and it's never as simple as the papal emperors like to pretend. I just want things to be right for you two—that yes or no to you as a couple doesn't have to depend on your yes or no to this baby."

"Thanks."

He stood up and shook my hand. "Whatever happens, keep me posted. If you need me I'm here. I'll marry you, bless you, counsel you, hear you out. Whatever you need. Don't forget that."

I walked out into the bright cold day and headed for the subway wondering what I would find when I got home.

What I found was what Justine said I would find. Bacon ready to sizzle and pancake batter ready to pour onto the hot griddle. Justine was chatty, almost giddy. She had gone out to the Korean grocer and brought home a few things, including a small bottle of real maple syrup. "I'm so glad they let you run a tab there," she said. "I didn't have enough cash to cover the syrup. The lady was adorable. 'Oh, yes, you are Mister Halsey's lover, of course I will put this on his account.' That was so cute— Mister Halsey's lover. With her little son standing right beside her, too. Maybe I'll paint a self-portrait with that title. You'd have to promise to buy it, of course—it would be for your eyes only." She looked seductively over her shoulder at me as she poured batter onto the griddle.

Had Justine made a decision in favor of having the baby? She had said she would stay home and play house—and she cooked me a big breakfast, went shopping, mingled with my finances. Mister Halsey's lover's eyes were bright and stress-free, so unlike yesterday morning. She was having fun, but I didn't know how to read it and I was not about to ask her any questions.

I went along with her flow. After talking to Father Steve I had made my way home gravely, expecting the worst, perhaps even that Justine would not be there. I ate my pancakes and said all of the right things, never mentioning the pregnancy, church, or any momentous decisions that needed to be made. We cleaned up the kitchen together and Justine said, "I've really got to get outside again. It was so beautiful out, even just going around the corner, after such a gloomy day yesterday." I told her I was game and invited her to lead the way. "I'll follow Mister Halsey's lover anywhere," I said.

We spent part of the afternoon browsing at the Strand bookstore. We were in different parts of the store for a while, and when I went to look for her I surprised her by turning the corner where she was in an aisle of books on pregnancy and childbirth. Justine pretended to be just passing through, and I pretended not to notice. I suggested we go to a coffee shop just down the block.

"I don't know anything about it," Justine said quietly as we waited for our waitress. "Are pregnant girls allowed to drink coffee? Does it make the baby hyper? I just don't know anything."

"I'm sure it doesn't matter this early."

"See, neither of us knows anything, neither of us is ready."

The mood that had prevailed all day seemed to be draining away. I reached across and touched her hand, wanting to slip around to her side of the booth, but resisting the impulse.

"We can find out. We can ask. That's what doctors are for. And books."

"Why did it happen, though? We were so careful," she said.

"Nothing's foolproof. Mister Halsey's lover is juicy and fertile."

She smiled but didn't laugh. "I haven't told anyone. Ellen and Jill weren't home on Friday when I got home and went to bed, and they were sound asleep when I left yesterday morning."

I didn't want to say anything about my chat with Father Steve, afraid she would assume the worst about that, so I asked, "How do you think we should figure this out?"

By this time we had ordered and the waitress had brought our drinks. Justine had opted for orange juice instead of coffee.

"Tell me what you want," she said.

I figured if there was ever a time for a direct statement this was it. "I want to marry you and start a family. Our family. I've wanted that since the day I watched you take your diploma from the SVA dean—you should have seen your face at that moment."

"My graduation?" Justine said. "That was the day we first kissed."

I was quite aware of that fact, and it felt good to know that she remembered as well.

"But when I walked on the stage and took my diploma, we hadn't even had that kiss. You knew *then* that this is what you wanted? Even before?"

"I got a really good seat at the ceremony," I said, "perfect for getting the best view of Justine Damont as she received her diploma. I saw something—I don't know how to describe it— when you took the diploma with your left hand and shook the dean's hand—firmly—with your right hand. Something. I saw the culmination of four years, and really more than that because of what it took for you to get there. I knew then, as I watched you—this is it, this is the day."

"The day? Like, the first day of the rest of your life, something like that?"

"Something like. Something like—it's corny as hell and romantic, but—this is the day, this is the day that love begins. That you would be part of the rest of my life. At least, I really hoped for that." I felt self-conscious saying all of that out loud, so I changed the tone. "One other thing I knew, really knew, was I couldn't go another hour without kissing you."

About twenty minutes after the ceremony I had found her in the hallway adjacent to the auditorium. Several small groups of people were squeezed into the narrow space, but we somehow managed to see each other. Justine held up her diploma, grasped in both hands and raised triumphantly above her head. We made our way toward an empty space about halfway between us. I took the diploma from her so that three of our hands would be free and I said "Congratulations-you-are-so-immensely-beautiful," two separate thoughts run so close together as to be indistinguishable, and I took her in my arms and kissed her gently, almost chastely, a miracle under the circumstances, but then as if with one mind and one desire we took the kiss far beyond congratulations and when we stopped to breathe I felt no doubt in myself, saw no doubt in Justine, and we held each other without words and then kissed again, putting a seal on the first kiss, acknowledging its reality and significance. Then, holding hands, we made our way from the ceremony to the theatre where I had to perform one last time in *Happy Birthday, Wanda June.*

And when the show was over we took a cab to my apartment and sipped wine and teased and nuzzled and groped and fell laughing into each other shyly proudly boisterously naked and fulfilled.

Now, though, sitting in that coffee shop, neither of us said anything. We both, I think, were remembering that moment at the graduation and the moments that followed it. Finally I said, "I know this is maybe not the smoothest way for that to happen, it's not a storybook, it's not love and marriage go together like a horse carriage, but things don't always play out that way. I *will* get down on one knee, though, if it helps."

Justine grinned. She slid around the table, squeezed in next to me, and rested her head on my shoulder. "I just never thought that far ahead, I guess," she said. "I mean, I'm just getting used to the idea of this being a long-term relationship. My old record was only about two months, and now we're at eight, nine. But that's still such a short time to be facing this stuff. Marriage. Baby."

I pushed my coffee mug away from me and asked her if she wanted to order anything else. I suddenly did not want to be in that diner, but I wasn't sure why.

"You need to know this, Justine. Whatever happens next, I'm with you."

"I do know that. I have faith in that. I understand that kind of faith. Confidence. Trust."

"Let's not lose each other in this. It's not as if the earth has split open and stranded us on opposite sides of some huge new ocean."

Justine pulled a five-dollar bill from her pocket. "This wasn't enough for maple syrup this morning, but it should be more than enough to cover coffee and juice." She put the bill on the table. She smiled slyly. "Let's go home. I don't know if this is natural for a girl in my condition, but I am suddenly very very horny."

"I'd say that's incredibly natural. But fortunately there *is* a cure."

"Is that so, Doctor Halsey?"

I sprung for a cab to rush us the seventeen blocks to my place and we made out like teenagers in the backseat all the way.

Justine stayed with me every night that week, going home to her place once in a while to check her phone messages and get clean clothes. At work I talked to Stuart, telling him that I wanted more responsibility at the agency. "And more pay, I suppose," he said. "Yes, I'm a master of subtext. But I think we can arrange something. Better that than lose you to some other schmuck in the business. Let's think about it for a couple of days and sit down to try and map something out."

About halfway through the week Justine sat down next to me on the couch with a sketchbook and a pencil. At the top of the page she had made two columns with the blunt labels "Yes Baby" and "No Baby." She suggested we try the age-old pros versus cons exercise to explore the issue of the baby.

"That might be asking a bit much of those two columns," I said. "This is not simple, or cut and dried. Two columns may not be enough."

"I'll make more if we need them."

I considered that and said, "Okay, well, you're the designer."

"I'm also the pregnant chick."

"And I've got a stake in this."

"Your poking your stake into me is what got us into this," she said, pinching me and giggling. "Now let's get to these columns. I'm trying to be mature and organized here."

She had obviously been thinking this over. In the "No Baby" column she wrote things like, "More time to work on my career" and "I will have time for kids later." She also wrote "Might regret it forever," "Damage our relationship," "Childbirth can have complications (but so can abortion)."

She was slower to start in the "Yes Baby" column. I suggested, "You're in better shape now for childbirth than you will be in, say, ten years." Then I said, "And I'm in better shape for fatherhood."

Justine suddenly scribbled all over the paper and tossed the pad across the room. "Charts and columns aren't going to work," she said. "This is a waste of time." She looked distressed. "My gut tells me to take responsibility. Have the baby. Be its mother. Be your wife. Raise it well. But then another part of my gut, at least that's what I think it is, tells me to think about my career, I've got a good start at the studio and if I have to take a break I may lose my place, you know, and I really love what I'm doing." She trailed off and slumped back into the couch. I took the pencil and pad from her and set them aside.

"I don't know what to tell you, sweetie," I said. "I'm afraid anything I say will be or seem self-serving, because I think we both know what I want here. I also want you to have a career you love, and I want you to feel ready, or as ready as anyone can feel. I want nothing more than to be right here with you, watching how it all unfolds. For better or worse, as the saying goes." I pulled her close to me. "Well, not right *here*. We'll have to get a better apartment."

"Damn straight about that," Justine said. She closed her eyes and in a few minutes fell asleep. After a while I carried her to the bed and undressed her. Still she didn't wake up. I tucked her under the covers and studied her sleeping face for a while, thinking about the day we would stand together beside the bed of our sleeping child, amazed about where it had come from and where it was going.

Early Saturday morning, lying in bed, I heard a rustling sound. Eyes half open, I saw Justine standing near the foot of the bed, looking at herself in the freestanding full-length mirror I had bought when she started staying over so regularly. She was wearing a pink flannel nightgown, frilly and feminine but warm enough for my chilly apartment. I didn't say anything. I just watched, curious. Slowly she pulled the nightgown up from her ankles to her waist, exposing her bare buttocks toward me. In the reflection I could see her belly and the triangle of soft red hair. She placed her hand over her navel and gently massaged her belly, down to the top of her pubic arch and then back to her navel. She seemed strangely transfixed. She pulled the nightgown up over her head and took it off, dropping it on the floor beside her. Naked, she extended the reach of the massage, up to her breasts, back down nearly to her vagina, then across her belly from hip bone to hip bone, up again to her breasts. She looked at herself for a few moments with her hands at her sides and then, almost demurely, bent at the knees and waist to pick up the nightgown, stood up straight again and slipped it back on over her head.

I closed my eyes then, feigning sleep, as she eased back into the bed and pulled the covers up over her. She turned toward me and rolled me onto my back. "I know you're awake, goof-ball," she whispered, "I can tell by your breathing. Reach here now and rub my tummy, nice and gentle and easy." I did as she said. "We're going to have a baby, Martin. Ready or not." I caressed her some more and watched as her face broke into a bright dancing grin and Justine said "This feels good, I feel so *good*," her voice emanating from deep inside her and perhaps, I imagined, being heard as well by the inscrutable presence growing in her womb.

I have never known, nor have I strived to learn, just how Justine made her decision, or when she made it—in those moments standing before the mirror, or in the moment she lay back down beside me, or at some other point unknown to me. I don't know if she felt, or imagined, a quickening, or if a child on the street triggered some sort of desire or anticipation. What I do know is that once the decision was made Justine never doubted it—not through morning sickness, not on the April morning we got married in City Hall, not during the hot golden October when her belly seemed big enough to burst, not in the early hours of the cold November morning when we made our way to the hospital and the miracle of Janet slipped wet and sloppy into our lives. The turns she took on the road to saying yes—to the baby, to our future—are hers to keep as private as she wishes. The sheer enjoyment of being beside her all the years since has been enough for me.

The performance of *Mary Poppins* ends at about eleven. We make our way backstage to offer congratulations but don't stay long. Though I slept late and didn't go to the office until after lunch, Justine was out to work by eight in the morning and I can see in her eyes that she is ready for a good night's sleep.

In the cab uptown she leans against me, head on my shoulder, and closes her eyes. I tell her that when I was a boy, Mary Poppins, as portrayed by Julie Andrews, was my first crush. "Especially on the picnic in the sidewalk paintings," I say. "She was irresistible."

"Feed the birds," Justine sings. "Tuppence a bag. So poignant. Is that where you learned compassion?"

I laugh quietly. "Could very well be. I don't recall hearing that word in my childhood church."

"You're completely a creature of the theatre, Martin Halsey." Justine tries but fails to stifle a yawn.

The cab pulls up in front of our building. I pay the driver and we get out. It is almost midnight. Justine takes a deep breath of the cold air. "Not even fresh air is going to wake me up tonight, I'm afraid." She starts up the stairs but I stand still, looking up at the three floors of our brownstone, thinking that it's more room than we need now, but unable to imagine any other place where I might feel at home. I fumble for my keys and follow Justine to the front door and unlock it.

She goes straight up to the bathroom and in a few minutes is in the bedroom, ready to get under the covers. I have changed into pajamas and a warm bathrobe. "I'm a little too wired to sleep yet," I say. "I'll watch some TV or read or something." We kiss goodnight. "Don't be a stranger," Justine says. "And don't stay up too late."

Downstairs I give up on television after only a couple of minutes, and none of the books on the coffee table capture my interest. Instead I sit alone with a memory, another memory, one of so many memories, of Celia. Baby Celia and mother Justine, a memory so present that I feel it happening here and now though more than twenty years have passed. I have just come home from the office and they are on the sofa, Celia sucking Justine's breast, Justine smiling and cooing as she easily and generously satisfies our daughter's need in a way that only she can.

I, too, am a beneficiary of Justine's ability to satisfy needs, and the image of the two of them in this posture of giving and taking—the image when first encountered, and now in memory—raises a need in me, and at the same time satisfies another. And the vision changes as Janet runs down from their bedroom, a toy car in her hand and shouting "Daddy home!" There's a leaping and sweeping and she is somehow in my arms and we are kissing each other with loud smacking sounds, and then the two of us are taken as if by a magnetic pull to the couch and nestle beside Celia and Justine. Despite the jostling Celia holds on to the tit and looks up at me when I kiss her forehead and breathe deeply the smell of her, of Justine, of Justine's milk. And Justine, with her free hand, touches my face and brings her mouth to mine for a generous sloppy delicious kiss. We hum together, a long "Mmmmmmmm," and then, nuzzling my ear she says, "I hope you're ready to cook or get some takeout, cuz honey babe it's been that kind of day."

"Whatever you want, boss," I say, but I stay put for the moment and there we are, the four of us, mother with baby at her breast, father with toddler in his lap, a family speaking simultaneous languages of words and babbles and touches and tastes and smells. Wholly a family, wrapped together like a single organism that comes together and goes apart and comes together and goes apart in irregular but ineluctable orbits of love.

We were vulnerable, too, like any living organism—we sometimes forget that, particularly when we are young and inexperienced. I was young then, just over thirty, and this little family of mine was like a garden teeming with flowers and vegetables at summer's height, a garden untouched by blight or adversary. Janet drove her toy car up my arm and over my head and down the side of my face jabbering the whole time about who was in the car and where they were going. Celia remained locked on her meal until she was satisfied and then, with gentle nudging from Justine, belched like a longshoreman and we all laughed, even Celia, who then lay happily on a soft blanket on the living room floor, surrounded by soft toys and Janet, still driving her toy car but now using her baby sister as her landscape. Justine returned to me on the couch and burrowed in beside me as we watched our little creations wiggle and roll and sing.

Justine spoke quietly and suggested that she, not me, go out and pick up some dinner. "Thirty minutes by myself and some fresh air will go a long way," she said, and she didn't need to say a long way to what for me to understand: Restoration. Being able to think her thoughts without constant attention to her little children. "Go ahead," I said. "I didn't spend any time at all today playing on the floor. I could use a change of perspective too." After a glance at the girls—and seeing everything was fine—Justine closed her eyes and put her mouth on mine to initiate another grownup and welcome kiss. "Be right back," she said.

I've heard a hundred stories over the years, maybe more, about the person who leaves the house on a routine errand and never comes back. An out-of-control taxi that hasn't had its brakes checked in six years careens onto the sidewalk. Something falls from a window several flights up. There's a robbery and a crossfire. A damaged and deranged person goes wild with an improvised weapon. Or she or he simply disappears: It is an idea so archetypal that our language includes figures of speech that describe it clearly and cleanly and, if you give it a moment's thought, frighteningly. Disappeared without a trace. Vanished into thin air. Missing in action.

None of that ever crossed my mind, though. In my memory Justine leaves and I get down on the floor with our daughters and talk baby talk to Celia and ur-English to Janet, and I think about and anticipate the grease-stained bag of falafel and hummus and pita bread that Justine will bring back from the Middle Eastern restaurant over by Amsterdam Avenue, a place where they know our takeout order before we even speak, we've been there so many times. I don't think about what she is seeing and hearing as she walks away from our building, or whether cars are running red lights as she crosses the avenue, or whether someone who is harboring ancient anger happens to reach a breaking point just as she walks by. We are young and vital and things like that don't happen to people like us.

I am still on the floor with the girls a half hour later when the door opens and Justine walks in and announces, "Falafel!" I'm grateful she is back, because I am hungry, but there is no sense of relief when I see her. Why would there be? She is a young woman coming home from a short walk; not an astronaut returned from the moon in a damaged spacecraft; not a patient returned from an operating room after having her chest opened and heart and lungs temporarily decommissioned. She is the love of my life and the mother of our children and she has merely been out for a short walk on the Upper West Side.

The memory dissipates like a wispy cloud in a windy sky, and the next thing I am aware of is Justine sitting on the floor next to the couch, her head close to mine, her fingers rubbing my scalp. I barely make out that it is morning. "I must have fallen asleep," I say, feeling ready and able to go straight back into slumber.

"You need to get up. It's eight-thirty," Justine says. "This is no time to be a slugabed. Force yourself. If that's what it takes."

I pull myself part of the way up. She leans toward me and grasps my face in her hands firmly and kisses me on the mouth, morning-breath be damned. "Force yourself," she repeats.

"I will, I will," I say, wanting it to sound like a promise but knowing that it doesn't. "You go. Go to work. I'll get out of here. Soon. I need a shower, that's all."

She gathers her things and puts on her coat. "There's coffee in the pot." She goes to the door and stands looking at me, one hand on the doorknob, the other slipped beneath the strap of her shoulder bag. "I need you, Marty. I need you." She is stern but not angry. I asked her to keep me accountable, and her eyes bore into me as she does her part. I stand purposefully so she can appreciate my effort. She nods, holds my eyes in her gaze for another few seconds, and leaves.

4

Third Sunday

I am thinking again about our daughters at Justine's breast, each in her turn, and how that image evokes in me a profound sense of safety and security. In Justine's arms our girls were embraced by comfort and solace, personified by their mother, who gave herself to them body and heart in that quotidian act of feeding.

It is another Advent Sunday morning and I imagine that in churches all over the city they are reading about an angel whispering in Mary's ear, asking her to mother a baby who would have worldly enemies even in infancy and grow to be a man who would live on the edge like an outlaw. No safety for him, but the churches are warm and no armies lay them siege today. I have not passed through those doors in a long time but I remember that being inside, during a particular period of my life, was a womb-like home from which I emerged in some way new after each eucharistic encounter.

That is gone now, and I have never regretted its absence—it was, I am sure, a construct of my own intellect and imagination, together with my needs, desires, and centuries of tradition that connected with my personal sensibilities. But there came a time when the poetic sense with which I understood and encountered my Catholic faith could no longer withstand the dissonance of dogma, doctrine, and a dictatorial church organization. Little children, my inquisitive daughters, were better than me at putting ideas to the test, and my mentor, even as he died, showed me something about seeing and discerning what had real value and what had just a false sheen.

I am up before Justine today, drinking coffee and reading the Sunday paper at the kitchen table. Another cold, clear day sends good light through the back window, inviting light, and my attention is split between the words on the pages of newsprint and more floods from the past that seem to invade my entire thinking process. I turn to the theatre pages hoping to find a solid distraction. I hear the sound of plumbing from upstairs, then Justine's feet as she descends the stairs. We kiss and hug and I make sure to show her as luminous a smile as I can muster. She pours coffee and sips, then sits across the table from me, never taking her eyes from me.

"You're up early."

"I forced myself."

"Good." She smiles. "Football with Ned today?"

"No. He and Molly flew out to L.A. on Friday. Last-minute call to shoot a commercial on Tuesday. The old coot who was supposed to do it dropped dead suddenly."

Justine looks stricken. "Don't talk like that," she says.

"Sorry. Just trying to, you know, keep it—real. Or whatever. Sorry."

We both realize we need to get out of the house and find a crowd that has nothing to do with Christmas or theatre or art or religion, so after consulting the sports pages I go out to a cash machine and make a withdrawal so that we will have enough money to pay scalpers' prices, if necessary, at the Jets game over in New Jersey. As we drive to the stadium I fill Justine in on the Jets season so far and the names of some of their key players. The walk from our parking space to the box office windows is an adventure as we maneuver among tailgating fans in various stages of pre-game inebriation. There are no official tickets available, but it's easy to find a pair at a reasonable price, and since we're not being choosy about seat location we are quite happy with what we get.

The game is entertaining, with an outcome that pleases the local fans, and I get a kick out of the instant camaraderie among the group of people clumped together in the seats adjacent to ours. We get into conversations with some of those people but manage to maintain a friendly distance. I don't say that I'm a talent agent—that always leads to questions about what celebrities I do and do not know—but that I am a business manager, which never inspires further interrogation. Justine shares that she is a designer, but steers away from naming specific book covers or movie posters she has done. But the excitement of the game carries most of the day and I am hardly even annoyed when, on the way out of the stadium, we see a player being interviewed on the jumbo TV screen and he praises God and Jesus for the victory. I roll my eyes as Justine laughs and pinches my arm. "Settle, settle," she says. "We both know this was really a Thor versus Zeus affair. Let's go home."

My mother used to say that even a blind man would have no trouble seeing that Janet and Celia were sisters. There was more to it, though, than physical resemblance. They were two sides of the same coin. Alike as they were at the core, they had opposite faces.

Janet was born skeptical. As a child, when she asked *why* and *how*, she really wanted to know why and how, and she refused to settle for made-for-children answers. I stood in line with her the Christmas season she was six, waiting to see Santa Claus, while Justine took Celia home from our shopping trip so they could both take a nap. After an hour's wait she finally climbed up onto the big man's lap and I could see, from fifteen feet away, that she was trying to have a serious conversation with him. She smiled dutifully for an overpriced photograph but was unimpressed by Santa himself. "I wanted to know about what it's like living at the North Pole," she said, "but all he wanted to know was what silly toys I want for Christmas."

"So what did you tell him?"

"Legos because I like to build things, but really I want a microscope."

"Did you tell him that, too?"

"Yes, but I'm not sure he knew what I was talking about." She rolled her eyes. "I really don't think he's real, anyway. Nobody lives at the North Pole and flies a sled." I loved how she said that—as if she were the only adult in the room.

When she got older Janet attended the math and science high school on Amsterdam Avenue, taking geology field trips to the Catskills, biology trips along the Hudson River, and frequenting the Museum of Natural History. After high school she went to Rochester to study environmental science, and then to Minnesota for graduate and doctoral work. Her research took her north of the Arctic Circle and she was better informed about global climate change than any of the celebrities or politicians who built second careers around saving the planet. She was an activist when activism made sense, but Janet's passion, for the most part, was to discover the facts and then make sense of them, preferably while remaining anonymous.

Celia was grounded and earthy, too, but she preferred to make images. Even as a little girl she had been fascinated by Justine's art and design work, especially her paintings and drawings. Celia created paintings and sculptures out of mud and clay and other elemental substances—activities much better suited perhaps to a suburban or rural lifestyle, but somehow we made do on the Upper West Side, and when Justine opened

her own design firm there was always room in the studio for
Celia. Between Celia's art projects and Janet's scientific research—no matter that it was the art and research of children,
students—our brownstone, even with the basement space and
the extra room resulting from the girls' choice to share a bedroom, always seemed like either the storage area of a museum
or the workshop of some fairytale cobbler or woodworker. As
Celia got older it helped that we were able to enroll her in the
high school of art—along with placing her near kindred spirits
in the visual and performing arts, she could indulge herself and
think on a larger scale than our apartment would allow. She
took after Justine in terms of talent, and was a brilliant drafts-
woman—she could render a landscape with the same precision
that Janet could define its underlying chemistry or geology—
but she always dared to take each meticulous line beyond its
natural beauty and make it mean something that no one but
Celia herself could ever expect it to manifest.

Toward the end of her last year of high school we went to
an exhibit of work by Celia and her fellow seniors. I was surprised by the breadth of Celia's work, in both medium and subject matter. Its quality, too, was remarkable, and I am not
merely bragging on my daughter when I say that. I knew she
was good but her work had so advanced that it was almost
frightening.

As we stood in the alcove display of Celia's work, Justine
said, "She's got a hard road ahead of her, if you ask me."

"How do you mean?"

"Celia's an artist. Pure and simple. She won't become a
graphic designer like me, limited by the dimensions of the
magazine page or the dust jacket or the billboard. You look
around on any street in the city and you see lots and lots of design, but very little art—you know, with a capital 'A'—but that's
what she'll need to be about in her life."

Justine continued to speculate, supposing that our early recognition of Celia's talent helped her to take it beyond a utilitarian ability. "I'm not saying sour grapes or anything, but I didn't have that kind of encouragement until relatively late. I love what I do, that's not an issue. But this work of hers tells me she's a purist, if that's even the right word—and that's a hard row to hoe."

I wondered whether Justine considered this to be a good realization or a bad one but she answered, sort of, without being asked. "We've been her patrons for this long, I guess it won't hurt to continue a while longer." She looked around again at the pieces arranged in the space and sighed. She took me by the crook of the arm and pulled me toward her, her excitement palpable in the strength of her grasp. Gesturing at the display she said, "Damn she's good. Damn!"

Many years before that, fifteen or so, Stuart Spender called me into his office. Martha was already there, along with Joseph McIlhenny, the agency's attorney. I shook hands with Joe, sat down in the proffered chair, and accepted a cup of coffee from Martha. Joe took a sheaf of papers from his briefcase and laid them on a bare spot on the edge of Stuart's desk. He looked at Stuart as if to give him a cue, and Stuart leaned back in his chair.

"Marty, I'm sorry to have to lay this on you like this, but the three of us, Martha and Joe and me, figure it's best to just put everything out there. About three months ago I was diagnosed with cirrhosis of the liver."

He paused. "Cirrhosis?" I said, stunned. Stuart was not averse to wine with dinner, but I had seen him nurse a single glass for an hour rather than chance losing his edge while negotiating on behalf of a client.

"We're managing it now, with medication," Stuart continued. "But it's in bad shape. And it's very possibly going to get worse." He paused. "*Probably* going to get worse. Honesty is required at this meeting. Probably going to get worse. That's what the signs are showing." He laughed lightly and seemed to want me to say something.

I didn't know what to say, so I asked, "Cirrhosis? You're hardly a drinker, Stuart, how the hell?"

"It's probably hereditary," he answered. "We never knew what killed my old man, he just got sick and died, and there was no autopsy. But I recognize some of the symptoms. Back then, in the fifties, he just toughed it out. Didn't like doctors."

"And if it's not hereditary," Martha put in, "there are several other possible underlying causes."

We are all silent for a moment. I ask, finally, "What's the prognosis? I mean, beyond that it's likely to get worse."

"Too soon to tell. As I said, it's medication now, but at some point they may have to try to get me a transplant. We're just keeping it at bay, slowing it down, but that's not the same as a cure."

Martha said, "The disease has its effects, of course, and the medication does as well. It's going to be harder and harder for Stuart to work fulltime, maybe even part-time."

"And the whole shebang just might do me in before the doctors can get a real handle on it. So the point today is that you've been my right hand for what, seven years now? Man, does time fly. That wad of papers Joe has in front him spells out the terms for making you an equal owner of this agency, with Martha and me, and what happens if I die. We'll call it Spender & Halsey, with an ampersand, because I like ampersands, and your first responsibility will be to hire that wife of yours to design us a new letterhead."

Joe McIlhenny tapped the legal papers with his index finger and said, "It's complicated, but I can walk you through it this morning."

"And you don't have to lay out any cash, Marty," Stuart said, "so don't worry about that. That would be asking too much. You've earned your equity. As an owner of course there are greater risks, but that's just a fact of business. I hope you'll go this way with me—the alternative is to release or sell off clients and shut the place down. But I built this from nothing and I'd like it live after me, whether I last another month or twenty years."

Everyone turned and looked at me, each with a quizzical look that seemed to be asking if I was willing to take this on.

"There's a lot to process here," I said, "but the business part is the least of it. You've never steered me wrong, Stuart. Martha. Both of you. Yes. Let's do what's right for the agency, for our clients."

Martha and Stuart gathered up some things and prepared to leave. "I've got to get poked and prodded for a new round of tests over at Mt. Sinai Hospital. Joe is all yours for the rest of the morning. Once it's all set, we'll make a public announcement. I want every last one of our clients to remain confident in the agency, with me or without me."

They left, and Joe and I went over the paperwork for the next hour, and later in the week Stuart, Martha, and I signed all the papers and made it official.

Stuart's condition was stable for the next three or four months, but then he seemed to reach the edge of whatever plateau he had been crossing and began an abrupt decline. He became more and more bound to the office, unable to come and go and attend meetings, the way he loved to, at theatres and rehearsal halls with all the bustle of performers, designers, and crew working behind the scenes to make the magic happen. Even at work, the medication eventually made him seem disengaged, though I could see that he was fighting to remain focused and on task.

A year after Stuart's diagnosis it was clear that the only way he might possibly survive was to receive a liver transplant. Evaluations were undertaken and procedures followed to get him onto the liver transplant list, a tedious but necessary process to ensure fairness and a level playing field for all potential recipients. "It's mind-boggling to think about," Stuart told us, the Spender and Halsey staff. "There's a list of people like me, all waiting for someone to die—someone who not only has the right liver but also has elected to give it away if he dies. It's amazing what can be done, but the circumstances that need to line up—just boggles my mind. Of course, it doesn't take much to boggle me, all these meds."

That was the last time we saw Stuart in the office. He soon started having trouble maintaining his equilibrium and was in constant danger of falling. A fall, and the potential damage it would cause, would very likely lead to complications in his condition that would move him down on the transplant list, or take him off it completely, if the doctors determined that his ability to survive transplant surgery itself had been too severely compromised. Nurses came to their apartment everyday to supplement the care that Martha could provide. We kept up a steady stream of visitors to Stuart's apartment—clients like Ned Flynn who had a long history with Stuart and who could handle seeing him in this condition, as well as his favorite barber and some of his friends and colleagues from other agencies and theatre organizations. I visited two or three times each week and gave him updates on the state of the business—deals signed, new clients, new opportunities—and as difficult as it might be for him, he worked at assimilating the information and acknowledged that we were doing well, that our trends were positive and the business was growing. I let him know everything about how my family was doing, how Justine was taking on enough freelance work that she might soon be ready to incorporate as a business and start hiring other designers to take on some of the workload. He always asked about Janet and Celia. Janet had been about three years old when Stuart became sick, and Celia was still a babe in arms then, and they were stuck at those ages in Stuart's mind even though nearly two full years had passed.

When I got the call from Martha that, in spite of all the precautions and home health care help, Stuart had fallen and broken some ribs, it seemed that such an outcome had been all but inevitable. Stuart was in intensive care, in an induced coma to manage the pain, but at the moment he was first on the transplant list. Standing at his bedside with Martha, Ned, and other friends, we spoke to him directly in case he was able to perceive us in his present state of consciousness. I doubted that he could, but it seemed to be right to make the effort amid the beeping and hissing machines that surrounded him.

We talked among ourselves as well, sharing memories of our times with Stuart and speculating about his chances for recovery. I heard stories from Ned and other longtime clients that I had never heard before—stories about Stuart's early days in the theatre, details about how he came to New York from Indianapolis wet behind the ears and ready to beat the world. Ned met Stuart when they were both cast in a production a Shakespeare's *Much Ado About Nothing*, Ned as the witless constable Dogberry and Stuart as one of his equally witless assistants. Their bond was instant and lifelong, personal and professional, with Stuart's first successes and ultimately his reputation as an agent coming from his ability to find work for Ned. Stuart was best man at Ned's wedding to Molly, and if Stuart had ever gotten around to marrying Martha in an actual ceremony Ned would have returned the honor in spades.

As Stuart breathed with the help of a respirator, not conscious of the world or people around him, I found it hard to imagine him recovered, back to even a fraction of his customary levels of energy and activity. At home one night I was updating Justine on his condition to prepare her for coming to the hospital with me the next day while Janet was at morning kindergarten and Celia with a sitter. Janet overheard and wanted to know what it was like seeing Stuart in the hospital. I wasn't sure how much to say, so I tried, "It's like he's asleep, and can't wake up until the sick parts of his body get better."

"But what if they don't get better?"

Justine looked at me, suggesting with her eyes that I try to keep it light. I wasn't sure I'd be able to do that.

"Well, sweetie, if his body doesn't get better, then he will die."

"My friend Carrie says her grandpa died because God wanted him to be in heaven." I tried to interject something but Janet kept talking. "But I don't think so. I think it's stupid for God to take Carrie's grandpa, because she only had one grandpa, like me, so that's not fair."

Justine said, "Yes, it's very hard when someone dies, but we can always remember them and all the good things we did together."

"It's still not fair, so I think God is bad," Janet said. "If God wants Stuart he should just make another one and leave ours alone."

I didn't want to address the God question, but felt I had to say something. Personally I had reached the point in my religious outlook where the inconsistencies were just too much for me to continue to tolerate. The mythology and ceremony were all fine and good, but I did not want my daughter thinking that people die because God or Jesus need them more than we do.

"Carrie says that her grandpa is happy up in heaven, up in the sky with God and angels and Jesus."

I flashed to when I was a kid and had imagined a cartoonish afterlife—dead people in white robes strolling around forever on puffy clouds, if they went to heaven, and dead naked people writhing in flames forever if they went to hell. I remembered how Sister Christopher taught us that heaven would be like sitting forever in the lap of your favorite grandfather. I grew up with only one grandfather, though, and couldn't remember ever sitting in his lap. Her analogy was lost on me, but when Sister asked if we understood what she meant I just nodded and smiled.

"Will Stuart go to heaven if he dies?" Janet's curiosity had no limits, and once she got started on a line of questioning it was hard to derail her.

Justine said, "Well, Janet, we don't really know what actually happens after we die. Different people believe different things about that. Like Carrie and her family."

"What does our family believe?"

I was afraid we were getting into waters too deep for Janet, at five, to comprehend—the difference between belief and knowledge, the many and varied ways of trying to make sense of the fact of death, the reality of grief and how we cope with loss throughout our lives. I took a deep breath as I tried to frame a response to Janet's question, but Justine spoke first.

"We believe that we just don't know. And we probably won't ever know. So the best thing we can do is to treat each other well and love each other. Like our family, we all love each other, even when we're mad or have hurt feelings. Stuart treated us all very well. He gave Daddy a job and taught him how to do it, and when Daddy and I got married he helped us find this place to live, and he also helped a lot of other people. So if he dies he'll still be with us, kind of—because Daddy and I will never forget how good and kind he was to us ever since we first met him. You and Celia won't remember as much because you're young, but you can always ask me or Daddy to tell you stories about Stuart and how much he cared about all of us."

Janet seemed satisfied, or her attention span had reached its limit for now, and she said, "I'm going to go play in my room now," leaving Justine and me on the sofa.

"Heaven, hell, purgatory," I said. "I look at Stuart in that hospital bed and I don't believe any of it. I don't think I ever really did, at least it never seemed important enough to think about when you're going to church and soaking up the ritual and then trying to help homeless and hungry folks." It was true—I had only ever cared about the afterlife when it was a matter of juvenile concern and when it was used to evoke fear-based conversion to Christianity. "The fundamentalists I used to know had a lot to say about hell—it must be one of their most effective promotional tools—but very little about heaven. Father Steve, though, never talked about the afterlife, just the kingdom of God, which made sense to me because he was talking about creating a better world today. Not pie in the sky when you die. But I don't think you even need God to live in the world the way you just described to Janet."

"Well, I am the wise woman of the Upper West Side." She smiled crookedly and crossed her eyes to give a full picture of her wisdom woman character.

I said, "I don't want our girls growing up believing in some kind of God who is a cosmic kidnapper, or heaven as a reward, or any of that."

"Do unto others. Isn't that all they really need? For its own sake."

The next morning we got to the hospital at nine o'clock and were surprised to see not only Martha but Ned and Molly and five or six others who had been visiting on a regular basis during the three weeks Stuart had been in the hospital. Martha asked us all to come with her to the waiting area at the end of the hall, where there was room for everyone to sit. She introduced us to the doctor who had been the lead physician on Stuart's case.

"I had a long talk with the doctor and nurses last night. Stuart's kidneys are failing now along with everything else, and his blood pressure can't be sustained at a high enough level, without medication, for him to survive transplant surgery." Martha's tone was officious, but I could see how hard she was working to hold herself together. "The transplant protocols dictate that because of these conditions he has to be removed from the list. He will not recover or regain consciousness." She looked at the doctor, unable to continue, and he cleared his throat.

He explained that Martha had, in consultation with the medical team, decided that they should, today, withdraw all the medications that were sustaining Stuart and let him peacefully go. "It's the most humane way to bring this to a close," the doctor said. "As if he were going into a deep sleep." Justine was standing closest to Martha, and took her in an embrace. We were all free to remain at Stuart's bedside, the doctor continued, for as long as it took.

Ned went to Martha and said, "I will be honored to stay with you today, Martha." His voice cracked and tears fell down his cheeks. "My best and oldest friend."

We all went to the room and made ourselves comfortable. Martha stood close to Stuart and kissed him on both cheeks, then sat at the bedside and held his hand. Justine and I sat with her. Ned and Molly were on Stuart's other side. After also kissing him, they took his other hand. The doctor stepped around the machines, touching a button here and there, explaining that the medication supporting Stuart's blood pressure would be withdrawn, his pressure would diminish, and "he will pass peacefully, just like going to sleep."

We talked and told stories, laughed and cried, sometimes addressing Stuart directly despite the unlikelihood that he was at all conscious. "You are surrounded here by great love, Stuart," Ned Flynn said, "and you're going to a place of even greater love." Though I could not believe the second part of that statement, I understood the impetus behind it and respected Ned's sincerity. But most of all I was humbled and glad to be part of the love surrounding Stuart, which had been surrounding him for years, since long before I came into the picture.

"Through all of this," I said, "these nearly two years with this disease, I never once heard Stuart complain or ask 'Why me?' The way he faced this, even when the odds were turning against him, is something I hope I'll be strong enough to emulate if the time comes." Beside me Justine wept quietly and tightened her grip on my arm. "It's a privilege to be with you all," I said. "Especially Martha. To mark this moment. A moment such as this needs to be marked, and remembered. I accept that responsibility."

"Such a sweetheart," Justine said, her voice slightly more than a whisper. Then she said again, "Such a sweetheart," this time as she kissed Martha and put her head on her shoulder.

The morning progressed until finally, just after noon, the doctor confirmed that it was done, that Stuart was gone, "Just like falling asleep," the doctor said again, "very comfortable," and we all began to take the steps needed to move into the next phase of our lives, absent our friend.

In the years since that morning we have often received news of other deaths—clients, old friends, acquaintances, relatives—some too young, some after long eventful lives. It is in some cases more challenging than others to find the sense in a death, other than it being the way of nature and there being no such thing as a guarantee of health or long life. I have learned, or perhaps just think that I have learned, to accept the idea that death is often as unfair as it is inevitable and that there is no answer to the question, Why?

Wednesday

One of the things we keep in the bedroom Janet and Celia shared is a painting Celia made in the spring of her junior year at Vassar. Just last spring, a season that seems sometimes so immediate in memory and at other times vague and distant. Justine prefers to keep the door to their bedroom closed. "At least for a while," she said to me back in September after Janet returned to Minnesota and our pain was still brand new and more acute than either of us could have imagined. I am sure that Justine opens the door from time to time and goes in to sit on Celia's bed or look at Celia's things on her dresser and bedside table. I am certain of this because I do that very thing sometimes when I am alone in the house, and for all the differences between the ways Justine and I have coped, this is one that I expect that we share. There is a splendid specificity to the way Celia ordered her world—the way she did not merely store her jewelry, say, but displayed it, and how she arranged her clothes so that the colors and shapes facing the viewer who might randomly see them in her closet were as carefully composed as any painting she had ever made. She was not self-conscious about it, nor was it accidental. Celia simply had an innate or instinctive tendency to treat the things of her life as artifacts in a gallery, and I have always loved being a viewer of that space.

The painting, though, the painting on that bedroom wall: In her junior year Celia and her advanced painting classmates were given an assignment to create a picture with the following parameters: the medium was oil paint; the size was to be 24 by 36 inches; the theme was to be taken from religion or mythology. It was an assignment designed to be completed over the course of two semesters, the work comprising not only painting but research, drafts, sketches, studies, and multiple sessions of peer and professor critique. Celia later told me, "I knew almost immediately that it would have something to do with Mary, the mother of Jesus. It took just a few minutes to settle on doing a portrait of the Holy Family."

When the paintings were exhibited in the student gallery toward the end of the semester, Celia's artist's statement included this paragraph:

My father is no longer a member of any religion, though he was a practicing Catholic for a number of years. But he still has—and it is something we have often talked about—an abiding fascination with Mary, the mother of Jesus. He says,

"I love her in the way that I love literary characters such as Rosalind in William Shakespeare's *As You Like It*, or young Esmé in J. D. Salinger's story 'For Esmé, with Love and Squalor.' Mary has a quality unlike any other biblical character. Her faith was born of a visceral connection with Jesus, literally from the womb to the tomb. No one else shared that continuum with him. The others—disciples and followers—came to Jesus through mere belief and a hope for something beyond this world. Mary loved him unconditionally, and was at the foot of the cross not because of anything she believed about Jesus, but because he was her son, and she was his mother. Although Mary has been twisted, trivialized, and sanitized by many who consider themselves her greatest devotees, I think there is no character more truthful anywhere in the literature of Christianity—or its history."

I hope I have shown that quality of earthy, instinctive love and faith in this picture of the Holy Family.

Though the assignment was given on the first day of the fall semester, almost a year and a half ago, it was several weeks before I learned about it. Late in the evening on the third day of nearly a week of cold October rain I came home from attending a showcase production at a storefront theatre downtown. The show itself had been more or less a disappointment, but there was a promising young actress who might fit the agency profile quite well, and I was still mulling over the merits of her performance. Justine was sitting on the sofa studying something on her laptop, which was propped on a couple of pillows beside her. She came to the door and kissed me—we hadn't seen each other since first thing in the morning—and asked, facetiously, "Raining out?" She took my coat upstairs and hung it in the bathroom to dry over the tub. We talked about our days as I dried off and changed into pajamas and my flannel robe.

Justine went back down to the living room and when I came back downstairs she was clicking around on whatever she was viewing on the screen. "Working late?" I asked. She held up a finger as she studied, her sign for "thinking right now, can't talk too," then typed some text, clicked a few more times, and finally looked up.

"No, just looking at something from Celia." She started to close the laptop.

"Wait, let me see." I loved being able to see Celia's works in progress on the computer—I had been able to watch her drawings evolve into paintings ever since she was a little girl, and missed having all that stuff right here at home. Justine closed the laptop all the way and shook her head. "No, no, not this time. Celia said specifically not to show it to Daddy. Yet." The computer made the sing-song sound that indicated it was shutting down.

She curled up on the sofa and tried to distract me with her best come-hither look. "I was stuck on the platform in Short Hills out in that cold for almost an hour coming back from a client meeting. I still haven't warmed up." We pulled a comforter over ourselves and snuggled in. "You'll see the painting when Celia says you can. She wants it to be a surprise."

I asked for more information, a few hints. Justine said, "I've been sworn to secrecy. But I get to advise on graphical matters. Don't look at me so skeptically. And don't let her know I said anything at all about it." She switched gears. "There must've been a breakdown on New Jersey Transit today. Almost an hour between trains in that rain and cold. How was the showcase?"

I talked about the play but kept hinting that I wanted to know more about Celia's painting. "Be patient, boy. It's not ready for your eyes. Soon enough."

Not that soon, as it turned out. I finally saw the painting in late April. Justine and I took a couple of days off and drove up to Poughkeepsie on a Thursday afternoon to attend the opening, in an improvised student gallery, of the paintings made over the past several months by the eight or nine advanced painting students. Each painting was accompanied by sketches and studies that led to the final work, and commentaries by the artists detailed their paths to the finished painting. It was an exciting event, attended by most of the art faculty and many students. We met Celia at the gallery door—we had last seen her in February—and she led us to her painting and watched as the final product of her several months of work took my breath away.

But I don't want to think about that trip to Poughkeepsie now—I want, instead, to enter the bedroom and view the painting itself, real and present, in the environment of Celia and Janet's bedroom, which somehow seems safer right now than memory. Home alone on this cold December evening I feel I owe it to myself to take comfort in the painting and the sense of Celia that it will offer me, even though that comfort will be accompanied by a deep familiar inescapable ache. I turn the doorknob deliberately, slowly, and cross the threshold in the way I might long ago have entered a church. The painting hangs over a dresser—I hung it properly, to both protect it and accentuate it, as soon as we brought it home after last April's commotion—but I avert my eyes from it as I enter the room. I don't want to encounter it first, or suddenly, upon entering the room. I work my way toward it, as I might save the Mona Lisa for last if I were touring the Louvre. I take in the rest of the room, the two beds with the autumnal bedspreads Janet had made them up with before she left in September, the closet with Celia's warm clothes that had never been packed for the fall semester, the odds and ends on the desk that Celia used, in contrast to the empty surface of Janet's. My eyes meander around the room until there is nothing left for them to encounter but the painting, so I finally direct my attention to it.

The colors, as always, are the first thing to strike me. The reds, ochres, and yellows that greet the eye, even before I discern shapes and figures, are a clear allusion to Henry Ossawa Tanner's painting of the Annunciation. But there is no angelic presence here, no ethereal source of light as in Tanner's work. The presence here is thoroughly human, earthy, and earthly, and the warm glowing colors that emanate from the three figures—Mary, Joseph, and the infant Jesus—originate from the candles and lamps burning above the lushly arranged pillows and bedding in which the family is found. Unlike the stark stone walls of Tanner's room, green and flowering plants rest upon multi-leveled shelves of the room Celia has painted. Where Tanner's Mary is seated upon a bed that is a jumble of blankets from which she has emerged upon being awakened by an angelic radiance, the blankets and sheets from the bed of Celia's Holy Family appear to have been kicked aside and out of the way. Where Tanner's Mary is covered in a long robe as one might wear to bed on a cold night, the three figures of Celia's Holy Family are uncovered, naked, their skin as vibrant as that of a Modigliani nude, but more muscular, and the contrast with the darkened corners of the room adds to the clear sense that it is a warm night, a night to sleep without cover.

Celia's Mary, leaning back on several pillows, cradles the infant Jesus in her right arm, nursing him at her right breast. Though she is naked her demeanor betrays no self-consciousness. She smiles as she looks at her son, and makes no attempt to cover herself. Joseph is also naked and lies beside Mary, kissing her neck. His left hand, a workman's hand, cradles her breast, at the same time lightly touching the baby's cheek. He, too, makes no attempt to cover himself, and the loins of this couple, this mother and father, lie visible in close and familiar proximity. Their bodies are in contact literally from head to foot—Joseph's left foot has engaged Mary's right, and the positions of their legs indicate that they are pressing their feet together, that Joseph is massaging the sole of Mary's foot with the top of his own as she suckles their son.

The image is realistic but the manner in which Celia has executed it is painterly—she always reveled in paint as paint, in the action of brushstrokes—and though there would be no mistaking this picture for a photograph, the figures have the substance of real bodies. It is an arresting image that continues to capture me the more I look at it and comprehend what I am seeing in the postures and details: On a hot night, a baby has awakened to be fed while his parents, this wife and husband, are in the midst of lovemaking, and he is welcomed into that moment with them while all their senses—and hunger and passion—are at their height. The mother and father are unashamed and even continue their afterplay—or perhaps their foreplay, or between-play—as the baby eats.

That the image is meant to portray the Holy Family, capitalized, that the image intentionally portrays the infancy of one whom billions consider their savior, and the parents who are thought of as saints and models of purity, is the ultimate arresting aspect of the painting. And of course it is the one that made it the center of a controversy.

❖

The exhibition of student paintings was open to the general public for a few hours each of the four days it was up. It was well-attended by students and faculty but did not initially draw much attention from the local community—there had been no advertising or formal announcements off campus. But what little attention it attracted turned out to be quite enough. The pastor of a local storefront evangelical church came in on Friday, advised to do so by one of his members who was a college employee, and, in violation of the prominently displayed "No Photographs" signs, took a picture of Celia's *Holy Family*.

The next morning the painting, with pixelized breasts and loins, appeared on the church's blog. It was accompanied by some of the text from a handout of the artist's statement, along with a poorly written condemnation of the painting and its creator, and of the college for allowing it to be exhibited. On Saturday afternoon a group arrived on campus with signs and placards saying things like "God is mocked here" and "Close this exibbit of smut and hate" and "Mary ever-virgin is not a slut." Campus police, citing private property laws, were able to convince the protesters to leave peacefully after a little while. By the time Justine and I arrived to pick Celia up when the doors were locked at three o'clock, there was no sign of the protest, but the student artists and their professor were still buzzing with it and on the phone with the college administration to provide overnight security for the building.

Celia's main concern was for the painting itself. "I know you guys are planning to leave tomorrow at noon," she said, "but I need you to stay till three or so, when the exhibit closes." She led the way out the back door of the exhibit hall and down a long hallway to a storage room. We stood just inside the doorway while Celia looked purposefully around the room, intent as a dog on a scent. "Ah, there," she said. "Daddy! A little help, please!" I took her instructions while she extricated a narrow wooden crate from a pile of what looked to me like junk. She eyeballed the crate and then measured it against the width of her own hand. "Perfect." She gathered some sheets of corrugated cardboard, along with a roll of brown wrapping paper, and gave them to me to carry while she hoisted the crate and led the way back to the exhibit.

"Tomorrow, as soon as the doors close, we pack up *The Holy Family* and you take it back to New York. It'll be safer there."

"Honey," Justine said, "this whole thing is bound to blow over in a day a two."

Celia smiled. "I wish. This is the internet, Mom—poor pixelized, censored Mary and Joseph are right now being copied onto all kinds of websites, for and against, but mostly against, and if the painting is not hidden away I'm sure that someone will try to get their hands on it and burn it or at least try to damage it. It's a sacrilege, you know. That's what they're saying, and that's what they do to sacrileges." I had never seen this sort of edge with Celia. She was thinking clearly and strategically, she was making sense, but she was above all extremely angry about the possibility that someone who disliked her depiction of the subject might go so far as to hurt the painting.

Students from the college's humanist club, free speech club, and arts club had volunteered to take shifts standing watch over the building for the rest of the day and overnight, and campus security brought on an extra guard for the same time period as well. Celia wanted to stay, but security was afraid that she would be a target herself if anyone snuck onto campus to try to do some damage. We all got into our car and drove across the river and up to Kingston to a little café for dinner, and by the time we returned to Poughkeepsie to the bed and breakfast Justine and I were staying at near the college, things seemed to have calmed down.

"You can stay here tonight," we told Celia. She really wanted to go back to campus and make sure everything was under control, but I persuaded her just to call a friend who was taking an overnight shift outside the building and find out what was going on. Everything was quiet, she was told. A few suspicious persons had been seen looking toward the building from a distance, but no one had tried to come close.

As we drove up to the college entrance in the morning we could see picketers at the gateway, with the signs from yesterday and several more. I told Celia to duck down in the backseat but she acted as though she hadn't heard me and stared directly at the protesters. "I've got nothing to hide," she said. "Anyway I need to memorize their faces. Maybe next year I'll do a crucifixion and they'll be the Roman soldiers." I couldn't help but smile at the piss and vinegar of Celia's response. We drove through and parked behind the exhibit building, then went in the back way. Celia's professor was overseeing a reconfiguring of the exhibit space—where before, viewers could step up just inches from each painting, now *The Holy Family* was behind a roped-off area and no one could get closer than ten or twelve feet from it. Sympathetic students were again recruited to stand watch in strategic areas around the space, and though no one got close to the painting there were several who got as close as they could and then shouted accusations of heresy. One tried to throw an egg at the canvas, but a bystander batted his arm just as he threw and the egg broke harmlessly on the floor while the thrower fled.

When the exhibit doors closed at three we wrapped the painting in protective paper and cardboard and then secured it in the crate. "My poor little lovemaking family," Celia said, "guilty of enjoying their humanity. All locked away and crated up." In a separate box she stashed her artist's statement and the sketches—many more than had been on display. "I want to keep everything together."

"Don't worry," I said, "I'll see that they are back out in the light of day before long. As soon as we get home." We hauled the crate to the shipping entrance at the far end of the building and locked it into the trunk of our car. Justine and I kissed Celia goodbye and drove off, still figuring that the whole thing was just a local affair and would quickly be forgotten. When we got home I hung the painting in the girls' bedroom where it remains to this day.

Celia was correct, though—this was the internet. On Monday the painting began to appear on countless Christian websites, complete with commentaries and condemnations. Few if any of these considered the painting as a painting—draftsmanship and composition were ignored—choosing instead to attack the concept of the painting and characterizing it with words like "desecration," "defilement," and "sacrilege." Celia herself was described as a witch, a heretic, and a "godless atheist evildoer." Someone found photographs of Celia and these were added to these vitriolic posts. In New York City our personal phone number was unlisted, but bloggers and reporters put two and two together and the phones at the Spender Halsey Agency started ringing with people looking for me and my comments.

Celia was trying to get through the last couple of weeks of school and exams, and the college faculty and administration did a good job of sheltering her from protests and individuals who tried to enter the campus and confront or interview her. Her college email address and cell phone number were discovered rather easily. "I'm not reading any of it," she said. "That's security and IT's job." She had a separate, private address to keep in touch with friends and family, so she rarely needed to use the college account anyway. I overnighted a prepaid cell phone to her with a new number so she could ignore the other one more easily and just turn it off. But I wanted to be sure she had a phone with her at all times in case of an emergency.

After a day or two of viral internet activity about the painting—which had developed two camps, for and against, and had begun to also rile up free-speech advocates—the story started to show up on the twenty-four-hour cable news networks. I was in my office on Wednesday afternoon when my assistant came in and said, "Martin, there's a guy on the phone who insists on talking to you. He says it's extremely important—something to do with your daughter. He says his name is Steve Rinaldo."

That was a name I had not heard in a while. My old parish priest had offered me a lot of good advice during the time we had known each other, even to the extent of not resisting when I chose to give up the church because that seemed to be the best course for my family. We had met for coffee or drinks from time to time in the years after that, and he had listened with patient intelligence as I shared with him that I had grown to no longer believe in God, and that I honestly felt happier in my state of "unbelief" than I ever did as a believer.

"It would impossible to come out of a long-term connection with the Catholic church without some baggage—both good and bad," I had told him. "I'll always have an attachment to the aesthetics, to the narrative. The paschal mystery—especially that. But I can no longer hang in there with the dogma and doctrine—the 'fantasy stuff' is how I think of it now, to be honest. Virgin birth as reality, not symbol. 'Real presence' as literal flesh and blood in the eucharist. Bodily resurrection—I mean, if you ask me to believe that a man was tortured and killed and buried in a tomb, and then after three days walked out, alive, then you're asking me to believe in a freak of nature, and believing in a freak of nature just, well, freaks me out. Ask me to believe in the *story* of this man, in what it teaches about how new life emerges from death, and how that reality plays out in our lives day in and day out, then you've got something for me.

But that's not what the church is putting out there, as far as I can see. The church dilutes all that with promises of life after death in exchange for dogmatic obedience *now*. I'm not willing to make that trade. It trivializes both life and death."

"I understand that," Steve had said. "I struggle with it too—how to bring that vivid symbolic level through in a context that emphasizes the mundane and literal. People don't usually characterize Catholics as fundamentalists, but in certain cases, like the virgin birth, if I were to teach that it's symbolic, and show how virgin birth was a fairly common literary motif that the writers of the gospels chose to employ for theological reasons, well, I'd be drummed out of church by the faithful themselves."

I said, "Yes, I can understand why—because the love of God gets conflated with love of the institution, and of doctrine and dogma, and marginalizes the love of neighbor. And love of self. It's so much easier to believe in the Virgin Mary floating off to heaven than it is to tolerate the people around you, especially when you think they're all bozos."

We talked for a while about the concept of cognitive dissonance and how difficult it was to stand simultaneously in the conflicting worlds of literal and symbolic understanding. I said, "It was always kind of like the human eye for me. You know, the image that comes in through the eye is upside down, but the brain corrects that, automatically. We don't have to think about it. But as a Christian, I had to constantly be on guard for ideas and statements that needed to be turned around—from dogma to poetry, say—and at the end of the day it just got to be too much. I couldn't recite the Creed without consciously turning it around in my mind, or say the Lord's Prayer without transposing in some image of God that wasn't so hung up on maleness. How could I honestly remain Catholic when I couldn't even say these words without internally editing them all the time?"

As for the Bible, despite the idea that it was an "all or nothing" book that could also be variously interpreted, I had always picked and chosen. I never believed it was in any way dictated by God to humans, and although the notion that it was "inspired" by God caught my fancy for a while, even that idea was not sustainable. The Bible, I came to understand, was a human reflection on life in a primitive and inhospitable world, and I took from it its radical expressions of justice and human dignity in the face of oppression and hardship. The Catholic tradition of teaching on social justice seemed to flow directly from the teachings of Jesus, as well as from the more enlightened and poetic passages of the Old Testament, but again, I had to pick and choose to put all of those connections together.

However, however . . . . The church itself was a bundle of contradictions. This was never far from the surface: its vaunted ideas about social justice versus its treatment of women; its openness to interfaith dialogue versus its intolerance of questioning "among the faithful"; its great reputation for education versus its generations of child abuse. "There are just too many howevers," I told Father Steve. "Even if I still believed, I could not support an organization that is turned so inside out upon itself."

The ultimate experience of cognitive dissonance came with the idea of God itself. I can't remember the day or time, but there was a moment when I realized that I simply did not believe in God—and that it was very likely that I never really had believed. Phenomena I had construed as "evidence"—the interior state during contemplative prayer, say, and the beauty of nature—were no longer compelling as evidence of God. They were plenty compelling as evidence of the capacity of the human mind and its physiological capabilities, and of the enormous splendor and complexity of the universe, but they no longer pointed me to a divine Creator or God underlying humanity and creation. I lost interest in the discipline of theology, which had for a long time fascinated me. It became as obsolete as alchemy, an artifact of bygone times and the limitations of human understanding now superseded by science and our expanding knowledge of the universe.

And once I was free of religious faith I felt that I was as free as a human being could be. I saw the world anew, as it is, without some sort of painted veneer or overlay that distorted reality by burdening it with divine justifications. I felt liberated.

But now, years after all that discussion, Steve Rinaldo was calling. I had heard that he had burned out after too many years as a pastor and had been assigned to a position in the archdiocesan office doing public relations. We hadn't talked in at least ten years. Obviously Celia and *The Holy Family* had reached the attention of the New York archdiocese. I nodded to my assistant and picked up the phone.

"Steve," I said, "This is Martin. I hope you're not looking for some sort of statement. How are you doing?"

"Martin, I'll get to the point. No time for small talk. A few hours from now I'm due at a TV studio in midtown. The archdiocese is sending me to be on one of those awful talk and opinion news shows. The Dave Leary Report. You know, all talk and opinion, but no real news. I guess I'm supposed to be the mainstream Catholic voice about Celia's painting. I'll be part of what they call a 'discussion' with an art professor from NYU and with the executive director of Defenders of the Faith. You've heard of them?"

"I've been out of that loop."

"A group of laypeople, more conservative than the pope. Talk radio and TV love them for this sort of story. They bring out the crazy and pretend to be representing 'all' Catholics. Whatever that means."

I didn't know what to say. "I'm sure you'll be able to hold your own, Steve."

"I'm wearing my Roman collar but I don't think it'll do me much good against the big-mouth Brian Driscoll of the Defenders. But listen, I just wanted to give you a heads-up. I didn't want to have you turn on your TV and wonder what the hell I'm doing. I can't stand this kind of manufactured, made-for-TV controversy. I just hope things aren't getting too ugly about this."

"It's unlikely I'd ever watch Dave Leary voluntarily," I said, "but I guess I will tonight. My only concern is about Celia's safety. And so far the college is taking good care of her. They at least still believe in free expression, Steve. This is still America."

"Just barely, sometimes. I don't know. But I felt like it was a necessary moment to reconnect. I'm relieved to hear that Celia is safe. I hope it stays that way." He paused. "I love this church, you know, Martin. With all its foibles and sins. And some of those sins are worse than awful. It's a life of contradiction, being a priest." He paused again and took a deep breath. "I love Celia's goddam painting, by the way. I just wish I could see a copy without all the pixelization. That's the Holy Family at its holiest. But the cardinal will have me dumped me in Long Island Sound if I say that on the air tonight."

"Do you remember where I live?" I asked. I said the address.

"Sure. The brownstone up in the west eighties?"

"Can you be there in a half hour?"

He caught on. "Really?"

"I'll grab a cab and see you there," I said.

Steve was already in the lobby when I arrived. We shook hands, then hugged. In the elevator he said, "Does anyone know it's here?"

I shook my head. "We snuck it down from Poughkeepsie for safekeeping. Once this all blows over we'll figure out what's next."

I led him to the girls' bedroom, switched on the light, and stood back out of the way so he could take it in. He shifted angles, moved closer and farther away, and after at least five minutes he said, "My, my, Martin, you and Justine have raised one hell of a daughter."

"Two, actually," I said. "But we can catch up about our climatologist some other time."

"Look at that," he said. He pointed to the potted plants placed on shelves around the room in which Mary, Joseph, and Jesus lay. "They not only carry your eye all over the composition, but look—green and flourishing, green and flourishing"—he pointed at each plant in turn—"but then this one, dry, thirsty, dead, and propped up by a cross-shaped stake. In all this luscious life, a *memento mori*. Marvelous. Just simply marvelous."

"Yes," I said, "a very Christ-specific reminder of death at that. That's just like Celia, to include that, just like her. She watched me looking at the painting the first time, waiting for me to see it." I chuckled. "I'm sure there are other meanings hidden among her brushstrokes, far less obvious. It's a challenge keeping up with her."

"No one knows the painting is here?" Steve asked. "Your secret is safe with me."

"Our technology guy at the agency is putting together a web site for the painting. Justine's photographer took some high-definition photos yesterday. I'm hoping the site will be up by the end of the week—the painting, Celia's artist's statement, the sketches and studies. I want people to be able to see it for themselves, without the commentary of talking heads and freak-show ministers. It will not have a section for comments. Or any pictures of Celia." I smiled. "I'm afraid that'll frustrate people who want to show support, but it would probably get hijacked by the opponents, so it's a trade I'll make."

Steve said, "Good idea all around. What's the web address? I'd love to see Celia's studies and sketches sometime." I told him. Steve jotted it down in a notebook and said, "But I really have to get going. That Brian Driscoll character gives me the creeps, and his voice is like fingernails on a blackboard, but I guess I have to toughen up for Christ's sake." He turned to leave, but stopped and looked back again at the painting. "Overwhelming. Good Christ. Overwhelming."

I went downstairs with him and we walked to the subway entrance. We promised to get together for lunch soon. "It's been too long," Steve said. "I always enjoyed our talks, but I didn't want to intrude—you're obviously a busy man, and I respect the choice you made. I hope you can watch this damn show tonight."

"I will," I said. "Justine too, and I'm sure Celia will be interested, so I'll let her know. She especially shouldn't be blindsided." We shook hands and Steve descended the stairs to the subway. He was not the Steve of old, I thought as I walked back home. He was more battered and worn down. I hoped, though, underneath all that exterior stuff he was relatively intact and contented.

When the Dave Leary Report came on, Justine and I sat through twenty minutes of partisan reporting on national politics before they finally got to the segment on "the controversial painting by a college student that is rocking the Christian world." The onscreen graphic showed the painting and was labeled "Her Say, or Heresy?" It began with Leary giving some background illustrated by stock footage of Vassar, Celia's high school graduation portrait, and a steady view of the painting, now censored by black bars covering the offensive body parts. Then Leary said, "With me in the studio is Denise Miller, professor of art history at New York University. To start with, is this painting any good?"

Professor Miller began by saying that she had only seen the censored version on the internet, but based on the clearest view of it she had been able to see, it was a beautifully composed and executed painting. "I sense that the artist, in her style and other choices, was making allusions to several other paintings—Goya's *Naked Maja*, for instance, and Lefebvre's *Mary Magdalene in the Cave*. Not to mention any number of Modigliani nudes and a touch of Gustav Courbet. But it's completely unlike traditional portraits of Mary or the Holy Family. It's a unique and lovely work of art."

She tried to comment on the triangular composition and the positioning of the three figures, but Leary cut her off. "Yeah, yeah, okay. Bottom line: Would you pay good money for it? Would you hang it in your living room?"

The exasperated professor said, "Well, I'm a historian, not an art dealer, so I have no expertise in how much this painting might fetch on the open market. Certainly more *after* this program than before. But I would most definitely hang it in my living room."

Leary said, "We turn now to Brian Driscoll, executive director of Defenders of the Faith. He joins us from our studio in Boston. Mr. Driscoll's article on the Defenders website today tells a much different story about this painting. It's junk, he says, it's pornography, and it's junk."

I had looked up the website and already knew the gist of Driscoll's point of view: In addition to his boilerplate accusation that it was pornographic, he said, Catholics everywhere should be offended by this painting because it denies the church's teaching about the perpetual virginity of the Blessed Virgin Mary. Driscoll began by saying that he did not care if the painting was beautiful or valuable, his only concern was that it was heretical and therefore had no place in an exhibition—even though the sponsoring institution was private, it or its students no doubt receive state and federal funds at the very least in the form of financial aid. Leary allowed him to state his position at length and without interruption and clearly enjoyed the strident theatricality of his guest. It was, if nothing else, good television for the network's target audience.

Leary said, "So, to sum up your view, the church says that arguments against Mary's perpetual virginity are wrong, and are therefore sinful? Even though, say, the gospel writers make references to Jesus' brothers?"

Driscoll said, "The church has always understood that the brothers of Jesus referred to in the gospels were actually cousins or other close relations. Mary remained pure, ever-virgin, from her own birth up until the moment she was physically taken up into heaven."

Leary nodded sagely at Driscoll's assertion that the gospel writers did not write what they meant, and let it go by unchallenged. It was finally time for Steve. "Also with us in the studio tonight to weigh in on this controversy is Father Steve Rinaldo from the public information office of the Archdiocese of New York. Father Rinaldo, as a representative of the official church, where do you come down on this painting of the holy family?"

"Well, first I'd like to say that I have to agree with Professor Miller, that it is a beautiful, even stunning, painting. Miss Halsey is obviously a very skilled painter—"

"But what about Mr. Driscoll's objections, and those of Defenders of the Faith? You represent the Roman Catholic Church, you're an ordained priest. Do you share his concerns?"

Steve said, "The church does in fact teach the perpetual virginity of Mary, but that is by no means a teaching that is subscribed to across the full spectrum of Christian denominations. Within Catholic teaching itself it is important to recognize that various teachings carry different weights in terms of their importance. Mary's role as Mother of the Church is extremely important, and her perpetual virginity is understood as a sign of her personal sanctity. But when compared to the teaching that Christ suffered, died, and was raised up by God to redeem humanity, it is clearly of lesser importance. This painting, this work of art, is merely one person's visual interpretation of the Holy Family, and as such it does not challenge the foundations upon which the church is built."

Driscoll interrupted. "It is provocative and offensive to the Catholic church and to the Catholic faithful. We believe in the perpetual virginity of Mary, and this painting denies that teaching in an obscene manner."

Professor Miller tried to insert herself back into the conversation. "The picture is hardly obscene. The nude human figure has been a mainstay of visual art for centuries—"

"Yeah, yeah," said Leary, "we don't have time for an art history lecture, Professor, with all due respect."

Steve jumped in quickly. "Dr. Miller is correct, Mr. Leary. With all due respect. As for being offensive and provocative, I've been Catholic since birth and a priest for almost forty years and I am not at all offended by this painting. Mr. Driscoll's self-described *job* is to imagine anti-Catholic bigotry hiding in every corner and to use that to incite people to contribute money to his organization, so of course he says the painting is offensive, and I'm sure donations are way up on his website today—along with the number of conservative Catholics who are getting an eyeful of the 'pornography' that Mr. Driscoll has prominently displayed on his front page." On the split screen we could see Driscoll turn red and Leary raise his eyebrows. But Steve kept talking with hardly a breath. "It's the job of the clergy, however, to be pastors to God's people, not to incite their anger. I can agree with Mr. Driscoll, though, that the painting is provocative, certainly. It provokes me to look at the Holy Family in a new and different light. I have been a pastor for decades and I have dealt with couples and families with all sorts of challenges and problems. To see the Holy Family depicted as vibrant, loving, and, yes, sexually alive and joyful, is quite refreshing."

Driscoll said, "I'm afraid Father Rinaldo may be falling into a modernist fallacy—"

"Mr. Driscoll," said Steve, "you can keep your fallacies and theories to yourself. Condemning this painting, its painter, and the educational institution that exhibited it simply because you disagree with what it says about its subject not only denies the place and role of the human conscience, which is central to the Catholic faith, it is also un-American and violates citizens' basic rights of freedom of speech and religion."

"The student who painted this, as I pointed out earlier," Leary said, "is a New Yorker by the name of Celia Halsey. She certainly hasn't taken advantage of free speech. She has not responded to our requests to comment or to come on this show."

Professor Miller jumped in again and said, "It seems to me that Ms. Halsey's work has been violated by being placed on the internet without her authorization—my sources tell me that there were several signs in the exhibit hall prohibiting photography, but that a Christian pastor chose to ignore those and illegally photographed and disseminated the painting. And, as Father Rinaldo has pointed out, even Defenders of the Faith has violated that copyright by including the image on its web site to motivate viewers to donate. I personally hope that in her silence Ms. Halsey is contemplating a lawsuit. One unfortunate consequence of this is that we are all sitting here judging her work based on a censored version."

Leary and Driscoll had been trying to interrupt, but Steve said, "Ms. Halsey expressed herself in her painting. She doesn't need to defend herself from people like Brian Driscoll. And to Professor Miller's point, I am fortunate enough to have seen the painting, in person and up close, and the censored image does not come close to conveying the breathtaking beauty of the work. I understand there will be a web site soon, maybe even in the next couple of days, presenting an authorized view of the work, uncensored and in high resolution." He gave the address I had told him. "The young lady is a college student at the end of an academic year, and I'm sure she has more important things to do than appear on television to defend herself against baseless and ignorant attacks."

"Okay," Leary said finally grabbing an opening, "We're out of time." Visibly angry, he thanked his guests and cut to a commercial.

Relieved that it was over, I pointed the remote at the screen and turned the TV off as if I wanted it to never come back on. Justine said, "Steve got the best of that exchange—from what I hear, that's a rarity on that show."

"He just burned some bridges," I said. "The cardinal and that Driscoll character have been bosom buddies for decades, according to Driscoll's website. Steve is toast in the archdiocese."

The phone rang a few minutes later. It was Steve. "Listen, I'm sorry."

I said, "Where are you?"

He told me he was in the green room at Leary's studio, about to leave. "I didn't intend to cross that line—you know, about seeing the painting, and the web site. It just got sort of, I don't know, hot in there."

I had put the phone on speaker, so Justine was listening too. She said, "That's all right, Steve. I think it was actually a good thing that it came out. We owe you a very nice dinner. I'm sure you'd love to meet Celia and Janet again after all these years."

"I would, yes, very much so." He paused, seeming at a loss for words. "One other thing I'm wondering. Denise—Denise Miller, the professor from NYU—is there any chance she could see—?"

Justine and I looked at each other and simultaneously shrugged a "Why not?" I said, "Listen, Steve, we were just about to pull the cork of a nice pinot noir. Go get a cab and we'll let the wine breathe while you're on the way. In the meantime we'll call Celia and see how she's doing."

"Thank you. Thank you. A glass of wine'll be perfect. It took everything I had going after Driscoll and Leary like that."

Justine said, "It'll be nice to unwind together. Now that we've hit the cable news cycle, maybe this whole thing can go away. I'm tired of the tension. And the worry." Justine had been checking in with Celia several times a day. "And maybe Celia will shift gears and only paint naked people who are *not* named Jesus, Joseph, and Mary."

I am still studying the painting when Justine gets home, but I don't hear the door open and can't make myself respond when she calls my name. She finds me in the girls' room sitting at the foot of Celia's bed, silently but intently gazing at the picture. "Oh, Martin," she says, and sits beside me, sees tears rimming my eyes. "Maybe you shouldn't be in here," she says, but she makes no attempt to get me to leave. She leans against me and wraps her arms around me, feeling like both a mother and a lover at the same time. I don't know which I need right now but my arms embrace her in return and we are lovers, plain and simple, our clothing partially shed and strewn about seemingly without conscious effort. Entangled on the bedspread of autumn leaves we kiss and touch. I feel her hands on me and I run mine along her familiar haunch, the small of her back, the inside of her thigh. I would know Justine by feel alone if that were the only sense I had, I would know her by taste or smell alone if I had to, but I am so passive that I would feel as though I have left my body if not for the warm moist calm that envelops me as she pulls me in and rocks us with her tender strength. When we are done she locks her eyes onto mine, just a few inches apart, our lips so close that when she speaks hers brush against mine.

She whispers. "Are you okay?"

"I feel like I'm in a dream." It seems to take five minutes to say it.

"Do you worry that this will never change?"

"I have no doubt that this will never change," I say. "But it will always be different, too." I don't know really if I'm talking about the lovemaking or the onrush of feelings that take me over any time I gaze at the painting or the sense that for the past several minutes, or half hour, I have been watching myself from outside my body. "Never change," I say.

Justine says "I'm cold" so we pull ourselves off the small bed and without bothering to gather up our clothes we turn to go to our room and our own bed made up with flannel sheets and a warm comforter. As I turn, my eyes again sweep the room, this room of our daughters, and settle again on the Holy Family. I stop and let my gaze linger and Justine's eyes follow the direction of my gaze and they lock onto the painting as well. We stand and stare, naked and entwined, until Justine without seeming to move touches the light switch and the room is dark and the painting just a black shadow on a black wall.

5

Fourth Sunday

Everlasting life.

The words are floating in and out of my consciousness as I struggle to wake up. My sleep has been fitful these past few nights, and the days, as a consequence, sluggish. But some dream in the early hours of the morning is delivering the words *everlasting life* into my awareness, and I grasp for any other pieces of the dream for clues as to why these words have come. An image flashes as I hear myself gasp for breath, but it is indistinct and out of view before I can identify it. Then I hear the words again, everlasting life, spoken in a familiar voice, like that of a southern preacher, and I know then that the words and perhaps the dream itself have something to with that most famous verse from the gospel of John, "For God so loved the world, that he gave his only begotten Son, that whosoever believeth in him should not perish, but have everlasting life."

I can't tell if I am awake or asleep but I feel like I am sliding down a snowy hill, toward a lake, toward a cove on a lake, and I recognize the place we rent upstate for summer vacation. I have never seen it in winter, but this is clearly the place and I am half walking half sliding on the snow toward the cove where normally I would find a rowboat and a canoe tethered to a small dock, but there is nothing there, just the shoreline and the surface of the lake frozen solid. Without hesitation I step onto the ice and walk and slide toward the opposite side of the lake. I notice that I am barefoot, that I am naked, but I feel no cold or pain, not even where my feet touch the rough cold ice.

Halfway across the lake I hear the southern-accented voice again, *For God so loved the world, that he gave his only begotten Son, that whosoever believeth in him should not perish, but have everlasting life.* Everlasting life. I begin to feel weak and cold but see, across the lake, amid the trees on the shore, the figure of a young woman, shrouded in white linen from head to toe, and she seems to float or glide among the stark tree trunks and leafless woods. Seeing her strengthens my resolve to move but I am now weak and cold and cannot feel my feet and I hear again, *Whosoever believeth in him should not perish*, and this time I recognize the voice as Scott Radner, from my year of college in Georgia so long ago, and I become angry at the thought of everlasting life and I shout, *I take no comfort in the fantasy that death is not death, that perishing is not perishing, that there will be some kind of other-worldly reunion of the dead, of the dead, of the dead.*

For a moment there is nothing but an echo. The echo of my own voice.

I catch another glimpse of the shrouded young woman. She has stopped on the shore and I know that if I could see through the shroud that covers her entirely, covers her eyes and the features of her face, I would see her looking directly at me, trying to tell me to stop, to go back to the other shore. If her arms were not bound to her sides by the gauzy cloth she would be waving me away, not beckoning me to come, but still I struggle to reach her while I rail against the proclamation of everlasting life.

There is a moment of recognition—I know who she is, I am sure of it, but I cannot pronounce her name with my cold blue lips—and I try to stride more quickly but fall hard to the ice and the cold and pain intensify. I look and gasp at the sight of my feet, bloodied from the sharp ice, my skin red and chapped from the cold. I am about to give up, about to give in to the ice and cold when I feel the touch of a hand and am covered by a quilt sewn with many colors, a rainbow of colors through which bright light now shines, and I cover my eyes and groan and know, from the touch, that it is Justine who covers me and holds me, almost holding me down, that strong, and saying "Marty, Marty, sweetie, what is it, you're having a bad dream, Marty, honey, Marty" in a soothing voice that slowly pulls me away from the dream and draws me back to wakefulness and finally I lie beside her and let her rock me and press against me and say my name and say my name and say my name until at last I am calm and certain that I am home.

For the last eleven or twelve years we have rented a small house on a lake up near Saratoga for two weeks every August. This past summer the four of us were together for the first of the two weeks, but Celia had to go Vassar for the second week as a volunteer for freshman orientation. The hullaballoo surrounding *The Holy Family* had largely died down, but since nothing ever really dies once it reaches the internet it continued to bubble up to the surface from time to time. Still, Celia had no desire to hide, and as a senior in the art department she wanted to be there to greet the new students in the department and help them get settled in for the semester. She saw the week in Saratoga as an opportunity to take a deep breath before diving into her senior year with all systems go.

The weather was nearly perfect at the lake, a bit humid, with periods of refreshing rain. Justine and I took a week here and there, and sometimes a long weekend, to get away alone while the girls were at school, but we still loved being a four-some with Janet and Celia at the summer place. While Celia was getting ready for her senior year, Janet was preparing for a long research trip in Alaska and Canada, above the Arctic Circle, that would begin in October and end in March. She was as excited about a project as ever, and she put on her most professorial demeanor as she described the goals of the trip and showed us charts of data and digitized maps and satellite photos of the areas in which she would be working.

Celia asked the most pertinent questions about the project. Justine and I tried to keep up with the science but were out of our element much more quickly than Celia was. This was not surprising, however, considering how close they had always been, but I had never given Celia quite enough credit for understanding her sister's work. And that depth of understanding was returned by Janet, whose appreciation of Celia's artistic projects went well beyond sisterly respectfulness. Like all siblings, they knew each other's sensitive spots and of course were not immune to the temptation to poke and prod to set the other off. What was closest to the bone for each of them, though—science and art—was off limits when it came to that sort of childish dynamic.

Janet and Celia spent a lot of time together that week. They took charge of our temporary household and did most of the shopping and cooking. Justine and I had both been intensely busy with work, so we were taking a lazy approach to the vacation, sleeping late and curling up together on the front-porch swing and just walking and talking and listening to the birds. Janet knocked on our bedroom door at about ten one morning halfway through the vacation and announced, "Celia and I are taking the canoe out for a while, to explore the cove across the lake. We'll be gone for at least two hours, so you two bunny rabbits can have plenty of time to get up to whatever you need to be getting up to on this lovely morning." Janet giggled while

Celia exploded with the throaty barroom laugh she had inherited from Justine, which set Justine off as if in response. All I could think to say was "Make sure to wear your life vests," which triggered even more laughter as their footsteps receded and the screen door slammed and their words as they chattered down the path became indistinct and finally silent.

When the girls returned a little more than two hours later they found Justine and me out on the patio, relaxed, satisfied, and grateful for the time we had had by ourselves. I asked about the cove but Janet responded by saying she was ravenously hungry and lit the grill, and we all prepared a lunch, Justine and Celia running up to the house to toss a salad while Janet and I grilled the kinds of spicy meats we only eat on vacation and at picnics. While we ate, our neighbor's dog ran into our yard, followed by the neighbor himself, a man we knew from previous summers here. He accepted the offer of a bratwurst and salad, and while he was there he took a picture of the four of us with the little digital camera I had in my pocket.

The next morning Celia packed her things and said goodbye to Justine and Janet. She was due at Vassar at three in the afternoon. We all planned to spend a night in Poughkeepsie at the end of the vacation, so it was not a big farewell moment. Hugs and kisses and a few inside jokes and chuckles with her big sister and we were ready to go. Being a city girl Celia didn't have many opportunities to drive on the highway, and she was hyped up about getting behind the wheel for the drive down. "You can sleep all the way there, Dad, I promise you I won't do anything wrong." I handed over the keys and got in the passenger side. I didn't plan to sleep—I would much rather use the time to talk with Celia about the past year and her expectations for this next one. And we did talk about those things, and about the crazy response to *The Holy Family* and whether there would be any recurrence of all that, or if she could just go back to being a college student learning her art. She wanted so much, she said, to just concentrate on painting.

"I really don't care what anybody thinks, whether they love my work or hate it," Celia said. "Honestly. But when they get all crazy and violent-sounding, well, I don't want to be anybody's victim. I also don't want to have to avoid subjects that might offend certain people." She said the words *offend other people* as if she were spitting them out of her mouth. "Do you know that some of the people most angry about *The Holy Family* believe that the so-called rapture is going to happen on a specific day next year, and they're getting their followers all riled up about that. No matter that they've predicted it before and it hasn't happened and won't this time, either, but it's their ilk that look at my painting and tell their minions to make my life miserable. I'm supposed to let those nutjobs define for me what's *offensive*? The pope in Rome will come out of the closet and march in the Pride Parade before I'll let them set the terms. They won't get their silly rapture, and they won't get me down. I can promise you that."

"Eyes on the highway, darlin'," I said. "Not to go all Joe Cliché on you, but if you work in the kitchen you know there's going to be heat. You've got a lot of company, though. Mom and Janet and I are right there with you."

Celia wasn't done. She had my attention and seemed to need to release some pent up frustrations. "And the Catholic church—the Catholic church!—is offended by a nude Virgin Mary? Really? The church with all the executives who looked the other way for decades, centuries really, while children were raped and abused by priests? By people they were taught to trust? The institution with all that stolen art in its vaults and galleries? If they were still burning people at the stake in the twenty-first century you know what they would've done with me. Because of a painting. A *painting*."

She stopped talking for awhile and we just watched the pavement disappear beneath us. "I thought it was great," she said, "when you put up the web site with the painting. No comments allowed, that was perfect. Talk amongst yourselves outside your computer, but I don't want to hear any of it!"

"I thought it would be best to just allow you and the painting to speak for yourselves. In this day and age there are plenty of opportunities for people to voice their opinions. But mainly I just wanted to make sure anyone could see the painting unimpeded. No censorship. No titillation by pixelization. And the sketches and your artist's statement, which no one had really paid attention to when they attacked you."

"Thanks for doing that. The whole thing. I don't think I ever thanked you." Celia turned toward me, her smile radiant. "I feel like I have a lot to live up to, and I'm looking forward to the challenge."

I told her not to forget to have some fun, and her smile turned mischievous. "I am definitely looking forward to reconnecting with a fella this fall," she said. "He's a math major, of all things, but, well, he just lights me up."

"Was he there in April?"

"Tennis team," Celia said. "They were on the road that weekend."

"And you've kept him secret all summer?"

She explained that he was spending the summer in Europe at his father's home. "He's half German, American mother, parents divorced, et cetera. You get the picture. We're up to about a million text messages."

"Well, good. Maybe we can meet him sometime?" I said. Celia nodded.

"Fun and careful," I said. "I suppose I can get more details from your sister." Celia nodded again.

We had lunch together at the college and kissed goodbye at the entrance to the dorm where she would be staying during freshman orientation. Celia looked so much like Justine when we had first met, the glinting eyes and facial expressions that always hinted at mischief about to be made. "Love you, Daddy-o," she said. "See you in a few days." I winked and said "Love you too. Be back soon. Be good." We squeezed hands and turned to walk in opposite directions, looking back for one more wave, and then I was in the car and on my way back north to the lake.

For an hour after I have awakened from my dream of the icy lake and the shrouded girl, Justine just holds me. We doze, in and out of light sleep, and each time I awaken our faces are so close as to be touching. Sometimes her eyes are closed, sometimes open, studying me as if she has just uncovered me in an archaeological dig.

This time when I open my eyes she is looking at me serenely, her eyes themselves a picture of steady composure. She told me the other day that she has been having, in her work, a creative blast, and feels as though she has broken through a ceiling to a new level of development as an artist and designer. I see that all in her eyes, I understand what she was telling me a few days ago about her eagerness to get down to work and explore this new stage of discovery. Each day had become for her a quest in which she had no goal and therefore all goals, and though she struggled to find words to articulate how she was feeling I could see it in her step, in her hands and eyes, in the way she performed the most quotidian tasks like switching on the light or turning the key and opening the front door.

Everlasting life, though. The words still stalk me, echoing, at once ominous and trite, from the distant dream. Not distant enough though, not by a long way. I don't want to think about everlasting life, or yesterday or last summer or tomorrow, but it takes great effort to pull away from past and future and forever, the memory of the ice and the voice and the shrouded girl.

"I need your hands on me," I say. It is neither a command nor a request, but Justine complies, whispers to me to be still, "I'll take care of you," she says, "just let me take good care of you" and she does, and beneath the dark tent of the quilted comforter she touches and kisses and explores without being overtly sexual but wholly loving, skin on skin, now pressing hard, now light, blood coursing unseen in rhythm with heartbeats, and we are poised absolutely in the present tense.

We extend the moment, the *now* that I am in and that I think Justine is sharing as much as causing. We burrow into the bed and don't speak, relying on touch to communicate, enmeshed in tastes and scents. I have lost all track of time. Justine whispers "I'll run a bath" and a few minutes later we slip into the aromatic bubbly hot water, the tub not quite built for two but adequate for two to become a wet slithery tangle of enwombed flesh, until finally we need breakfast and move on to the kitchen, though I try to hold on to the present tense, no more last summer, no more everlasting life, just today and now and us.

It can't last, of course, and I know that. At some point I have to tell Justine about the dream, about what it was that reduced me to a shivering mess beside her, disturbing her sleep. I stall for a while, slice an orange into quarters, slice a banana into a small bowl of yogurt. I eat some, I feed some to Justine, I kiss her. I finally tell her that I had a dream, a winter dream of our summer vacation place. I describe the snowy view of the yard sloping down to the lake. I pause as I start to see it all again, hoping maybe to chase it away. Justine sits beside me at the table and says that the dream means nothing, really, and that she is not surprised about that image, that place, occurring in my dream.

"Everlasting life," I say, "That's what set me off. The phrase. The idea."

We are quiet for a minute. Then I tell her about the lake, the ice, the shrouded girl in the dream.

"And then the voice. I was scared of it in the dream," I try to explain. "Scared of the idea that death is not death, and just believe in God and there's no perishing, there's everlasting life."

"You rejected all of that twenty years ago," Justine says, a gentle reminder of fact. "It didn't scare you then. You turned your back on it." She reaches and turns my face directly toward her and looks intently into my eyes. "You rejected all that."

"Maybe life would be easier, this whole thing would be more bearable, if I hadn't done that, rejected that."

We are quiet again, but the pause is a full one. The sun coming in the back window glances off the silver tea kettle on the stove and reflects on the opposite wall, a trapezoid of light created millions of miles away.

"I was here, you know, before and after," Justine says. "I loved you before and I love you after. But after has been the better part. You know that—after has been all of us, our girls, our lives together. And you know that death is death and final. As hard as that is. You know that." She looks out the kitchen door, toward the stairway that leads up to the bedrooms. "I know that."

"I don't know what I know," I say. "But I never thought I would arrive at a place where I would doubt my unbelief."

"You may think you doubt your unbelief," Justine says. "But I'd stake my last dollar on this: you do not believe in God." She looks at my eyes, my face, as she searches for words, some idea in her memory and finally finds it in the cusp of the before and after of my belief. "You said it yourself—way back then— everlasting life, you said, eternal life, makes a mockery of the paschal mystery. The gospels taught you about the struggle to grow through loss and pain, but God's promises, religion's promises, cheapened that whole dynamic. Made religion into a guide to chasing after an imaginary forever. Too easy an answer for the hard reality that is life, you said, a sappy greeting card, and a promise that can't be fulfilled." She swallows hard and her jaw clenches. "I remember. I was listening to you all the while."

She reaches across the kitchen table, grasps my hands and pulls me forward so we are both leaning in, on the edges of our seats, close together. Justine smiles, a compassionate smile that salves wounds more effectively than any medicine or doctrine, a smile that could, and did many times, turn a toddler's cry into giggles on sight. I can't help but pick up the infectious smile just inches away from my face, and after another moment we burst simultaneously into laughter.

"That's what I said," I say when we have quieted down. "You're right, that's what I said." The pause is pregnant. "Everlasting life." It is a scoff. "And once everlasting life was gone, there was no need for God."

And I never felt more alive. I think it first, then say it, looking straight into Justine's eyes: "And I never felt more alive."

"What you loved about your religion was all about telling a story, that's what you said. Always the story of how to be alive in the present."

That is how I used to describe to Justine why going to Sunday mass appealed so much to me. We, the congregation, were telling and enacting a story of a life, a death, and a resurrection. For all the inconsistencies in the sources—the gospels—we had an adequate account of the teachings of Jesus, and I had bought into his essential ethic about how to go about being a human being. The accounts of his birth, death, and resurrection don't match up in the details, but that never surprised me—those are aspects of the legend, not biography. The lesson remains largely consistent even if the details are inconsistent, and playing around with the details gives the story credibility in different times and places. Read the Gospel of Matthew in church on a Sunday morning, and see *Godspell* on Broadway in the afternoon. But the story has the most power when its irrational ingredients and demands for an unreasonable fealty are put aside and forgotten.

Years ago, in the months after Janet was born, I had been uneasy about not having her baptized. But I was even more uneasy about trying to force the issue with Justine. In her opinion, subjecting a baby to a religious ritual that committed the infant to something, in this case membership in a church, was simply unfair. "She can be baptized when she's grown up—if that's what she wants." I was still an active member of St. Luke's then, and Justine and I talked a lot about maybe becoming more involved as a family. She read a few books on Catholic teaching, and even met privately two or three times with Father Steve to explore her questions. In the end she decided not to take it any further, and I had no choice, as Father Steve was quick to remind me, but to respect that. "Your family comes first, that's your primary commitment. Love, not doctrine, is the measure. Give them a foundation of love."

Ned Flynn took issue with this kind of thinking, and he was not afraid to tell me about it. He spent plenty of time at the Spender office when he was not working out of town. He liked to gab with Stuart about the plays and movies on his wish list, and sometimes he would run lines with me between rehearsals or shoots for whatever script he was working on. He had no patience for what he called Father Steve's progressive ideas. "I don't think you should be listening to that guy, that Father Gautama the Buddha. You've got to get that little girl baptized," he told me, with a hint of panic in his tone. "It's a matter of her immortal soul, Martin, you have a responsibility here. It's about the Catholic belief, you know, we believe that if you die, you can't go to heaven without the sacrament."

I said, "I'm more concerned, I guess, with my earthly responsibilities, care and feeding and nurturing." I shrugged and chuckled, trying to lighten the mood. "Besides, I've never been very interested in the whole afterlife thing, really."

"What do you mean?"

"I'm more concerned with the here and now. Being a better human being, making a better world. We don't know what comes after this life, or even if anything does."

Ned let out one of his long sighs. "So you're some kind of Buddhist? Be here now?"

"Consider the lilies of the field?" I tried to counter. "Look, Ned, I guess that I just have to believe, if there is an afterlife, that our fates will depend on something more substantive than whether we poured water on a baby's head. It's like those fundamentalists back when I was in college, trying to scare me into accepting Jesus Christ as my personal lord and savior so I wouldn't burn in the fires of hell. Life is not that simple, and if there's an afterlife, it can't be that simple either. I'd rather base my religion, my life, on taking care of my family and loving my neighbor than on following a crazy list of rules and being afraid of what God will do if I don't. And if that means I essentially do not have a religion, am not even Catholic, or don't even accept the existence of God, then so be it."

Still, I had to admit I liked the baptism ritual. It provided the whole congregation with a chance to affirm our commitment—to strive to be better people—in the presence of a baby, so palpable and immediate.

When Celia was born, and Janet was just over three years old, I raised the question with Justine one last time. "I can't do it," she said. "I can't be a person who looks at life that way. That's not how I'm wired, I guess. You know?"

I had to answer yes, I knew. And I had taken the leap into loving her and marrying her with that knowledge. She had hidden nothing from me, not even her reticence about the Christianity I carried with me—and had given herself to me despite that difference between us. If I had been hoping that over time this would change and she would join me on my path I would have been disappointed. But instead I found myself growing toward Justine, and the more I thought about it, the more certain it became that I could not embrace and affirm those "I believe" statements of the baptism ritual. It made absolute sense to choose Justine over amorphous spiritual ideas. It was she, after all, and not a character in a book or an idea in a theologian's imagination, who nestled against me night after night and kissed me in the morning and loved me and our daughters fiercely and tenderly, no questions asked.

As trades go, I have never doubted that I made a sweet deal.

And I've never needed the strength to fight through loss more than I do right now.

On the third morning after I had taken Celia to Poughkeepsie I was lounging on the patio of our bungalow facing the lake when my cell phone rang. Justine had just brought me a cup of coffee and was across the yard with Janet, examining something that had bloomed at the start of the path that leads to the lake. I didn't recognize the number on the little screen, and almost decided to ignore it, let it go to voicemail, but finally pressed the button to answer.

"Mr. Halsey?" A woman's voice.

From that point on the day becomes a blur, mostly, with occasional moments of clarity, but in my memory it is never a memory, it is present tense and it happens over and over, sometimes with as little impetus as the closing of my eyes or the whisper of the name Celia somewhere along the edges of my mind.

The call is from Vassar, from someone, dean somebody, and it's about Celia. The dean in a calm and motherly voice says something about Celia, and I hear the word *collapse*, and then *hospital*, and then *serious*, and it's clear she wants us to come to Poughkeepsie as quickly as possible. She says Vassar Brothers Medical Center and I say yes I know where that is and I'm running down the stairs and across the yard to Justine and Janet, trying not to shout. I somehow tell them that Celia is in trouble, in the hospital, and they spring into action, running to the house and throwing things into suitcases at random and ordering me to take this to the car, something else to the car, and in a matter of moments we are on the road.

Janet in the backseat takes my phone and calls back the dean but gets no answer and leaves a message, saying we are on the way and to please call us again as soon as possible. We have reached the Thruway and I am reading signs for Albany and then we are beyond Albany and the phone chirps twice and Janet answers. I'm hearing words like *intensive care* and *very serious* and then the dean puts the doctor on the phone and somehow I am not the fastest car on the highway even though I feel like we are flying. The doctor wants to talk to the mother or father so Janet puts the phone on speaker and holds it between Justine and me in the front seat with the volume all the way up. Again I hear the words *serious* and *intensive* and then he says *aneurysm* and I see a sign for the South Albany Airport and I press the gas pedal a little harder. I search my brain for anything I have ever learned about aneurysms but cannot find anything even though I know I have read about them before. I want to ask Janet because I know she will know, but her face in the rearview mirror is dark and I am afraid she is already lodged in the depth of whatever she knows. Justine reaches and takes my hand gently but says nothing and it takes only a glance at her eyes for me to see that she is in a dark place too and I try to focus on the road.

Just before I see signs for Kingston, Janet starts pushing buttons on her phone and tells me to stay on the Thruway, that it'll be faster to go down to 299 instead of getting on 9W the way we usually would. I do as she says and still feel as though this is a dream as we drive onto the Mid-Hudson Bridge and then we are in Poughkeepsie on the other side of the river turning south again to Vassar Brothers Medical Center.

We were greeted first by a distressed looking dean of students who maintained her composure with obvious effort as she handed us over to the doctors. I know that the doctors, a woman and a man, both very young to my eyes, spoke to us in clear and measured tones and that I took it in with whatever native intelligence I possess. I know that Justine did the same, and that Janet's presence of mind was both sisterly and analytical, because she is always, no matter what, a scientist. We sat in an isolated room apart from patients and other families while the doctors explained that Celia woke up this morning complaining of a headache. She went outside for a walk with her roommate and the headache became worse and Celia vomited into a flowerbed and then dropped to one knee. Her roommate caught her before Celia could hit the ground and eased her down onto the sidewalk and called 911.

Police and an ambulance arrived in just a few minutes and Celia was brought to the hospital. There was no question of triage or priorities as they wheeled Celia past the sick, injured, and dazed patients who had been waiting their turn. Workers in scrubs flew like sheets loose from a clothesline, clearing the way for the gurney to critical care.

It had been nearly four hours since Celia collapsed.

The next words are spoken and I hear them but my own blood seems to be pounding so loudly through my head that I can't really remember the sensation of hearing them. The words *are nothing we can do, brain death, respirator, life support, do not resuscitate.* Through it all I understand that my

Celia is gone, and I can tell by the way Justine and Janet are looking at me and holding me, and how I am holding them, that they understand it as well.

We have the chaplain here, I hear a doctor say, If you wish to speak with him, and I see that a paunchy man about my age in a Roman collar has come in through a door at the back. I hold up my hand, I, no, I say, that won't be necessary, we're not—but I stop there and Justine says loudly Forget about priests, I need to see my daughter and the chaplain disappears the way he came while the doctors usher us down a hallway to a curtained room in which Celia, surrounded by machines that beep and hiss, is incomprehensibly smaller and more fragile than I could ever consider her, especially when we bear-hugged goodbye just three days ago on campus a couple of miles from here and she was all smiles and refreshment and life-force itself. Now I am supposed to understand and accept that the girl embodied in that flesh just three days ago is no longer there, is nowhere, and that the body before us is a proverbial empty vessel—I actually hear myself think those words, a proverbial empty vessel—that only appears to be living, and that barely, because a machine pumps air into her lungs.

I see in my peripheral vision that the priest has followed us to this room and is waiting outside with a woman, younger than him, who I assume is a chaplain of another denomination, just in case. The doctor says again We did everything we could do, it was a massive hemorrhage and the other says It is rare for this to come on so suddenly I am so sorry. Justine and Janet and I are wrapped up together, like we are one person, pressed up against the bed and both of them weep into my chest as I stare, in shock, at Celia flat on her back covered in a hospital gown and a sheet, with tubes running in random-looking patterns. The doctors point to instruments, explaining what each one signifies, but the key thing is that the machines are doing the work, that her brain is not functioning, that the flat line on this monitor demonstrates . . . .

Justine has been listening but now pulls away from my chest and looks at the doctors, an imploring look, a begging look, and says Everything? Everything you could?

The doctors nod and one says Yes, her brain function is—

Everything everything everything? There is nothing else, nothing, nothing?

I'm sorry, Mrs. Halsey.

Justine stands beside the bed and leans close, inches from Celia's face, holding Celia's hand and arranging the wisps of hair that escape from the band some nurse must have used to tie back its usual wild nature. Janet goes to the opposite side of the bed and strokes her sister's forehead and cries silently. Justine says, her voice barely a whisper, Oh Celia Celia my Celia lovely Celia and I stand beside Justine and pull her to me again as a I touch Celia with my right hand, tracing the lines of her cheeks and chin, the slope of her nose, her throat, her neck. It is as if I have never seen her before, am seeing her for the first time, first time, last time, alive, not alive, brain death, breathing not breathing, machines, hemorrhage, massive, massive, so much more massive than these doctors will ever know.

The doctors clear their throats. They stand at the foot of the bed and look at each other. The woman indicates a plastic bag in her hand, in which I see a small purse. She says, Mr. and Mrs. Halsey, your daughter, your Celia—these are the personal effects she had with her when she was brought to emergency. Her effects include a—in her wallet, with her driver's license— an organ donor card.

The doctor holds the card out for us to see or take, I'm not sure which. I don't know if you were aware of that, the doctor continues.

I take the card and read it front and back. Justine continues to look intently at Celia and touches her face, just as I had been doing a moment before. I didn't know, I say.

Janet says, Yes, Celia and I both have donor cards. We talked about it a few years ago and signed up for them. Janet buries her face in her hands and sobs loudly then inhales sharply and says But no one would think she'd—

Her knees seem to give out and I catch her and guide her to a chair and kneel beside her kissing her cheeks and the tears that glide down until she composes herself and looks up and stands again beside the bed.

The doctor haltingly explains—detach life-support, medications, then nature takes its course, nature takes its own time.

And there's nothing—? Justine says again, and the averted eyes of both doctors are all the answer any of us needs.

Our chaplains are ready to assist you if you need to discuss—the doctor cuts herself off as Justine shakes her head.

Please, Justine says, with all due respect, I don't think any of us wants talk of god's will or heavenly comfort right now.

Justine is speaking for all three of us, and the doctors know it. Her tears have stopped and she is clear and cogent. Do what you need to do, just let us stay with her until—for as long as we can, Justine says. We just need to stay together here now as a family, four of us, one last time, before you can—before she can help you save other lives.

The doctors confer, voices hushed, and then the female doctor approaches a couple of the machines that surround Celia and touches buttons. Beeping and hissing instruments go quiet and the doctors withdraw from the now-silent room, silent except for our breaths and sobs and heartbeats, they close the door behind them, and we encircle our beloved daughter sister friend for the final time, and after a moment Janet begins to sing the lullaby they sang to each other many nights when

they were girls in school, an old song Justine learned somewhere along the line, and Justine and I sing with her.

> Baby's boat the silver moon
> Sailing in the sky
> Sailing o'er the sea of sleep
> While the clouds float by.

> Sail, baby, sail
> Out upon the sea
> Only don't forget to sail
> Back again to me.

> Baby's fishing for a dream
> Fishing near and far
> Her line a silver moonbeam is
> Her bait a silver star.

> Sail, baby, sail
> Out upon the sea
> Only don't forget to sail
> Back again to me.

We are all weeping as the song ends and we know that our
time is up, that there will be no more sailing back, that it is time
to give our daughter, our love, our Celia to whatever parts of
the world she can now affect. I don't know if it is minutes or
hours before nature has taken its merciless merciful course and
we each take our one last moment to hold Celia close. I kiss her,
forehead, cheeks, lips, tip of the nose as one kisses a child, I
whisper something, I don't remember what, in her ear and
snuggle her and smell her neck and her hair. I can't bear to
watch as Janet and Justine each approach Celia and, I assume,
do much the same as I did. As we turn to leave Justine whispers

something to the nearest nurse, who immediately opens a drawer in a cabinet near the door to the room, takes out a pair of scissors, and hands them to Justine. The nurse rummages some more as Justine stands beside Celia once more, and, careful not to do so in a way that would mar the remaining beauty of the way Celia's hair frames her face, snips away a generous long lock and, holding it against her cheek, backs away from the bed. The nurse hands Justine a small plastic bag, which Justine takes as she hands the scissors back, but she keeps the lock of hair in her own hand, still against her cheek, and we stand aside to allow the doctors and nurses to do what they need to do that will give this ending a palpable meaning by making it part of some unknown beginning.

Justine held the lock of Celia's hair for the rest of the day, twined between the fingers of her own right hand, but eventually stored it in the bag the nurse had given her. We would, not too much later, take the lock and divide it into three, each of us taking one to have for our own private secret moments of recollection and remembrance.

The doctors gently briefed us about the organ-removal protocols. I felt as though I were at a play that requires extensive backstage apparatus that the audience never sees. I understood, though I did not want to think about it, what was happening to my daughter's body. I knew that in corridors unseen to us, personnel from hospitals all over the northeast would have arrived via flights on small planes carrying small coolers no different than the ones you might see at a picnic, and they would carry pieces of Celia away as quickly as possible. I knew that, as we sat grieving, making hard phone calls to relatives, friends, and business associates, hardly able to comprehend what was happening, that other families at other hospitals were gathering with new hope as their loved ones were being prepared to receive the organs intended to repair or even save their lives.

We chose, the three of us, to maintain silence regarding the donation of Celia's organs. None of us wanted to hear about making a noble, heroic choice in the face of a tragic loss. We were simply following Celia's wish, and could not imagine that she ever considered herself a hero for signing a donor card.

The dean of students had been at the hospital throughout and offered us a large room at the Alumnae House. They could ensure privacy and quiet there, and she was right that we all needed that. By late in the afternoon there was nothing more for us to do at the hospital so it seemed best to go to the room and get some rest. The next morning we would go back to New York, visit with family and friends, and make further arrangements.

We all lay down together on the larger of the beds. Sleep was elusive, but we were, at least for now, cried out and emotionally exhausted. "I guess it was about four years ago or so," Janet said. "That we got organ donor cards." Justine reached across my chest to rub Janet's arm.

"It's okay," Justine said. "It's a good thing."

"That's what Celia said, we might as well so there could be some good from it. If it ever happened." Janet stopped and I could feel her jaw clench. "I had this boyfriend, Ben, for a few months back then in Rochester. I never even told you about him, it was that short-lived. He was pre-med, wanted to be a surgeon, and was really interested in organ and tissue transplants. I was telling Celia about Ben, and what he was into, and she got curious and checked it all out and suggested that we do it. Get the cards. I guess we never mentioned it to you guys."

I held Janet more tightly and kissed her again on the forehead. "Like Mommy said, sweetheart, it's a good thing. One good thing out of a very awful thing." Despite the words coming out of my mouth I knew I was beyond consolation.

We remained in our little cluster of grief and mourning until dinner was brought to us. I made more phone calls to discuss harsh realities like the disposition of the body and its transportation from Poughkeepsie to New York City. I called the funeral home that had handled Stuart Spender's death and made an appointment to come in the next day, while they arranged to bring the body to New York once the hospital released it.

The body. "It." No longer Celia, no longer "she" or "her."

The three of us talked about how to mark Celia's life and death. There would be art—Celia's—and we would talk about art, which was another of Celia's favorite activities. There would be music and tears and laughter.

There would be no prayer, no talk of "a better place" or of the will of God or of reuniting in some sweet by and by.

Back in April and May, when Celia's painting was a viral sensation on cable TV, the internet, and in pulpits, and our phones rang with calls from people seeking comments or pointing accusing fingers, we were all concerned with safety, particularly Celia's. We came through it unscathed and took from it whatever lessons we could. Celia steeled herself for a career that would be in part, at least, defined by *The Holy Family*, no matter what else she might produce. At the same time, she felt confident that the painting would permanently remain up to her standards.

We could not have known, of course, that the severest danger to Celia was a tiny flaw in an artery in her brain that would grow to colossal significance suddenly and without warning. That those who attacked her so viciously in the spring of the year would take our tragedy as a sign of their righteousness was so unthinkable as to be outside the realm of predictability. But Steve Rinaldo called us on the second morning after we returned from Poughkeepsie and asked if he might drop by after lunch. He had aged visibly since we had last seen him, on an evening in June when he had come to our apartment for another private viewing of the painting and a festive dinner prepared by Celia and Justine to thank him for his defense of Celia and *The Holy Family* on the Dave Leary show. Immediately after the show the cardinal had placed Steve on administrative leave and then, a few weeks later, assigned him to be assistant dean of admissions of a small Catholic high school in Queens.

When I asked how things were going, though, Steve brushed off the question. "That's not important," he said. "I'll survive, and I'll keep making waves. His eminence the cardinal forgets that I've got nothing to lose and I won't allow him to make me miserable. But, as I said, that's not important. I hope you haven't been subjecting yourselves to television and internet since—since, well, you know."

We assured him we had not, except for the most necessary emails, "I feel that I should tell you—there are sharks in the water. The clergy grapevine is vast and often indiscriminate, so I hear things—these people," he told us, his voice soft and measured, "the ones who made all the noise about the painting, are not finished." He explained that the perpetrators of the attacks last spring, led by the local minister who had initiated the controversy over the painting, were planning new celebrations and protests. "He's clergy, you know, probably has chaplain credentials, so he heard about Celia within an hour of the call to 911. There are no secrets or privacy, really, where the clergy are involved." The minister and his followers revised and reposted their original internet attacks on Celia and *The Holy Family*, they contacted the media, and they wrote gleeful obituaries in which they claimed that God had heard their prayers and had struck down the heretical Celia Halsey in the prime of her life. They started promoting her death as a sign that God supported their entire agenda, which included fighting everything they considered to be evil, from abortion to gay marriage to atheism.

"The worst thing," Steve said, "is that they're planning to create a disturbance, as they put it, at Celia's funeral or memorial or whatever you plan to do. I think you need to know about that. You wouldn't want such an event to be—marred—by that kind of ugliness."

His concern was obviously heartfelt, and we thanked him for making us aware of it.

"We'll be planning a memorial service," Justine said, "but not a funeral." Justine seemed unable to say any more. The next morning, I told Steve, the three of us would view Celia's body for the last time, after which her remains would be cremated. My statements were matter-of-fact, but it felt as though I had to push each word separately through my larynx and into the air.

Janet said, "I know that's what Celia wanted. Sisters, you know. My sister. We talked about every goddamn kind of thing over the years. Our wishes, our dreams, men we think are hot, our deaths." Steve took her hands in his as she began to cry quietly.

We sat together in the living room for a while longer, not uneasy about the silence that engulfed us. Sometimes there is nothing left to say, and the worst thing to do in that moment is to say something. It was almost like being at prayer, but when a truck horn blasted out on the street I was brought straight back to the reality that we are earthbound, dust, pieces of carbon, short-timers on this planet who need to make our own meanings.

Celia had made hers, I was sure.

Eventually I said, "We will mark this privately, as a family, for now. When the time is right we can include others. In a couple of weeks, say. If there's controversy to manage, we'll manage it."

Steve approached each of us in turn and grasped us firmly by the shoulders and kissed our foreheads. "Anything you need, you know you can count on me. I love you all," he said, and he left.

I spent the rest of day looking at Celia's sketchbooks—she had had so many and I had seen only a few—and thinking about the donation of her organs. I thought about how, at this moment, patients were recovering from surgeries in which they received those organs, and how much I hoped they would all go on to live long and fruitful lives.

"I'm going mix up batter for some everlasting pancakes," Justine says as she looks into the refrigerator. Going from the hot bath to the relative cool of the kitchen has really enlivened her. "You know, the ones where you don't need to eat again until the third day."

I laugh and swat her on the butt, let my hand linger and knead that superb flesh while with the other I touch her face and she turns to me and we kiss as we stand in the chill light that comes from the fridge. I breathe deeply, feeling as though I am inhaling Justine's essence itself, and every nerve ending seems to go on alert. She closes the fridge behind her, slips her hand under my waistband, and says "You want something, mister? That'll cure your theological problems once and for all?"

We grope and tumble our way into the living room, slipping out, as we go, of the sweatpants and t-shirts we had pulled on after getting out of the bath. I feel beastly, in a way, there is a fire in me the likes of which I can only remember from much younger days and I feel almost violent as I steamroller Justine toward the sofa. I know I will not hurt her, that I don't have it in me to hurt her, but I am plainly ungentle as I pin her beneath me and spread her legs and move to enter her with an urgency that feels more animalistic than passionate. I realize suddenly that it is anger that is moving me, a rage I have never acknowledged, and this rage is joined by horror as I look at my wife beneath me, naked and vulnerable as I attack, that is how it feels to me, *attack* her, and for split second I hesitate. Justine, though, sensing my need to expel this fury—and maybe she even shares the necessity—pulls me to her, emphatic, and bites me hard on the shoulder, emitting a vocalization like that of a mother protecting her young. I answer with a guttural sound that empties my lungs as if I've been hit from behind, and I don't know if I am reacting to the pain of her teeth in my flesh or to the pleasure of being trapped by her strong loins and legs. She releases my shoulder and inhales sharply and I hear a determined shriek, repeated, repeated, repeated as she imposes an ideal rhythm, like an orchestra conductor, and we rock in and out, toward and away, until our mirrored movements give way to release and we can do nothing more but collapse and pant like sprinters at the end of a full-speed run.

My eyes are closed now and I try to open them, but can't until the moment I smell blood, which shakes me alert like smelling salts, and I see blood dripping from my shoulder onto Justine's chest, and it mingles there with sweat that trickles onto and between her breasts. Justine sees it too, and looks at me, her eyes seeming to smile and ask for more, and I kiss and lick her nipples and the blood and sweat as it pools together, and she looks for my mouth with hers and we devour each other as anger fades and transforms into something sweet the way fruit ripens to its perfect flavor. We arrive at a moment of rest and press together, stretched along the length of the sofa, giving mutual shelter.

Moments of silence.

"Better?" she asks. A gravelly whisper.

"A little scared." I look at the blood on my hand, feel my eyebrows raise.

Justine laughs, a gut-laugh, but speaks soothingly. "Beasts, we are just little beasts." She kisses my shoulder. The blood has begun to congeal but still leaves a smudge on her lips. "Demon exorcised?" she asks.

"I didn't know it was there," I say.

"I did." She buries her face in my non-wounded shoulder and I feel a slight shudder and sob. "Our little girl is gone, Martin. You are entitled to your anger. Your despair." A silence. "We both are." Another pause. "But we can't let anger or despair become what defines us."

I am certain of only one thing, that Justine and I alone hold the keys to the restoration of our hearts. And though that will never be complete—I can no longer imagine such a thing as a perfect, restored heart—neither of us will ever take the easy but unacceptable answer of everlasting life. We choose taste and touch, sight and sound, smell. All the senses radically and humanly engaged, pursuing love and knowledge.

Death indeed stings, and no redeemer beckons us. We will face, every day, the hard reality that the end is the end, that our Celia is gone except in memory and artifact. I feel a rush of gratitude for the paintings, the drawings, the earrings left on the dresser. The lock of her hair. The sensuous, finite love embodied in *The Holy Family*. All of that is something, not nothing, and meshed with the forces in us—body and heart—that created and nurtured Celia, leaves us with no alternative but to go on.

Ten days after Celia died we held a memorial.

It was unmarred by actions taken by any who considered her their enemy—either they had lost interest in the interim, or our attempts to keep the details about the service private succeeded.

We assembled—family, friends, Celia's key teachers, classmates, and associates from Vassar—in a theatre in the West

Village. It was a Monday, late afternoon and going into evening, and on the theatre's traditionally dark day it had been made available to us by colleagues from the business. Earlier in the day the lighting director and a technician had met us—Justine, Janet, and a few friends who wanted to help—at the door ready to assist in any way. We brought paintings and drawings, easels and tables, and set up a gallery of Celia's work on the stage. *The Holy Family*, of course, was at the center. I had known the lighting director for decades, since my early days in New York. She quietly directed her assistant, a young woman fresh out of college, in making subtle and brilliant adjustments so that by the time the guests arrived each work of art was visible in, literally, its best light.

In addition to Celia's work, a small table held photographs of Celia, from birth to just weeks before she died. The picture taken at the lake, the last picture of Celia, had not yet been discovered, the camera stashed in the pocket of a suitcase where I would find it weeks later. Janet provided several photos we had not seen before, most of these showing Celia with Janet in various locations they had visited together. Janet herself seemed to have a hard time helping with the setup, taking a break several times to sit in the empty rows of seats with her head down or eyes closed. When some musicians arrived—friends Janet and Celia shared—she was finally able to shake loose of her distracted state and help them get situated at the side of the stage.

By 3:30 everyone we expected to see had arrived. All took seats despite the temptation of the thrust stage extending into the audience, and spoke in hushed voices. The theatre was nearly full. Justine and Janet and I went to the front of the house and stepped up onto the stage. I held hands with both of them and thanked everyone for coming. "This is not going to be a traditional or religious service, by any means, and I'm sure that comes as no surprise. No one is designated to officiate and we do not have a program to follow." I gestured toward the paintings and drawings. "This is Celia's legacy, and we'd like to celebrate and remember her life simply by sharing it with you."

Justine said, "We're not in church—so please wander and mingle and take some time to come up here to the gallery. Martin and Janet and I would love to speak personally with everyone. We have all the time we need. Our musician friends will play, I've been told they may even break into song from time to time with some of Celia's favorites, and refreshments are being assembled in the lobby. Make yourselves at home. Our love for Celia goes on and on, and our grief is acute, but we thank you for your friendship and support, yesterday, today, and tomorrow."

6

Christmas Eve

We traditionally spend Christmas Eve in New Jersey with my family. Unlike Thanksgiving, it is the one occasion where everyone has always been together, and we have a gift exchange among my siblings and our spouses and among all the grandchildren. This year it has been awkward for everyone. There is one less name on the list of grandchildren, and Janet is far away. Justine and I have talked about staying home. I think it might be easier for everyone else to enjoy the holiday if we just stay put. Justine disagrees, saying we need to move forward in every way we can, even within the bounds of our new normal.

We wake up on the morning of Christmas Eve still undecided about whether to go or stay home. The evening is usually festive but not religious, and we have always enjoyed it. In between showering, dressing, and eating breakfast Justine and I talk about the pros and cons.

"Wouldn't it be nice to get out of the city for a bit?" she asks. "Maybe we could stay overnight at your sister's—she said that'd be okay—or get a hotel room, or come home late and check in with Janet online?"

"You may be right, I don't know." I am in my worst frame of mind, the one in which I avoid making a decision until it has to make itself. I try to justify myself. "I feel like, the other day, I finally managed to achieve some bit of equanimity. I guess I'm just afraid of rocking the boat—I mean, I have no idea how long this even keel will last, or how little it might take to knock me off course."

Justine says, "I'll look out for you, I'll tie you to the mast if I have to. And we have gifts to take—I did all the shopping for the gift exchange, and I'd hate to have to lug them all the way to the Post Office to ship them after Christmas." Justine puts on her mock pouty face and bats her eyelashes, which forces me to smile.

"You really do want to go."

"I feel like I need to, chancy as it might be," she says.

"I'm afraid I might lose it," I say. "Ruin it for everyone."

Justine wraps herself around me. "I don't think anyone could fault you if you did. And it wouldn't ruin it. It's going to be hard for everyone. And different. Celia was always—the life of the party, ever since she was a little girl."

"I wish Janet were here. I worry about her, too, so isolated."

"She's part of a team up there," Justine says, "and she says she's getting a lot of support. You heard what she said about that last time we talked to her."

"Yes. But it's Christmas now. That changes things. Days like this, events like this, set things off. Time bombs."

Justine guides me to a chair and starts massaging my shoulders and neck. "We have to take that chance. It's called being alive. We'll call Janet before we leave, and again later or tomorrow. We're part of her support system, and she's part of ours."

"Give me a little more time."

At 10 o'clock our mail arrives. Along with a handful of greeting cards and bills there is a large envelope from the agency that administered the transplantation of Celia's organs. As part of the process we had chosen anonymity but allowed for communication with recipients, with the agency as intermediary. If we wished to respond, we could do so through the same channel. This is the first time we have received anything from the agency other than administrative-looking business envelopes.

We are standing in the entryway, and after some hesitation I slip my index finger under the seal and tear open the flap. Inside is a second envelope, still sealed, addressed simply "To the family of my heart donor." The handwriting is soft and feminine, careful but easy. Justine and I look at each other. She has gone pale. I feel the blood has drained from me as well, and I have a sudden need to sit down. I go to the sofa and Justine follows me. We sit and lean toward each other, the envelope frozen in my hand. I drop it onto the coffee table and we stare at it. Justine links her arm in mine, kisses my shoulder, and whispers, "No time like the present." I pick it up and open it quickly, like ripping a bandage off skin, and the letter, a single sheet in the same handwriting as the envelope, is finally open before us. We pore over it as if it is a scroll of holy writ pulled from an ancient jar.

To the family of my Heart Donor,

My name is Erin and I live in Bangor, Maine. I am
27 and I am alive today because of your misfortune.
I know that your grief must be strong, and I want
you to know that I think of you and your loss every
day of my life, and I expect that I will for as long as
I live. Your daughter's strong and healthy heart
beats in my chest, replacing my damaged and
broken one.

When I first found out about my heart condition I thought it would take a miracle to survive. I understand now that it was not a miracle but a tragedy that has given me new life, given my son his mother back, and my husband his wife back.

Your tragedy is a burden that I carry willingly.

I would like to know about your daughter. Whatever you are comfortable telling me will be enough—I want to know her better so I can honor her better every day. If you prefer not to respond, I understand, but please know that I hold her in highest esteem.

I wish you healing as deep as your grief. Thank you for listening.

Respectfully,

Erin

Justine and I collapse back onto the sofa, not sure whether to feel relief or revitalized grief or anger at this unexpected message, and neither of us is sure what the other is feeling. When I look at Justine I see tears in her eyes, but other than that her expression is not sorrowful.

Then she says, "Celia will never stop making me proud."

"Let's write back to her right away, we need to." I am surprised at how sure I am that this is what we must do. We will write today, now, and we will write again and again in the months and years ahead if that is what is needed. Justine finds writing paper and her favorite pen and we go to the dining room table and prepare to write. We agree that we will email copies of both letters, Erin's query and our reply, to Janet as soon as we are done. We will mail the letter today on the way out of town for Christmas Eve. Tonight at my sister's house we will read both letters out loud to our family—we have never told them about the transplants, at first because it just seemed like too much to add to the fact of Celia's death, and since then because there never has been a moment that seemed right—and that will be, in a way, our gift to them, this knowledge that there is something of Celia still in the world in addition to the walls of drawings and paintings that shout her name.

We will do all of this knowing that all may never again be fully well for us, but we will make it well enough, that although tragedy will color the rest of our story it does not have to dominate or define it.

We sit at the dining room table, cream-colored paper before us, a pen laid beside it, and breathe in deeply as we gaze at each other before we both look to the paper and I follow the motions of Justine's fine hand as she begins to write.

Dear Erin,

Our daughter's name was Celia.
She was a painter

Alan Michael Wilt is a writer and editor.
He lives in Massachusetts.